COYOTE RETURNS

Thirty feet away sat a coyote. Something limp hung from the animal's mouth.

The coyote cocked his head to one side as he studied the human. Gabe didn't make any sudden moves.

After almost three minutes, their joint scrutiny was interrupted by a howl coming from a nearby hill. Both of them looked in the direction of the sound, then back to each other.

The coyote dropped what he had in his mouth and looked at Gabe. Neither moved. The coyote leaned forward and nudged the object with his nose, toward him. The animal gave Gabe one more look, then trotted off in the direction of the howl.

Gabe walked over to the object and picked it up. It was a man's belt with a sheath. A heavy bowie knife was stuffed inside. . . .

Also by Micah S. Hackler

Legend of the Dead

COYOTE RETURNS

Micah S. Hackler

A Dell Book

Published by
Dell Publishing
a division of
Bantam Doubleday Dell Publishing Group, Inc.
1540 Broadway
New York, New York 10036

ISBN: 0-440-22094-7

Printed in the United States of America

Published simultaneously in Canada

July 1996

10 9 8 7 6 5 4 3 2 1

RAD

For Sabyn and Stuart

ACKNOWLEDGMENTS

Although it sometimes feels like it, authors don't work in a vacuum. First and foremost, I want to thank my greatest supporter, Suzie, my wife. I need to thank friends like Al and Sue Suess and Bill and Bobbie Riggle for their moral support and spelling acumen. Sincere appreciation goes to The Factory, George Sewell and Dan Baldwin, for the steadfast encouragement and marketing assistance. Continued thanks to Nancy Love and to my editor, Jacob Hoye, and his excellent staff.

The author wishes to thank Alfred A. Knopf/Random House for permission to use an excerpt from The Plague by Albert Camus (Stuart Gilbert translation), copyright 1948.

I would also like to thank Mr. Wayne Ude for permission to adapt his story "Coyote Learns a Lesson" from his book Maybe I Will Do Something: Seven Coyote Tales, copyright 1993, Houghton Mifflin Company.

THIS STORY IS FROM WHEN THE WORLD WAS STILL young. It was just after the animals emerged from the *Sipapu* and before they spread out to occupy all the land. There was only one great herd of buffalo. There was only one flock of crows. It was in the time when there was only one small huddle of deer.

Coyote, who was always greedy and selfish, decided he was hungry, so he devised a trick. He would teach the deer how to dance. He would tell them this dance was to honor Mother Earth and that she would rejoice at hearing their dancing hooves.

So Coyote went to the deer and taught them how to dance. Then he told them to close their eyes and follow him. He would lead them to the secret Holy Place where they could dance forever. The deer followed but they did not know Coyote was leading them to a cliff. Coyote's plan was for all the deer to fall from the cliff and die. Then Coyote would have all the meat he wanted to eat.

All the deer fell from the cliff and died, except for one. This was a young doe, so pregnant with two foals she could not keep up with the other deer. When she saw what had happened to the others she begged Coyote not to make her dance off the cliff. If she did, her children would die with her and there would be no more deer in the world.

Coyote's heart softened when he saw the doe's tears and he let her go.

Mother Earth did rejoice that Coyote taught the deer how to dance. But Father Sky had seen what Coyote had done to the deer and He told Mother Earth. She became very angry with Coyote because he nearly killed all the deer and because he did not give thanks to his brothers for giving him nourishment. So Mother Earth sent a pestilence to rot the deer meat. It became so rancid that Coyote could not eat it and he almost starved to death.

To this day, because of Coyote, the deer still dance. It is also because of Coyote that we give thanks to the spirits of the animals that feed us. For without the gift of their lives we would surely starve. We are also taught, through this story, that we should never take from the earth more than what we need.

—*Coyote Legend*

COYOTE WAS HUNGRY. COYOTE WAS ALWAYS HUNGRY . . . or thought he was. As a three-quarter moon shone brightly in the cold, crisp night he kept his nose close to the ground, sniffing. Constantly sniffing. Looking for some small morsel of food to fight off the pain in his stomach.

Coyote's hunger was an ancient memory. It was his first memory. It was from when the world was new, almost at the beginning of time. It was from the time when only Coyote and Badger existed, before the other creatures emerged from the great hole in the earth. It was before the age of Man.

The snows had not completely melted. Great patches of white still clung to the northern sides of hills. Smaller divots huddled under the scanty shade of the New Mexican sage, jealously guarding their meager moisture, refusing to melt. Father Sun was still making His lazy trek from the southern sky and His warming rays had not reached their full potential.

Coyote couldn't remember the last time he had been in these mountains. His little cousins talked of two springs earlier. The deer mice had been so plentiful, they nearly leapt into your mouth. You could barely walk without stepping on one. The mere thought of that cornucopia made Coyote's stomach hurt even worse.

This year he could find almost nothing.

He had dug through the compost pile of a ranch a few miles back, but the pickings had been slim. He remembered there was a town of white men to the south. Their garbage cans were always full of palatable things, things he couldn't find in the scrub or in the mountains. But the town was too far away and he was hungry now.

Maybe he had come back too early. If he had stayed to the south one week longer the deer mice would be scurrying. Maybe the birds would be building nests. Birds were easy to trick.

Coyote quit thinking about his hunger when he heard the screeching of tires on pavement. A moment later there was a thud . . . maybe a door being slammed? Coyote's ears searched the night sounds, trying to pick out a direction.

Another sound. More tires grinding on gravel.

Two voices. Men's voices. Yelling at each other.

Coyote began a cautious trot toward the sound. It came from the other side of a small hill. If there was one thing more overpowering in his life than hunger, it was his curiosity.

A beam of light silhouetted the sagebrush along the top of the hill. Coyote stopped and waited to see if the light came any closer. It didn't.

The two voices began yelling at each other again and the light they had been shining disappeared. There were two more thuds, similar to the first one. Doors again. Two engines roared. Then came the frenzied sound of gravel being crushed and kicked by tires.

Coyote had to know what this was all about. He decided, however, to go around the knoll so he could avoid where the light had shined. He kept his nose high so that he could smell the night air better. Almost all the other smells of the high desert were smothered by the odor of the metal monsters the humans used. The gaseous cloud gradually started to dissipate and Coyote began to discern another scent—strong, human. It was the smell of blood.

A new day was beginning to stir. The eastern stars were being wrapped in the pale blue cloak of dawn. In an hour, Father Sun would stretch His arms above the horizon and pull Himself into the morning sky.

To Coyote it made little difference. His realm was the night. Even if there had been no moon, he could see as well as Brother Owl. His yellow eyes searched the low brush on either side of him, looking for the source of the scent.

As he rounded the bottom of the hill, he spotted the still body of a man behind a small tuft of sage. The man was hiding, Coyote guessed, so he could not be seen from the road.

Coyote sniffed the air once more. There were no other humans around.

Using all the caution he could muster, he approached the man. Coyote was impressed at how well the man could stay motionless. It reminded him of a rabbit hunkering in the weeds.

Coyote circled the body, stopping occasionally to sniff. Finally, after several minutes of hesitation, he let his cold, damp nose touch the man's finger. Coyote immediately jumped back when the man's eyes sprang open.

At first the eyes registered fear and surprise, then bewilderment. The man raised his head ever so slightly and blinked as he tried to focus his gaze. The eyes . . . the eyes dissolved from bewilderment to realization to recognition.

"You . . ." The man's voice was barely a whisper as he locked his stare on Coyote's eyes.

Coyote had seen the stare before. It was the stare of a man who, standing on the brink of eternity, had just had all things revealed to him. He had no more fear of dying, because a part of him had already crossed over. In that one moment before complete surrender, he could see all things as the Great Spirit had created them. He could see Coyote.

"You must help . . . your children," the man gasped. "It is . . . in . . . your . . . power." The last word was no more than a breath escaping as the man's head dropped to the ground.

Coyote watched the life force drift into the starry sky to become part of the cosmic ocean. The chilly air became pungent with the smell of death. It had been a long time since Coyote had been near a dead human. He had nearly forgotten the odor.

Cocking his head to one side, he stared at the body. He pondered what he should do. There were all sorts of humans in the world: white men, black men, red men. Only red men were true human beings. Coyote knew that from his ancient memory. Only red men told the true stories of creation. (At least some of them still did.) Only red men remembered Coyote: Coyote, who had been there at the beginning; Coyote, who could change shape at will; Coyote the Trickster.

The man Coyote now stared at was a red man. Coyote knew the rules of the true human beings. It was important that the dead be buried. Even though the life force was gone, the spirit remained. If a man wasn't buried, his spirit might never rest. His spirit would hide in the shadows of the night and terrorize the living.

Humph! Coyote thought. Help his children, indeed! He was Coyote. He would do as he pleased. Still . . . the red man did ask for his help.

It would be daylight soon. Men in their metal monsters would travel up and down the black ribbon of road just a few feet away. But they would never see the body, hidden behind the bushes as it was. If they couldn't see the body, how could they take it away and bury it? If they did not bury him, his spirit would be restless for all time.

It was against Coyote's nature to perform an act of kindness. Still, the red man did recognize his great power. He did ask for Coyote's help.

Coyote took the man's jacket collar into his teeth and began to pull. The body was heavy. The loose gravel beneath Coyote's feet didn't offer much traction and his paws kept slipping. But he had made up his mind to do this, so he kept on pulling. Coyote considered changing shape. He could take human form if he wanted to. That would give him hands, but only two feet. Four feet were much better for this kind of work, so he remained in his coyote form.

He had no idea how long it took, but eventually he reached the edge of the asphalt. The traction was much better there and he began to make good progress. He tugged at the collar and the body inched forward. He backed up a few steps and tugged again.

Halfway across the pavement Coyote stopped. He wondered if other men would find the body now. It was at this pause that he felt the rumble. He looked first to his left, then to his right. Down the strip of asphalt, and not too far away, were the approaching lights of a metal monster. Coyote could tell from the vibration of the earth that it was a big one and it was coming fast.

Coyote glanced at the body. Surely they'll be able to see the body here, he thought. He trotted quickly to the side of the road and hid behind a sage brush.

As the strains of the music died away, Clarence pushed the rewind on his tape player. He loved listening to Bonnie Raitt singing "Angel from Montgomery." He loved that song and wanted to hear it again. He could listen to it all night. In fact, he almost had.

Clarence Brooks and his eighteen-wheeler had been on the road for three days: Albuquerque to Denver, Denver to Salt Lake City, now back to Albuquerque. Normally he took I-70 to Highway 191, then south to I-20. If he had gone that route he would have been home already. That is, if he hadn't had a delivery to make in Grand Junction. There weren't any good roads between Grand Junction and home. Still, he was making good time.

He glanced at the clock on his dashboard. It read six o'clock. He did a quick calculation. Hour and a half, two hours at the most to Santa Fe. Another hour to Albuquerque. He'd be able to drop off his load by the nine o'clock deadline. The roads were clear and the weather was fine.

The trucker pushed the PLAY button on his tape deck. The guitar lead-in started up. After a couple of measures, Bonnie started singing to him again.

"Son of a bitch!" Brooks bellowed, slamming on his brakes and simultaneously grabbing his gearshift.

The monotony of the straight, two-lane road had left him in a complacent mood. The all-night drive had dulled his senses. It took a second too long for him to realize the dark form in the road ahead was a man.

Brooks could hear and feel the sickening thump of his tires making contact.

The giant semi skidded to a halt a hundred feet past the lifeless form. The trucker grabbed a flashlight and jumped from his cab. Running back down the road, he finally found the victim.

Brooks turned his head to fight off a wave of nausea. The body was crumpled and lifeless. If it weren't for the clothing, it would be nearly impossible to tell it had once been human.

Shaking uncontrollably, Brooks stumbled back to the cab. In a daze, he shut off his tape deck and reached for the CB microphone. It took a few moments before he could clear the lump in his throat.

Coyote watched as the man from the big metal monster lit red sticks, then threw them on the asphalt. The bright red fire hurt Coyote's eyes, forcing him to look away.

It appeared the man was going to stay. He had found the red man. Coyote guessed he was waiting for other men to come so they could bury the body.

The Trickster was a little disappointed. He had done this good deed and no one would ever know. Oh, well, he thought, there was plenty of time for pranks that he would be given credit for.

Coyote turned and trotted away. He had important things to do. The dead man had distracted him and he had forgotten he was hungry.

It seemed like he was always hungry.

2

SHERIFF CLIFF LANSING SPED NORTH ON HIGHWAY 15 with his blue and red lights flashing. There was no need for the siren. The paramedics had already radioed that they were at the scene of the accident. Lansing was confident the lights were warning enough. Other travelers on the highway would know he was in a hurry.

The first streaks of sunlight were pushing their way over the peaks around Taos. Lansing tried his sunglasses, but it was still too dark to use them. He stuffed them back into his pocket.

The sheriff got the page on his beeper around six-thirty. He had been up for an hour already and was in the barn feeding his horses when the call came. Peters, the night deputy, reported he had gotten a CB call from a trucker about fifteen miles north of town. The trucker had hit a pedestrian. He was afraid the man might be dead.

Following standard procedure, Peters had notified the paramedics at the volunteer fire department first, then called Lansing. Lansing was glad to learn that after four years on the force, Peters was finally learning "standard procedure."

Lansing saw the highway flare first. The silhouette of the eighteen-wheeler, just beyond the flare, began to be filled in with details as he drew closer. Beyond the truck he could see the flashing red lights of the ambulance. He stopped on the shoulder of the highway across from the truck and turned on his flashing amber warning lights.

It was cold outside. Cold enough that Lansing could see his breath. The truck driver sat on the step of his cab, his heavy coat draped over his shoulders, his face buried in his hands. He looked up as the officer approached.

"I . . . I didn't see 'im," the trucker sobbed. "I mean, like, he was layin' in the middle of the road. There was no way I coulda stopped in time."

Lansing looked toward the paramedics. "Is he dead?"

"Yeah," the trucker said, burying his face again. "Yeah, he's dead all right."

The sheriff nodded. "Stay here. I'll need to get a written statement."

The trucker nodded, but said nothing.

Lansing walked back to where the paramedics waited. They sat in the open back door of the rescue unit. The sheriff cringed. Carlos Gomez and Willy Sutter had grown up together, graduated high school the same year, even went to paramedic training together. They both had jobs at the Western Auto, and when they weren't drinking or working, both hung around the fire department. Lansing admitted they were halfway decent paramedics, but they had a morbid fascination with blood, broken bones, and other tragedies that can befall a human body. Their gallows humor was something the sheriff couldn't quite understand.

The body of the pedestrian still lay where they had found it. It was covered with a black plastic tarp.

"Mornin', Sheriff," Carlos said, blowing out a lungful of cigarette smoke. He nodded toward the body. "It's a bad one. Bad as I've ever seen."

Cliff stopped next to the plastic sheet, hesitating a moment before lifting it.

"Hope you haven't had breakfast yet," Willy, the other paramedic, joked.

The sheriff ignored him. Bracing himself, Lansing lifted the cover. The legs, somehow, had escaped damage. The head and upper torso hadn't. The arms were contorted, bent at angles never intended by nature. The chest was crushed. So was the skull. There were not enough identifying features to prove the head ever had a face.

Lansing dropped the plastic sheeting, grateful the sun wasn't any higher than it was. He returned to the grinning paramedics. "What the hell do you think is so funny?"

"Nothin', Sheriff," Willy admitted. "It's just that—"

"That's a dead human being over there."

"We know that, Sheriff!" Carlos protested.

"Then wipe those dumb-assed grins off your faces."

"Yes, sir," the two said in unison. They stared at the ground, trying to show a little shame.

"I have to take some pictures. When I'm finished, wrap him up and take him to the mortuary."

"Or what's left of 'im," Willy whispered to his partner.

The remark was just loud enough for Lansing to hear. Willy shrank under the officer's icy stare. "And show him some respect," the sheriff growled.

"Yes, sir."

Lansing slowed as he approached his patrol Jeep. The trucker sat motionless, his head still buried. Cliff wished he had a thermos of coffee with him. He'd give the driver a cup. As it was, he had nothing to offer the man.

As he opened the rear door to the Jeep, the sheriff heard the distant wail of a siren. That would be the highway patrol, he thought. He could use the company.

The sheriff was already taking pictures when the patrol car pulled up.

"Morning, Cliff," the patrolman said, grimly surveying the scene.

"Hi, Marty."

Marty Hernandez helped Lansing patrol San Phillipe County. They had coffee together at least three times a week and Cliff genuinely liked the younger man. They had a good working relationship and neither tried to interfere in the other's jurisdiction. Unfortunately, the highway patrolman wasn't always available. Besides San Phillipe, Hernandez had to cover the two adjoining counties. It was purely coincidence that he was around that morning and Lansing was grateful for whatever help he could get. The sheriff pulled the Polaroid photo from the dispenser and got ready to take another picture.

"Need any help?"

"Yeah. I'm afraid so. I need to get a written statement from the driver and I still have to walk off the skid marks."

"What's the scenario?"

Lansing sighed. "The driver said the victim was lying in the middle of the road. It was still dark. By the time the driver saw him it was too late to stop."

Hernandez looked back at the driver. Brooks sat motionless, staring at the ground. "What do you think?"

The sheriff shrugged. "I checked the bumper and the fenders. No sign of impact. I think he's telling the truth. My guess is some poor soul got drunk and decided he needed to lie down and take a nap."

"Got an ID?"

Cliff shook his head. "No wallet. No driver's license. Could be a local. Could be a transient." He clicked off another photo, then signaled to the paramedics to remove the body. "I got a missing persons report from Burnt Mesa Pueblo about three days ago. A guy by the name of Jonathan Akee."

"You think that's him?"

"Hope not," the sheriff admitted. "I liked Jonathan."

Hernandez nodded. "Well, let me grab my clipboard and take down the driver's statement."

"Thanks."

Lansing solemnly watched the paramedics as they bundled the dead man into a body bag. The more he thought about it, the more sure he was that they were carting off the body of his friend. Jonathan hadn't had a drink in six months, and now this. The sheriff didn't relish the thought of driving up to the pueblo, but he knew that's where he'd have to go once he was finished at the scene.

As the rescue unit pulled away, Lansing returned to his Jeep to retrieve the tape measure. He hoped the day would get better.

3

IT WAS NEARLY NINE O'CLOCK WHEN DEPUTY GABRIEL Hanna got to the office. He had been on patrol past ten the night before. He wished he was getting paid by the hour. Even at minimum wage, it seemed like working sixty hours a week would make him a millionaire by the time he was thirty.

"Good morning, Gabe," Marilyn sang from behind her reception desk/communications center.

"Morning, Marilyn." Gabe liked Marilyn. She was the plump, soft, earth-mother type who made you feel good whenever she smiled at you. And she always smiled. He had been in Las Palmas less than four months, but she made him feel as if she had known him all his life. "I see it's yellow roses this morning."

A vase of bright yellow silk roses sat at one end of the reception counter. Marilyn always had flowers on her counter. In the winter, when freshly cut flowers weren't available, she used silk flowers and potpourri incense. To enhance the illusion, Marilyn used a different set of faux flowers every day. "Yes," the receptionist sighed. "I thought for sure my tulips would be up by now. Maybe in a week. You just wait, though. When things start blooming, this office will look like a florist's shop."

Gabe smiled. "I don't doubt that a bit."

"Can I get you a cup of coffee?" she offered.

Gabe held up the Coke can he was carrying. "I told you. I never learned to drink coffee."

Marilyn shook her finger at him. "That stuff will kill you. All that is is acid and sugar. It'll give you diabetes. I know that for a fact."

Gabe shrugged her off. He knew he'd lose any argument with her. "I didn't see Sheriff Lansing's Jeep outside."

"He had to go to an accident this morning. Around six-thirty."

"Anyone hurt?"

"Evidently some poor man was killed. Hit by an eighteen-wheeler. Just walking along the side of the road and *bang* he was gone."

"Damn," the deputy said somberly. He had been on the job only fourteen weeks. In fact, he had been a law enforcement officer for only fourteen weeks, not counting the ten-week academy. This was the first time he had been even remotely involved with a death. He didn't know how he would have reacted if he had been called to the scene.

"Here are the notes Deputy Peters left." Over the top of the counter she handed Gabe a half dozen sheets of paper torn from a stenographer's pad. "I haven't typed them into the computer log yet, so I need to get them back."

Gabe glanced at the neatly printed words. Peters was so damned meticulous, he thought. He wondered if all deputies were expected to be that tidy. He glanced up from the papers. "Do you know if the sheriff wants me to go out on patrol?"

"He radioed in about seven-thirty," Marilyn said, after putting on her glasses to check the telephone log in front of her. "The note here says he'd like you to hang around the office until he gets in. Around ten. Of course, that is unless something comes up."

"Thanks." The deputy picked up the stack of newspapers from the counter and went back to the dayroom.

The sheriff's department occupied the south end of the San Phillipe Courthouse. It was divided into the reception area, a private office for the sheriff, a dayroom for the deputies to use when they weren't on patrol, and the lockup. The lockup had two cells, which were seldom used.

The dayroom was sparse. It had three desks, a coffee bar, and an ancient Teletype machine. The Teletype mostly gathered dust since Marilyn's computer was tied to the Law Enforcement Comfax. The Comfax was on-line twenty-four hours a day. Their secretary/receptionist downloaded the bulletins three times a day. If Sheriff Lansing was in, she would give him the hard copy. Otherwise, it was put in the dayroom for the deputies to review.

Gabe shared the dayroom with Jack Rivera, the other full-time deputy, and Danny Cortez, the part-time deputy who worked on the weekends. Larry Peters, the night officer, worked from Marilyn's station.

Gabe tossed his baseball cap on one desk, then sat at another. He picked up the Comfax printout from that morning. New Mexico had thirty-three counties. If anything important in law enforcement happened in a given county, the sheriff's department would feed that information into the Comfax. That way other counties and the highway patrol would be aware of any pertinent information. The big-city police departments, Santa Fe, Albuquerque, Farmington, anyplace with a population over twenty-five thousand were also tied into the network.

The printout looked fairly routine to Gabe: Albuquerque listed three gang-related shootings and one drug bust. Santa Fe had a barroom brawl that left three injured and one dead. Lincoln County listed a hit-and-run accident that injured a woman. No automobile description was available.

The highway patrol had only one APB. Six gang members affiliated with the Cobra Motorcycle Club were wanted in connection with the brawl in Santa Fe. Officers were warned that the six involved should be considered armed and dangerous. Approach with caution.

Gabe popped the top to his can of Coke and turned his attention to the newspapers. He didn't pay much attention to the *San Phillipe Epitaph*. He already knew everything that was going on in the county. However, Lansing made sure their office also got papers from the surrounding counties. If a brouhaha occurred with the Apache Indians in Sandoval County to the south, the sheriff wanted to know about it. Something like that could easily spill into San Phillipe, since the reservation straddled the county line. Or if cattle rustling was going on to the east, around Taos, Lansing wanted his officers to know about that. No halfway intelligent rustler would try to sell livestock in the same county from where they were taken. The cattle, in all likelihood, would end up in San Phillipe or one of the other neighboring counties. The deputies had to be aware of such business.

It all made sense to the novice lawman. He was almost positive he would have the same policy if he were in charge.

The headline on the front page of the *Farmington News* proclaimed TRIBAL COUNCIL SPLIT ON LOGGING PROPOSAL. The subheadline warned NAVAJO DECISION COULD IMPACT CITY ECONOMY.

Even though he was supposed to be scanning the paper for items of police interest, the deputy was drawn to read the article. Gabe was Navajo. At least he was half Navajo, by blood, on his father's side. In the great scheme of things, being Navajo meant very little to him. He didn't grow up Navajo. He wasn't raised in the Native American traditions. He wasn't even born in the United States. He was born in an army hospital on the Korean Peninsula.

Despite his ambivalence, Gabe was compelled to read the article. He told himself his interest was because the piece dealt with land conservation and ecology, important topics. He was motivated by another feeling, something deep inside that he couldn't identify. Whatever was stirring, he suppressed. Since he hadn't had breakfast yet, he decided it was hunger. That was all. He'd grab a bite at the diner later. For the time being, he took a sip of his Coke and read the article.

AP—FARMINGTON—Mabel Ooljee, chairwoman of the Navajo Tribal Council, announced in a press conference Friday that the council still has not reached a decision regarding the logging of reservation lands. Over 100,000 acres of virgin spruce and pine forests located in New Mexico, Utah, and Arizona are under consideration in the proposal. The single largest tract of land under consideration is 75,000 acres of forest around Coyote Summit, 75 miles southwest of Farmington.

Pro-logging advocates, lead by Tribal Councilman Edward Hania, believe the timber harvest alone could generate over $5 million in sales annually. Hania maintains that more than 150 jobs would be created for tribal members, infusing another $500,000 into the reservation economy each year.

Walter Tallmountain, a noted tribal ecologist and the outspoken leader of the anti-logging camp, maintains that timber cutting of any kind will tip the balance of nature against the reservation. Citing recent archaeological evidence, Tallmountain claims that the tribe's predecessors, the Anasazi, destroyed their own civilization by stripping away the native vegetation to make way for farming. "The pinnacle of the Anasazi civilization, the

era of the cliff dwellings, lasted only one hundred years,"
Tallmountain explained. "In that time they destroyed
the natural habitat around them, depleting the thin layer
of soil that supported their crops and reducing the landscape to a barren desert. That's the lesson they taught
us. That's the lesson we can't forget. That's why we can't
afford to lose what little forest we have left."

Tallmountain has no official standing in the council.
Pro-logging advocates feel the debate should be limited
strictly to council members only. Further, Tallmountain's views are controversial, and as Councilman Hania
points out, not all archaeologists agree with the theory.
Additionally, several Native American groups disagree
with Tallmountain and believe his theories fly in the
face of tribal traditions. They maintain the Native people of North America have always believed in the sanc-
tity of the land and have historically treated it with
respect.

Despite their disagreements, Navajo traditionalists
have sided with Tallmountain on the logging issue. They
believe the forests are sacred and should be left undis-
turbed for future generations.

Insiders close to Ms. Ooljee say the eighty-four-
member council is split over the debate. They suggest,
if a resolution is not reached soon, the issue may be
placed on a tribal-wide referendum.

If the proposal is approved, a new sawmill will be built
northwest of Farmington, just beyond the city limits.
County commissioners have already rezoned the property
for industrial use in anticipation of Navajo actions. The
sawmill will be built by Rocky Mountain Resources
(RMR), a logging and mining concern headquartered in
Denver. RMR's regional vice president, Samuel Elverson, said the proposed sawmill could be operational by

the end of the summer and will employ fifty full-time workers.

Gabe knew almost nothing about the Navajo reservation. He knew it was big, covering thousands of square miles in three states. He knew most of it was in Arizona.

He had driven through a portion of the reservation a couple of years earlier. What he had seen was parched desert, barren mesas, and abject poverty. He couldn't imagine what kind of forest in that desolate terrain would be worth fighting over.

On the second page of the paper the deputy found another small article about the reservation. This one, at least, had something to do with law enforcement. The Arizona and New Mexico state police were forming a joint task force with tribal authorities to investigate the rapid rise of illegal drugs on Navajo lands.

Before Gabe could get too deep into the article the phone rang at his desk.

"Deputy Hanna," Gabe announced into the receiver.

"Gabe." It was Marilyn. "I've got Kelly on the other line. They're having a problem at the diner and she's pretty upset."

4

SHERIFF LANSING TURNED OFF HIGHWAY 15 ONTO THE
asphalt patchwork called Burnt Mesa Road.

The road was a continual point of contention between
the Tano Tribe of Burnt Mesa Pueblo and the San Phillipe
County Commissioner's office. The tribe wanted a smooth
blacktop all the way from the highway to the reservation,
fifteen miles. The county didn't have enough money for
road improvements. The commissioners thought the tribe
should pay for the upkeep, since they were the only people
who used it. Because Burnt Mesa Road was a county road,
the state sided with the tribe. San Phillipe was obligated
to maintain the full stretch, at least to the reservation limits.

The commissioners grudgingly kept the road open, but
barely. Whatever was left over from some other job got
dumped onto Burnt Mesa Road, a dump truck of asphalt
here, a couple of yards of concrete there, whatever it took
to cover the potholes. (The state never declared that the
road had to be smooth.)

It was early spring. No highway projects were under way
and the road had suffered significantly over the winter.
Lansing gritted his teeth as he dodged holes big enough to
swallow a small child. Even with the high suspension on

his Jeep, he was afraid he might rip out the transmission if he wasn't careful.

While he tried to concentrate on the obstacle-laden road, Lansing's thoughts kept drifting to two other matters. He couldn't help thinking about the dead body on the highway. He kept telling himself it wasn't Jonathan Akee. The more he told himself it wasn't Jonathan, the more convinced he became that it was.

Lansing's other concern was Margarite Carerra, the public health physician who handled Burnt Mesa and San Francisco pueblos. They had known each other for a year and a half and had been seeing each other on a fairly regular basis for the last nine months. It had not been a smooth relationship.

Lansing knew what his problem was. He had been divorced for five years and it was still painful. He knew the relationship with his ex-wife was over. She was already remarried. Had been for three years. But he still saw her once a month when he went to Albuquerque to pick up Cliff junior (or C. J., as he was better known). He still loved her, or at least a piece of him did. Whenever he was alone and had time to think about it, he promised himself he would never hurt like that again.

Margarite knew what the problem was too. She knew it better than Lansing. Though they never spoke about it, he could sense her appreciation of his feelings. (She had been through a similar situation, although there were no children involved.) She put up with his stubborn silence and his armor-plated defenses. She never insisted that he talk about it, unlike other women he had dated.

What Margarite did want to know was where *she* stood. Lansing had a hard time with that. She was a beautiful woman. He enjoyed his time with her. He even found himself admitting to himself that he wanted to be with her. But his damned defense mechanism kept popping up, warning him to be careful. If he admitted his feelings, he could get hurt. She tolerated his response: that he cared about her, that she was the only woman he was seeing.

Lansing felt he was a good sheriff and a reasonably decent man. Professionally, publicly, he knew he had his ducks in line. His personal life was not so orderly, though. Margarite hadn't talked to him in a week. They were supposed to go to Santa Fe the previous weekend, but he had had to cancel the trip. He had forgotten all about the Spring Scout Jamboree at Philmont and he had promised his twelve-year-old son they would go together. He saw C. J. little enough as it was. He couldn't afford to break that promise.

Lansing knew it was a mistake to break the news to her over the phone. The least he could have done was drive to the reservation and tell her in person. The sarcasm of her response before she slammed down the receiver made him shiver: *I hope you have a good time!*

He had been back two days and still hadn't called her. He wondered if her Spanish temper had calmed any. He hoped it had as he pulled into the parking area in front of the pueblo clinic.

The clinic was small. The large outer room served as the reception area and secretary's office. Margarite had a small cubicle for her things plus there was one examination room. A two-bedroom trailer in back of the adobe clinic was what the pueblo doctor called home.

The only vehicle in the parking area was Margarite's faded green pickup truck. It was still too early for patients. Even so, the sheriff found the front door to the clinic already unlocked.

Margarite looked up from the file cabinet she was sorting through. "Well, Lansing, what brings you all the way out here?"

Lansing didn't mind her addressing him by his last name.

She always addressed him like that, or with "Sheriff." In fact, he couldn't recall her ever using his first name, except when introducing him to someone.

"Business, I'm afraid," he said, smiling weakly as he removed his hat.

"Oh."

Lansing wasn't sure if he'd caught any sign of disappointment in her voice. "I was wondering if anyone had heard from Jonathan Akee recently."

"What do you mean?"

"Susan called the station last Friday. Evidently she and Jonathan had another one of their big rows and he took off. She was afraid he had wandered into town and got drunk."

"Jonathan's been on the wagon for six months, Lansing."

"I know he has. It's just that . . ." He squirmed at having to explain. "There was an accident out on the highway this morning. It looks like one of the tribal members went to sleep on the road and got run over by an eighteen-wheeler. I was afraid it might be Jonathan."

Margarite had managed an aloof attitude until that point. The news cracked her facade. "Are you sure it was Jonathan?"

"No," Lansing admitted. "The guy's features were pretty messed up. But this wouldn't have been the first time Jonathan ended up on that stretch of highway passed out drunk."

Margarite closed the drawer she was rifling through and reached for the pueblo phone directory on the receptionist's desk. "There's one way we can find out."

The phone directory was nothing more than a dozen sheets of paper stapled together. With only twelve hundred people on the reservation, there was no need for anything fancier. Margarite turned to the first page of household numbers. Keeping her finger on the page for reference, she quickly dialed a number. A moment later she spoke into the phone. "Susan? Dr. Carerra. I'm sorry to disturb you this early. . . . Good. Listen, I was wondering. I heard that you had reported Jonathan missing last Friday. . . . Yes, Sheriff Lansing told me. I was curious if he had returned home. . . . Oh, he did. Last night." The doctor laughed. "He was hiding out in the clan kiva." She gave Lansing an indifferent glance. "Yes, I do think that's a good idea. You should promise not to throw things at him anymore. . . . But he is home now? Good . . . Yes . . . Yes, I can pass it on to Sheriff Lansing when I see him. All right. Good-bye."

Lansing let out a sigh of relief as the doctor hung up the phone.

"You should *try* to use the phone more often, Lansing."

There was just enough acidity in her tone to tell him her words had two meanings. "Yeah, well, I just left the accident scene," he said sheepishly. "It was just as easy to drive out here as it was to call from town." Margarite's silence was icy. "I'm glad that wasn't Jonathan this morning."

"Yeah. Me too."

Lansing could tell he was nowhere close to getting off the hook. "Listen, Margarite. I really am sorry about last weekend. I guess I need to do a better job about keeping my schedule straight."

"I got over that the day after you canceled our trip," Margarite snorted, turning back to her file cabinet. "But you've been back for two days and I haven't heard from you. I didn't know if you got hurt or if something happened to C. J. I almost drove into town yesterday to see if you were all right. If I hadn't been so busy, I would have."

"Oh," Lansing responded lamely. "It's only . . ." He let the words fade. He didn't know how to explain why he hadn't called. He knew it had to do with talking to her face-to-face, about canceling their trip, about her intimidating temper. The bulletin flashed through his mind that he was particularly inept at dealing with women. "Ah, the hell with it," he mumbled, putting on his Stetson and turning toward the door.

"Where are you going?" Margarite asked, surprised he was leaving so quickly.

"Since that wasn't Jonathan out there on the highway, I have to find out who it was. I'm going to stop by the council house and see if anyone else might be missing." He started to open the door.

Lansing had no idea how well Margarite could read him. She saw his frustration at not being able to express his feelings. She knew this "man's man" had emotions that ran deep, and to protect those emotions he put up barriers. When his shields went up, she knew it was time to back off.

"Lansing," Margarite said, interrupting his exit. "I'm still making a list, but I have to drive into town this morning for supplies. Would it help any if I took a look at the body? I know every man, woman, and child in the pueblo."

Lansing's disposition brightened considerably. "Sure," he responded, grateful for the offer.

"I'll be ready to go by the time you finish at the council house. I'll follow you into town."

"Great." Lansing forced a smile. "I'll see you in about twenty minutes."

Lansing slowed his Jeep as he approached the scene of the accident. Once he was clear of the area he pulled over and parked on the gravel shoulder. Margarite parked behind him.

"This is the spot?" Margarite asked as she stepped down from her cab.

Lansing nodded and pointed up the road. "He was hit

about a hundred feet farther up. The truck stopped about where we are now. The victim didn't have any identification on him and it was too dark this morning to see much. I thought we might look along the shoulder for a wallet now that the sun's a little higher."

It was nine-fifteen. Lansing's plan was to walk along the side of the highway to beyond the point of impact. If they didn't find anything, they would walk back on the opposite shoulder.

"What happens if we don't find anything?" Margarite asked, searching the ground in front of her.

"We'll make a press release. See if anyone can help us identify the body. We'll check missing persons reports. Probably send fingerprints to the state crime lab. Of course, that only works if the guy was ever arrested. Since most people don't have jail records, that'll be a waste of time, but it's all part of the procedure."

"What happens if no one claims the body?"

"After a week, if nobody comes forward, we'll give him a burial at county expense. Not much else we can do." He stopped and pointed at the asphalt next to them. "That's where they had to scrape him up."

Margarite inspected the spot closely. "Where was the initial point of impact?"

"What do you mean?"

"This is where the body came to rest. Where did the truck first hit him?"

"As far as we know, he was hit right here. The truck driver said he was just lying there. I'm afraid he wasn't much more than a speed bump."

Margarite walked around the stains on the highway. There was a little blood. There was even a small blotch of gray gelatinous matter she recognized as brain tissue. "You said the truck ran over the man's head?"

"Yeah."

Margarite knelt to examine the stains. They were still slightly wet. She looked up at her companion. "There's not enough blood here."

Lansing had no idea what she was talking about. "What do you mean, 'there's not enough blood here'?"

"There should have been a big pool of blood after the skull was crushed. The heart would have kept beating for several seconds, maybe even minutes, after the brain ceased functioning. Blood would have been squirting all over the place. And after the heart stopped, the blood in the rest of the body would have oozed out through the trauma area." She stood and pointed toward their vehicles. "The truck tires would have tracked blood down the highway, but there are no tracks."

"So what are you telling me?"

"That your victim didn't die here. That's my guess. I can give you a better opinion when I see the body."

"That can be easily arranged, Doctor," Lansing said, turning toward his Jeep.

Margarite looked around her. "What about that wallet you wanted to find?"

"I can send out one of my deputies later. Right now I want to find out about this dead body I have on my hands."

"Okay." Margarite started toward her truck. "I'll follow you into town."

As Lansing reached his Jeep, a warble came over his radio. Someone was trying to reach him. "Lansing here," he reported into the microphone.

"Yes, Sheriff. Dispatch," Marilyn said over the speaker. "There's some trouble at the diner. A half dozen motorcycle hooligans. Deputy Hanna went over there about five minutes ago, but I think he's going to need help."

"Right. My ETA is fifteen minutes." Lansing shoved the microphone into its cradle and started his engine. A second later his tires were tearing up the highway shoulder as he rammed his transmission into first gear and sped toward town.

Margarite tried to fan the dust away from her face. She was certain Lansing had a reasonable explanation for pelting her and her truck with dirt and gravel. At least, he'd better have.

5

THE LAS PALMAS DINER FACED WEST. DURING THE morning hours the shades on the plate-glass windows were raised so patrons could view the picturesque little town. Sitting across the street from the town square, they had an excellent view of the park and the ninety-year-old courthouse.

The eating establishment, built in the 1940s, had never been through a major renovation. The walls were plastered with twenty layers of high-gloss paint, each strata representing a change of ownership or change of style. The chrome-and-Formica counter could serve a dozen customers on swivel stools. The Formica tops of most of the chrome-legged tables and the six booths along the north wall matched the faded gray of the counter. Three of the tables had been repaired in the past. Their tops were yellow.

Kelly Martin, the fortyish chief waitress with a beehive hairdo dyed a strange orange-red, tapped her foot impatiently behind the counter. She was waiting for an "Order up!" from the cook and some sign the sheriff's department was coming to her rescue. Her regular customers were gone, run off by six unkempt, rowdy, and offensive motorcyclists.

Velma, the other diner waitress for the day shift, was hiding in the back. That surprised Kelly. Velma was always flirtatious and enjoyed bantering with the male customers, especially banter that involved vaguely disguised sexual innuendo. Evidently there was nothing vague about the desires of her current customers. Two of the men started pawing at Velma as soon as she filled their coffee cups. A third tried to corner her in the rest room. (That was a switch for Velma, who had cornered a few customers of her own that same way. Of course, that was before she started dating John Tanner, the town physician.) Velma considered herself respectable now. The encounter in the rest room had sent the waitress scurrying in tears to the safety of the kitchen.

The bottom of the diner's windows sat three and a half feet off the floor. They were designed that way so tables could be pushed against the front wall. The low wall blocked only the view of the sidewalk and the parking spots in front of the café.

Standing behind the counter, Kelly could see the top portions of the six motorcycles. She could also see the street beyond and the passing cars. There was no sign of help.

Velma peeked through the order window. "Is the sheriff here yet?" she asked in a hoarse whisper.

"No," Kelly snapped, upset that he wasn't. "Are you about finished back there? I could use some help with these pigs."

"I'm not coming out there."

"You will or I'll dock you a week of tips. . . ."

"Hey! Sweet buns!" one of the cyclists shouted. "How 'bout some more coffee over here?"

"Yeah, and hurry up with those breakfasts," another one added.

"You just get your fanny out here," the senior waitress ordered, grabbing the pot from the coffeemaker. "And tell Ernie to hurry up with those eggs."

As Kelly approached the table she noticed one of the sheriff's patrol Jeeps cruise slowly by the front of the diner. The new deputy, Gabe Hanna, was driving. The Jeep didn't stop. In fact, once past the diner, the Jeep speeded up and continued down Main toward the southern part of town.

"That little snot," Kelly said under her breath. "That little chicken snot."

"Who you talkin' to?" a biker called Buck asked.

"Not to you, honey," the waitress growled.

Buck put his hand on Kelly's behind as she poured the coffee. She slapped the hand away and continued pouring the coffee without spilling a drop.

"Would you look at that?" Snake said. Snake was the man who had cornered Velma in the bathroom. "She didn't miss a beat. . . . You must like friendly customers, huh, Red?"

Kelly filled another cup. "Just used to them. That's all."

Snake looked around Kelly toward the counter. "Where's my little sweetie? I miss her."

"She's busy getting your breakfast. That's what you wanted, isn't it?"

"Yeah, for now." He reached over and nudged one of his buddies. "When I finish eating . . . that's another matter." The two men laughed.

A bell rang at the counter. "Order up!" Ernie announced from the window. Kelly hurried back to the counter. The sooner she fed that group, the sooner they'd leave.

Velma emerged from the kitchen, still wiping her eyes. "Have you seen the sheriff yet?" she asked in a subdued tone.

"That new deputy, Gabe, drove by. He took off out of town as soon as he saw all those bikes sitting outside. He's a damned chicken, if you ask me."

"What are we going to do?" Velma whimpered.

"First off, we're going to feed these boys," she said, putting plates of ham and eggs on a large serving platter. "While they're eating, I'll call Marilyn and tell her what's going on. Maybe she can get Cliff here. That new deputy's worthless."

Kelly led the way to the tables at the center of the diner where the bikers sat. Velma stayed a few paces back, refusing to get within arm's reach of any of the men. Kelly, after setting down her plates, had to retrieve the platter Velma was carrying.

"Some more toast," one biker with a long beard ordered. He didn't bother looking up. He was too busy sopping up egg yolk with a handful of singed bread.

"Yeah, and orange juice," another commanded.

"Keep the coffee coming too," Snake instructed. He looked directly at Velma. "You bring it this time, sweetie pie."

Kelly pushed her coworker toward the counter. "She has work to do in the kitchen. I'll get it for you."

The six bikers stuffed themselves in reasonable silence. The snorting and lip smacking reminded Kelly of her father's hogs. At least they were momentarily distracted from the women.

Kelly snuck into the kitchen to use the phone. Marilyn had no explanation for Deputy Hanna's actions, but she assured the waitress that Sheriff Lansing would be there within the next ten minutes. As Kelly hung up the phone, trying to figure out what she could do to ward off the heathens in leather, a commotion started in the outer room. She looked out the order window.

The bikers were knocking over chairs and pushing tables out of their way.

"Hey, you out there!" Snake bellowed toward the street. "What the hell you lookin' at?"

All six bikers were rushing toward the front door. On

the sidewalk stood Deputy Hanna, studying one of the parked Harleys.

Kelly rushed from the kitchen to observe the action.

Once outside, Buck approached the deputy menacingly. "You got a problem there, Barney Fife?"

Gabe Hanna stood a respectable five-foot-eleven. His cowboy boots gave him another inch in height. Buck, obviously the leader of the group, still towered over him by two inches.

The deputy smiled pleasantly at the pack gathering around him. He had no problem recognizing the Cobra colors the bikers wore. "I don't have a problem, bud, but somebody does."

"Oh, yeah?" the man with the beard asked. "How's that?"

Gabe pointed at the Harley closest to him. "Looks to me like somebody's got a busted cylinder head. They're leaking oil all over the place."

Snake pushed past the deputy. "That's my chopper. There's nothin' wrong with it." He knelt for a better inspection. Oil was dripping down the manifold and gathering in a puddle beneath the cycle. "What the hell?" He checked his pants leg to see if oil had splattered his denim. The pants were dry. Snake took a threatening step toward the deputy. "You tryin' to pull somethin'?"

"What do you mean?"

"I'd have oil all over my jeans if the head was cracked."

"Not if it cracked after you parked. I don't know how far you guys ran this morning, but it was cold last night and it's still kind of chilly this morning. If your head gasket's worn, even a little moisture's going to crack the head if you're not careful."

"Who are you? Harley-Davidson junior?" Buck snorted.

"I've had my share of bikes," Gabe admitted. "My first

one was a '59 Knucklehead. I had to tear that thing apart once a month to keep it running."

"Yeah, well, this ain't no '59," Snake growled.

"I know," Gabe agreed. "It's a rebuilt '72 Super Glide: twelve hundred cc's, V-twin with overhead valves. It can probably hit sixty in under six seconds. I modified one like this down in Las Cruces."

"Las Cruces, huh?" Buck snorted. "Where in Las Cruces?"

"Ted Morley's Harley shop. We did a lot of work for bikers."

"Yeah, I know Ted." Buck nodded. He eyed the deputy for a moment, then glanced at Snake. "Start up your bike."

"What for? I ain't finished eatin' yet."

"I said start it up!" Buck snapped.

Grumbling, Snake straddled his motorcycle. He set his throttle to neutral and hit the kick-start. The engine sputtered for a second while he worked the gas feed. The motor revved higher, accompanied by a loud *whap-whap-whapping* sound. It resembled the noise of an engine without a muffler. Oil began leaking down the manifold. Snake shut off the engine.

"It didn't sound like that before!" he complained.

"Well, it sounds like that now!" Buck shouted. "When was the last time you even tuned that thing?"

"Six months ago."

"How old is that head gasket?" Gabe asked.

"I don't know," Snake whined. "It's the one they put on there when the engine was rebuilt, about four years ago."

Gabe shook his head. "Man, I tear mine apart and put a new one on at least once every two years."

"I heard you only had to replace those every fifty thousand miles," one of the other bikers observed.

"Yeah, if you're riding a Triumph or a Harley built after

'86. But the older models like these . . . I don't care what the books say. Twenty-four months, twenty-four thousand miles. Otherwise, you're going to be stuck out in the middle of nowhere like this."

"What do you mean?" Buck asked.

"There's no place around here that can fix that." The deputy gestured toward the leaking engine. "Where're you guys heading?"

"We're going to Durango."

Gabe thought for a moment, then shook his head slowly. "You may find somebody up there to help you, but you're talking about almost two hundred miles. And that's all mountain riding. I wouldn't do that to my bike."

"Can you fix it?" Snake asked eagerly.

"I probably could, if I had the parts. Trouble is, it would take a day or so for them to come in and I wouldn't have time until the weekend to get to it."

Buck studied the puddle under the cycle. "Where's the closest shop?"

"Santa Fe. A place called Centurians, down on Rodeo Road on the south side of town."

"Yeah, I know where you're talking about."

The biker with the beard pulled Buck aside. He hoped the deputy couldn't hear his whisper. "We can't go back to Santa Fe. Not after last night!"

Buck pulled himself away from the pleading grasp. "Relax. The cops will be looking for us everyplace but Santa Fe." He turned back to Gabe. "How far is it to Santa Fe from here?"

" 'Bout sixty miles."

Buck pointed at Snake's motorcycle. "Will it make it that far?"

"It should. He has a gallon capacity in the oil reserve. But the way that thing's leaking, I'd get a couple of quarts of oil anyway. I'd check the level every twenty-five miles or so."

The leader of the pack nodded. "Come on, boys. Let's go."

"What about breakfast?" Beard asked.

"It's probably cold by now," Buck said, throwing his leg over his chopper's seat. He noticed Kelly standing in the doorway. "Snake. Pay the lady."

"Why me?"

" 'Cause you don't know how to take care of your hog, that's why." Buck turned the starter and revved his engine to drown out any more protests from his companion.

Snake stomped over to Kelly and pulled out a roll of bills. He pealed off two twenties and stuffed them in the breast pocket of her waitress uniform.

By the time Snake started his engine, the other five motorcycles were already roaring. Buck nodded toward the deputy, his reluctant way of saying thanks, then turned his motorcycle toward the street. A moment later he was heading down Main Street in the direction of Santa Fe, followed by his companions.

6

AS THE COBRAS SPED TOWARD THE SOUTH SIDE OF town, Gabe could hear the wail of a police siren coming from the opposite direction. A second later, Sheriff Lansing came to a screeching halt in front of the diner. Right behind him a dented, rusting public health service truck with faded green paint skidded to a stop.

"What's going on?" Lansing shouted above the subsiding whine of his alarm.

"Not much, Sheriff." Gabe smiled.

Margarite came running over from her truck. "Is anything wrong?"

"Marilyn said there was trouble. Bikers or something," Lansing explained. "Why were you trying to keep up with me?"

"There might have been a medical emergency. I didn't know. You might have needed my help. You didn't say anything. You just took off."

Lansing turned back to his deputy. "I got here as fast as I could."

"Thanks for the backup, but nothing really happened." The deputy waved the sheriff's comment away. "They didn't stay very long."

Kelly stepped onto the sidewalk followed by Velma. "Don't let him kid you, Cliff. That group was bad news.

One of them almost raped Velma. I don't know how Deputy Hanna did it, but he got them to go away. That's all I wanted."

"Do we need to put an APB out on them?" the sheriff asked.

"The highway patrol already has." Gabe pulled the Comfax printout from his pocket and handed it to Lansing. "They're wanted by the Santa Fe police."

Lansing read the printout, then looked at his deputy. "If they're wanted in Santa Fe, why are they heading in that direction?"

Gabe shrugged. "I convinced them one of their bikes had a broken cylinder head. I told them the closest place to get it fixed was Santa Fe."

"I thought it was broken," Kelly interrupted. "There was oil all over the ground. And his engine sounded awful when he started it."

"You get the same effect when you loosen a spark plug." Gabe pulled a socket wrench from his pocket.

"What about all that oil?" Velma asked over Kelly's shoulder.

Gabe pulled an empty jar from his other pocket. The glass was streaked with a black, oily residue. "I just poured a little of this down the manifold and the rest on the ground. I got it from the Phillips Sixty-Six station."

"That's where you were going." Kelly nodded. "I owe you an apology. I thought you were hightailing it out of town 'cause you were chicken."

Gabe smiled sheepishly. "I suppose you're right about that. I certainly wasn't brave enough to try and arrest them by myself."

"No lawman in his right mind would," Lansing commented.

"While they were eating I crawled under the windows and tinkered with that one bike. When I was finished, I crawled out of the way, then walked back down the side-walk so they could see me. I knew they'd come out. Guys like that love their hogs better than their women."

"You really weren't kidding when you said you knew about motorcycles," Velma gushed.

Kelly could tell her coworker was already making designs on the young law enforcement officer. Velma's smarmy adulation was a prelude to eventually trapping her unwary prey in some dark corner, probably the rest room. Kelly said nothing for the moment.

Gabe shook his head. "No, I wasn't. I also know that half the guys who ride these things don't know anything about mechanics. I lucked out and found one who didn't."

Lansing couldn't hold back his smile. He was proud of his deputy's resourcefulness. "If it wasn't still breakfast time I'd buy you a beer. How 'bout a cup of coffee instead?"

"You can make that a Coke." Gabe nodded. "I think I'd better contact the state police first. Let them know their suspects are headed back to Santa Fe." He started for the Jeep he had parked around the corner.

"I'll wait for you in the diner." Lansing turned to Margarite. "Have you had breakfast yet?"

"I ate earlier," the doctor commented. "I thought you wanted me to look at that body, Lansing?"

"I do," Lansing admitted, "but he can wait until I've at least had my first cup of coffee."

Lansing and Margarite followed the waitresses into the diner.

"How old do you think Deputy Hanna is?" Velma whispered to her redheaded partner.

"Honey," Kelly cracked, "whatever it is, it's ten years younger than what you should be running around with."

"Humph!" Velma snorted, shaking her head indignantly. "What do you know?"

7

AS EDWARD HANIA STUDIED THE CONTRACT IN FRONT of him, Thad Berkeley glanced around the expensively decorated office. The room was cavernous, and despite the many times he'd been there, Berkeley always found something new to examine. The room was decorated in an eclectic mixture of modern art and Navajo relics. It reminded him of a Santa Fe art gallery, not a Farmington business office.

Berkeley knew he should be in no hurry. Hania was thorough. He would take as long as he wanted to read the material.

Thad couldn't complain. As the personal lawyer for one of the richest men in northwest New Mexico, he had done quite well for himself. That's only because Hania had done quite well for *himself*.

Edward Hania was an exception to everything that was considered normal in New Mexico. He was full-blooded Navajo and still lived on the reservation, but he had cut himself a sizable niche in the white man's world. Starting in his early twenties with ten used cars he sold on consignment, he opened Navajo Motors. Within ten years Navajo Motors expanded from one used car lot to five automobile dealerships in three states.

In the mid-seventies Hania started buying land on speculation and opened High Desert Realty. Berkeley could only shake his head in wonder over that coup. Hania had grabbed every piece of available real estate within fifty miles of Farmington. When the boom times of the eighties hit, he sold off almost all of it, despite Berkeley's protests. Hania told him, "Don't worry. I'll get it all back."

Son of a gun, if he didn't.

When the bottom dropped out of the market in 1986, Hania was there with ample cash reserves. He bought back his former properties at a quarter of his original selling price. Then when interest rates dropped in 1990, he began selling again, doubling his money.

Berkeley could only marvel at Hania's business savvy. And the rewards Hania reaped went well beyond the confines of his bank account. He had been a sitting member on the Navajo Tribal Council for ten years. He was a former president of the Farmington Rotary Club and cochairman for the Governor's Council on Economic Development.

Despite his many public and business obligations, Edward Hania always had a new project under development. His current enterprise was to create a shadow company to manage the proposed logging on the Navajo reservation.

Hania looked up from the contract. "According to section two, you have RMR retaining all financial rights to the timber. I thought we were going to buy the raw timber, then deliver it to RMR and sell it ourselves."

"I've already convinced the tribal lawyers to go with this. It's pretty standard stuff," Berkeley said, setting down his cup of coffee. "By signing over the rights to RMR from the outset, you won't be seen as an unnecessary middleman out to skim the profits. This is simply a management package. We supervise the operations. We run the books. We do the hiring and firing. We arrange the transport of the timber from the cutting sites to the sawmill."

Hania smiled. "And as the management company, we couldn't, in good faith, recommend that the Navajo Nation sink good money into logging trucks."

"Exactly." Berkeley nodded, echoing his employer's smile. "We'll subcontract that out . . ."

". . . to ourselves," Hania completed the statement, "and set the fees." He closed the cover of the contract. "I think we have a winner here. If you think the tribal lawyers are satisfied, let's get copies out to the council members this afternoon."

"I don't know," Berkeley said doubtfully. "Don't you think we're jumping the gun? Half the reservation is still against the proposal. There may not be any timber cutting at all."

"I know there are some traditionalists. There are also tree-huggers and bark-eaters like Tallmountain floating around. But what's going to tip the balance in our favor is this proposal. Nobody on the reservation knows how to run an operation like that. They're scared. If we can show them that we'll run the business and all they have to do is rake in the bucks, it will be a done deal within a week."

The lawyer gave his client a skeptical glance. "Are you sure the rest of the Navajo Nation is as motivated by money as you?"

"Everyone's motivated by money, Thad. That's what makes this such a wonderful world to live in. You can always count on everybody else's greed and laziness."

The buzzer sounded on Hania's intercom. "Yes?"

"I have Mr. Elverson on line two, Mr. Hania," the secretary reported. "Should I tell him you're in conference?"

"Not at all. I'll be with him in just a moment." Hania looked up at Berkeley. "That's all I have for you right now. My only worry had been the tribal lawyers and you've taken care of that. I'll talk to you later."

"Sure." Picking up his briefcase, Berkeley left the office.

"Sam," Hania said into the telephone, sounding as cheery as he could, "this is a surprise. I thought you were going to be in Denver this week."

"A few things came up around the office, but I'll be leaving in the morning," Elverson commented.

"So, what's going on?"

"I need to tell the board of directors something tomorrow, Ed. They're getting tired of this wishy-washy stance your tribal council is taking. Are you guys going to cut trees or not?"

"I'm working the issue," Hania snapped.

"So am I," Elverson snapped back. "I've pulled out all the stops on my end. I've done everything I can physically do to get this project going. But the board wants an answer and soon."

"Listen, Sam," Hania stalled, "there's a management proposal going to the council this afternoon. It's going to take a day or two for the council to study my plan. When they see what a good deal it is for the reservation, they'll have to vote in favor of logging."

"What if you're wrong?"

"I'm not wrong," Hania huffed. "These are my people. I know how to handle them, but it takes time. Tell your board of directors we'll have the deal ready in a week."

"I'll stall them if I can," Elverson said wearily. "But I'll tell you right now, you're running out of time. Rocky Mountain Resources has twenty-five million set aside for logging operations and that money has to start flowing soon. If the Navajo Council can't get off its collective ass and make a decision, we'll take our business somewhere else. We're already talking to the Uintah Tribe. They have plenty of timberland east of Salt Lake City."

"All I'm asking for is one week." Hania hoped he didn't sound like he was begging.

"It's already been six months!" Elverson snorted.

"Then one more week shouldn't matter, should it?"

There was a long silence on the other end of the phone. "Fax me a copy of your management proposal," Elverson said finally, with a sigh. "I need to show the board something tomorrow. If it's a solid plan, something that will get your council to sign our contract, I can probably buy you another week."

"That's all I ask," Hania said, relieved. "My secretary has your fax number. You'll have it in your hands in ten minutes."

"Right. I'll let you know the board's decision." Elverson hung up the phone without bothering to say good-bye.

Hania studied the phone he was holding. He wasn't sure how much bluff was behind the threat of RMR dealing with the Uintah Tribe. He'd used the same tactic himself: Work with me now, or I'll take my business elsewhere. With millions of dollars at stake, it wasn't a threat Hania wanted to take lightly. He hung up the phone and pressed the intercom button.

"June, I have a contract in here I need faxed."

"I'll be right in, Mr. Hania."

Hania stood and straightened his tie. He knew the council would see things his way. All it would take is a little arm twisting and he was a master at that.

8

THE LAS PALMAS MEMORIAL FUNERAL HOME WAS SEL-
dom a busy place. With barely twelve thousand residents
in the entire county and with two other funeral homes
vying in competition, Burt Sellers just managed to keep his
parlor in business. He was secretly grateful when the rescue
unit arrived with the unfortunate pedestrian. It had been
two weeks since his last customer had passed through.

Sellers turned on the light to the refrigeration room. The
fluorescent tubes glowed dimly.

"Would you like for me to move the body to the embalming room?" Burt asked solemnly. "The lighting is
much better in there."

"I think that would be a good idea." Margarite nodded.
"Sheriff, could you help me shift the body onto the gurney?"

"Yeah, no problem."

Sellers rolled the stainless steel gurney over to the wall
that held six two-foot by two-foot doors. The mortician
locked the swivel wheels on the gurney, then opened the
door to the chamber containing the deceased. Pulling out
the long tray that held the body, the funeral director motioned for Lansing to grab the feet. The dead man was still
encased in the body bag the paramedics had used that
morning.

With a single heave the dead man was transferred to the gurney. Sellers unlocked the wheels and began pushing the cart toward the adjoining room. Margarite and Lansing followed.

The embalming room resembled an operating suite in a hospital. The walls and floor were white tile and numerous exotic-looking devices were situated around the chamber. Lansing knew the different apparatuses were used for removing blood and injecting embalming fluid. The place had an antiseptic smell to it.

Sellers wheeled the gurney under a bank of incandescent lights suspended from the ceiling. Locking the wheels again, he turned on the lights. The body was showered with an intense yellow-white glow. Despite the brilliance, Lansing found the bulbs gave off relatively little heat.

"Would you like for me to remain behind?" Sellers asked.

"No, I think we can handle this," Margarite replied.

Sellers indicated a supply cabinet in one corner. "You'll find gloves, masks, and instruments in there. There's an intercom on the wall. If you need anything, you can buzz me in my office."

"Thanks, Burt," Lansing said. "We'll let you know when we're done."

Sellers left the chamber, pulling the door closed behind him. Margarite retrieved operating gowns, gloves, and masks from the cabinet. When she and her less-than-willing assistant were properly attired, she unzipped the body bag.

Lansing noticed Margarite's involuntary shudder when she first looked at the head. He couldn't blame her. It was a grotesque scramble of blood, bone, and tissue loosely held together by shredded skin. The sheriff did his best to avoid looking directly at the mess.

Margarite recovered quickly. "Help me get the body out of the bag."

In a matter of seconds the body bag was draped over the sides of the gurney. The dead man was dressed in denim jeans, cowboy boots, flannel shirt, and a leather jacket.

The doctor unzipped the jacket, then unbuttoned the shirt.

"Let's see if we can get the coat and shirt off," she directed.

Early signs of rigor mortis were setting in and the man's fingers were already stiff. The arm and shoulder joints were limber enough that they could be moved. Rolling the body toward Lansing, Margarite removed the jacket sleeve from the arm. She stopped and examined the coat.

"Are you going to remove the shirt?" the sheriff asked, hoping to let go of the body as soon as he could.

"Can you see this?" The doctor indicated the dead man's back.

Lansing looked over the top of the body. The lining of the jacket was soaked with dried blood, as was the shirt.

"Let's roll him onto his stomach," Margarite suggested.

The gurney was narrow, and rolling the body onto its stomach sounded easier than it turned out to be. Eventually they managed the maneuver. Margarite gave the material on the shirt a little pull. The cloth was securely plastered to the skin by dried blood. She then examined the jacket. After close scrutiny she found two small holes in the leather. She showed them to Lansing.

"These could be bullet holes," she observed. "Judging from the saturation, it looks like your victim was shot and bled to death." She looked up at Lansing. "Do you want me to do a formal autopsy?"

Lansing shook his head. "No. Not yet. I need to get blood and tissue samples, photos. . . . I don't want to disturb anything else on the body if we can help it." He studied the body for a moment. "I'm going to need some help from the crime lab boys."

"Do you want to put him back on the slab?"

"In a few minutes." Lansing stepped to the wall and pushed the intercom button.

"Yes?" came the tinny response.

"Burt, this is Cliff. Call my office and have Marilyn send over a fingerprint kit."

"Sure thing."

Margarite gave him a quizzical look.

"It'll be a week before anyone from the crime lab shows up," Lansing explained. "In the meantime we might as well try to find out who this is."

9

"A TABLE FOR TWO?" CHRISTINE ASKED.

"No, we'll need something bigger," Lansing said, removing his hat and hanging it on a peg along the front wall. "Deputy Hanna's going to join us."

"I'll get you one of the big tables in the middle then." The hostess smiled, grabbing three menus from behind her counter. "This way, please."

Lansing and Margarite followed Paco's daughter into the dimly lit dining room of the cantina.

Las Palmas did not have a wide variety of cuisine. The Dixie Queen, a relic from the early fifties, had burgers, shakes, and carhops. The Las Palmas Diner had good breakfasts and halfway decent open-face turkey sandwiches drenched in gravy. And then there was Paco's Cantina. The sheriff had done his share of traveling and he knew for a fact it was the best Mexican food in northern New Mexico. It rivaled anything Albuquerque or Santa Fe could offer.

There was another restaurant building in town. Unfortunately, it rotated from being a steak house, to being a barbecue house, to being closed. Rumor had it that it would reopen as another steak house that summer. The sheriff knew it was destined for failure. Not that the food wouldn't be any good. It probably would be. In the first month it would do a booming business as people checked it out.

Then, after the newness wore off, people would settle back into their old habits and frequent the established eating places. In a county of twelve thousand and a city of twelve hundred, the economy could support just so many restaurants. Three seemed to be the optimal number for Las Palmas.

"Can I get you something to drink?" the hostess asked as her two customers sat.

"Iced tea, please," the doctor said.

Lansing looked at his watch. It was five o'clock. "It's been a long day. I think I'm ready for a beer."

"Corona?"

"Yeah, with a lime."

It was fairly early for the normal supper crowd and the cantina was almost empty. Lansing felt comfortable that there were no prying ears close to them. When the hostess left, he leaned toward Carerra. "You sure you have to go back tonight?"

"You know I do, Lansing. I have to be at San Francisco Pueblo by nine tomorrow morning. Besides, I still have to put away my supplies tonight."

"I know," the sheriff said, trying not to sound disappointed. "But it was a shot."

Margarite had planned on spending only the morning in Las Palmas. The inspection of the body in the funeral home delayed her plans. Having to wait for the second Greyhound Bus to retrieve her medical supplies prolonged her stay even further.

Fortunately, it had been a quiet day at Burnt Mesa Pueblo. Margarite's receptionist/secretary was also an LPN qualified to handle minor emergencies. Margarite called her clinic to see if anything significant was happening. The only mishap was a cut hand that required three stitches. Her nurse handled that with no problem. Margarite left a number where she could be reached, but her nurse evidently didn't need the help.

Margarite found other things to occupy her time. While Lansing went about his official duties, she spent the afternoon at the Las Palmas clinic helping Dr. Tanner and reading his most current medical journals. She had arranged for an early dinner with Lansing so that she could start back for the pueblo before dark.

"You know, Lansing, the public health service owes me a couple of days off." The sheriff perked up at the news. "I was thinking of making it a three-day weekend."

"How are you going to work that? I thought you had to be on call."

Margarite smiled. "After I helped him all afternoon, John Tanner asked me if there was some way he could return the favor. I asked him to be on call for the three days I want to take off. I'll work tomorrow at San Francisco. Thursday, I'll get everything squared away at Burnt Mesa. That will give me Friday through Sunday to do anything I want."

Although neither one of them seemed to be ready to make a lasting commitment, their relationship had been anything but platonic. Images of a nice hotel in Santa Fe equipped with room service flashed through Lansing's mind. The sheriff smiled warily. "And what would that be?"

Margarite pointed her finger at him threateningly. "You've been promising for six months to take me on a fishing trip by horse pack. I'm ready to go."

The vision of the hotel exploded in Lansing's brain. "What?"

"You promised me."

"I know I did," he stalled. "But I said we'd do it as soon as it got warm."

"It hit sixty-five today. How much warmer does it have to be?"

Lansing had to think fast. As much as he enjoyed camping, he didn't consider it his avocation. Once a month was all right with him and he had already spent the previous weekend in a tent with his son. "For decent fishing, we want to hit the mountain streams. At night it's still getting well below freezing up there."

"We can always build a big fire and"—she smiled seductively—"zip our sleeping bags together."

As much as he hated fishing, Margarite's last suggestion forced the sheriff to rethink his position. There was a lot to be said for body warmth. "Margarite, the best I can offer you right now is a firm maybe."

"Oh?" The word sounded more like an expression of anger than a question.

"I don't know how much work this homicide investigation is going to be. The longer I wait the colder the trail gets, and I have a full-time job to take care of on top of that."

Christine brought their drinks and set them on the table. "Would you like to order now?"

Lansing said, "No."

Simultaneously, Margarite said, "Yes." There was a touch of impatience in her voice. "I'll take the taco platter."

Christine wrote down the order. "Sheriff?"

"I'll wait." He took a sip of his beer and waited for the hostess to leave. When they were alone again, he asked his partner, "Are you in a hurry?"

Margarite snapped her cloth napkin to shake it straight. "You have an investigation. I shouldn't keep you from your business." She spread the napkin on her lap without looking at him. She took a sip of her tea, then glanced casually around the room as if she were bored.

Lansing wondered how he always ended up on Margarite's bad side. "Well, if you're finished manipulating the situation . . . Can I call you tomorrow and let you know?"

Margarite gave him an icy stare. "I don't manipulate. I just get angry."

"You were trying to get me to feel guilty, weren't you?"

"Yes," she said, trying to maintain her stoic expression. "Did it work?"

Lansing gave her a half smile. "Yeah."

"Good." The expression on her face softened. "In that case, yes, you can call me tomorrow."

"Even if I come up with the wrong answer?"

Margarite hesitated. "I'll have to think about that."

Deputy Hanna entered the dining room from the hostess's reception area.

"Over here, Gabe." Lansing waved, grateful the fishing issue was momentarily postponed.

Gabe removed his jacket and hung it on the back of his chair before sitting. "Dr. Carerra" he nodded toward her— "I thought you were leaving early today."

"Circumstances beyond my control." She smiled. "Any word about your motorcycle gang?"

"Oh, yeah." He pulled a piece of paper from a jacket pocket and unfolded it. "This just came over the Comfax." He handed the paper to Lansing.

The sheriff studied the note. "It looks like those were the felons the Santa Fe police were looking for. Two of them were injured in a shootout with the highway patrol. The other four surrendered." Lansing looked up from the printout. "Damned good work, Gabe."

The deputy smiled sheepishly. "Thanks."

"You keep that up, the state police will be begging you to join them. You may not have to wait for an opening."

"State police?" Margarite asked.

"Yeah," Gabe admitted. "I've got an application in to them, but the waiting list is, like, two years."

"I knew that when I hired Gabe," Cliff explained. "He was fresh out of the academy and I needed a deputy. He'll fill in here until something better comes along. He gets the experience and I get the help."

"But why the state police?"

Gabe shrugged. "If you want to know the truth, Doctor, it's the only job in the world where they pay you to ride a motorcycle. That's why I got into law enforcement to begin with."

Margarite looked at Lansing. "You knew that?"

The sheriff nodded. "I'll take a deputy who loves motorcycles over a deputy that loves guns any day of the week."

Christine, who had been busy with other customers, approached their table. "Can I get you something to drink, Deputy Hanna?" She sounded almost embarrassed to ask the question.

"Yeah. A Coke, please."

"Okay." She giggled, hurrying from the table.

"I think you have an admirer," Margarite observed.

"Christine? Aw, she's just a kid."

"I think she's a senior this year," Lansing thought out loud. "That makes her . . . what? Seventeen, eighteen."

"Come on, Sheriff." Gabe felt his face flush with embarrassment. "She's in high school. I'm twenty-three. I'm way too old for her."

"I don't know if you've noticed it yet, Gabe," Margarite commented, "but Las Palmas is pretty small. The pickings are kind of slim around here." She nudged Lansing. "Sometimes you have to settle for what's available."

Lansing gave her a what's-that-supposed-to-mean look, but said nothing.

Gabe missed the exchange going on in front of him. "I think I'd better stick with learning my job for now. Besides, with the hours we have to keep, there's not much time for dating anyway."

"Yeah," Margarite joked. "I'll second that statement."

"You're pushing it, Doctor," Lansing snorted.

Margarite decided she had teased Lansing enough and changed the subject. "Well, if you get hired by the state police, are you going to try for Farmington or Gallup?"

"No. Why would I ask for those towns?"

"They're close to the reservation."

"So?" The question was curt.

Margarite was taken aback by the response. "I'm sorry. I had heard that you were Navajo. . . ."

"I am." Gabe suddenly became very apologetic. "I'm half Navajo, but I don't have any ties to the reservation. I don't even know if I have any relatives there." He thought for a moment before continuing. "My father left the reservation when he was eighteen and joined the military. I grew up as an army brat. Got to see a lot of the world. Got to do a lot of things. But I never learned a damned thing about being Navajo. My dad never talked about it."

"How'd you end up in New Mexico?"

"The old man died about five years ago. When he did, Mom moved us to Mesquite . . ."

"South of Las Cruces," Margarite completed. "I know the town."

"Yeah. She had family down there and we didn't have anywhere else to go."

Gabe's story was interrupted when Christine brought his Coca-Cola. "Here's your drink, Gabe," she tittered. "Are you folks ready to order?"

"Just a few more minutes," the sheriff suggested. "And I'll have another." He held up his empty bottle.

"And could you hold my order until the others are ready?" the doctor added.

"Certainly, Doctor."

After Christine left, Gabe continued, trying to sound a little more chipper. "Anyway . . . I tried community college for a couple of years, but me and the books just didn't get along. I had helped my dad mechanic on things since I was old enough to hold a wrench, so I knocked around at auto and cycle shops for a couple of years. When that got old, I thought I'd try the police academy." He picked up his drink. "And here I am."

"Hi, Gabe!" Velma sang.

The three looked up to see Velma and John Tanner approaching the table.

"I mentioned to John we'd be eating here tonight," Margarite explained. "I suggested they might join us."

"No problem," Lansing said, standing as the new arrivals neared. "How's it going, Doc?"

"Fine, Sheriff."

As the two men shook hands Velma hurried and commandeered a chair next to the deputy. Gabe had her full attention.

"Evening, Velma."

"Oh, hi, Cliff," Velma said rather offhandedly. "So, how was your day, Deputy Hanna?" she cooed.

Tanner rolled his eyes as he took a chair next to Margarite. There was nothing permanent in his relationship with Velma, so he was used to her being distracted by a new pair of pants in town. Her infatuation would last a week at best. Velma didn't carry on with other men to make him jealous. They both knew he would finish his contract with San Phillipe County and be on his way to some big city back East. She just liked men in general and couldn't help herself. After her obsession waned, they would get back to their standard routine, which consisted mostly of sex.

"Looks like your deputy has more than one admirer in this town," Margarite whispered to Lansing.

"Yeah." The sheriff nodded. "Fortunately, I make him wear a gun, so he at least stands a fighting chance."

10

"YES, ROGER," LANSING SIGHED INTO THE PHONE. "I understand it's costing you money, but there's not a damned thing I can do about it right now. . . ." He listened for a moment while the complaint continued. "I know. I know where you're coming from, but this is the sheriff's office, not the animal control shelter. . . ."

The sheriff was interrupted by a series of threats from the other end of the line. "You do that, Roger," Lansing said, breaking in on his caller. "Call the county commissioners. Call the governor. You can call the president, for all I care. If you want to run against me next election, go ahead. Then you can handle calls like this and I'll go fishing!"

Lansing slammed down the receiver. The clock on his desk read nine o'clock. He had been at work for an hour and that was already his sixth phone call. Picking up his coffee mug, he went to the dayroom to refill it. He was starting to lose his temper with his callers and that was something he never did.

After he filled his cup, he walked out to Marilyn's reception counter. Marilyn was on the phone talking to yet another complainant.

The receptionist looked up from her desk. "One moment, I'll see if the sheriff is still here. . . ."

Lansing shook his head vigorously.

"I'm sorry. He just stepped out. . . ." She paused while the caller explained the situation. "Okay. I understand. I'll see that he gets the message." She hung up the phone.

"Coyotes?" Lansing asked.

"Coyotes," Marilyn confirmed. "That was the foreman up at the McGaffrey ranch. He claims a coyote unlatched the barn door *and* the corral gate and ran all their horses off."

The sheriff was exasperated. "A coyote can't do that."

"He claims the only tracks they could find were coyote tracks."

Lansing shook his head. "That's the seventh call this morning and every last one of them had to do with coyotes. . . . It's mid-April. Everyone around here knows that's when the coyote pups start showing up. The parents are out looking for food."

"Well, there must be a gaggle of pups this year," Marilyn observed, "because we've never had complaints like this before." She picked up her telephone log to review the calls. "Two calls for overturned garbage cans; one dead cat; one dead dog—and a German shepherd at that; a raided chicken coop; three missing calves; and now a herd of scattered horses."

"Roger Kellim wants me to get up a posse and hunt down the varmints," the sheriff complained. "Hell, he has horses. He has traps and he knows how those animals operate. He sure as hell doesn't need me."

"Well, you know Roger," Marilyn said, shaking her finger. "If there's some way he can get someone else to do his work for him, he'll find it. Especially if it's going to save him some money."

The sheriff took a sip of his coffee. "Yeah, I suppose."

Gabe entered the office carrying a Coke can. "Morning, Sheriff."

"Hi, Gabe." Lansing nodded. "Anything go on last night?"

"Naw. It was pretty quiet." He thought for a moment. "Although, I did see a strange thing. . . . I was on patrol north of town. . . . I guess I wasn't paying enough attention driving down the road. There was a coyote in the middle of the highway, right there in the middle of my headlights. . . . God, I can still see those eyes glaring at me. I slammed on my brakes, but it was too late. I hit the poor thing."

Lansing shrugged. "There's nothing unusual about that. Evidently there are plenty of coyotes to go around this year."

"That wasn't the strange part," Gabe continued. "I stopped and went back to pull the carcass off the road . . . but there wasn't a carcass."

"You probably knocked him clean off the highway," Marilyn interjected.

"I looked . . . both sides. Finally, I said the hell with it. I turned around to go back to the Jeep and there was that coyote, standing right next to the car, staring at me again."

"You sure it was the same animal?" Lansing sounded doubtful.

"I know it was the same animal," Gabe said adamantly. "And he wasn't the least bit afraid of me. You know what he did?" The other two shook their heads. "He lifted his hind leg and pissed on the front tire. Then he turned around and trotted off into the brush." His eyes were wide with amazement. "Sheriff, I don't know much about coyotes. Do they all act like that?"

Lansing couldn't help himself. He looked at Marilyn and started snickering. Then she started snickering. In a matter of seconds they were both laughing out loud. Gabe had to wait for an answer.

"I've heard a lot of good coyote stories," the sheriff finally said, wiping a tear from his eye, "but that's one of the better ones."

"You don't believe me?"

"Oh, just the opposite." Lansing sighed. "That sounds exactly like something a coyote would do. That was his way of telling you he didn't care for the way you almost hit him."

The deputy wanted to argue the point. He *had* hit the animal. He was sure of it. Of course, if he had, the coyote couldn't have peed on his car. He decided to drop the matter.

The phone on Marilyn's desk rang. Lansing waved his hand, indicating he was still not in the office. "Gabe, I'm going out on patrol. You're going to sit here in the office and field the next hundred complaints."

"San Phillipe Sheriff's Office," Marilyn said into the phone. "May I help you?" She listened quietly for a moment. "Yes. Sheriff Lansing is in. Just a moment and I'll transfer you." Lansing gave Marilyn a dirty look that she ignored. "It's the state police. They have an ID on those fingerprints you faxed them yesterday."

"Oh!"

Lansing hurried to his office and picked up the phone. Gabe stood in the doorway and listened to the conversation.

"Sheriff Lansing . . . You do? That was quick work. . . ." He picked up a pen and began scribbling on a piece of paper. "Yeah, yeah, I've got it. . . . Do you have a current address?" He continued to write. "Yeah, I've got it all written down."

He put down the pen and leaned back in his seat. "Right now I don't have anything. Just a D.B. . . . Well, at least I have a name. It'll give me a starting point. . . . Yeah, whenever you guys get the chance I'd like you to pick up the body for an autopsy. . . ." He listened for a moment. "Okay

. . . and thanks for the help." He hung up the phone and stared at his notes.

"What'd you find out?" the deputy asked.

"Evidently he's some guy from the Navajo reservation. The State Bureau of Investigation had his fingerprints on file. All they had to do was run a computer cross-check. He spent eighteen months in prison back in the sixties for possession of marijuana. I can't figure out what he was doing around here, though. The reservation's a hundred and twenty miles from here."

"They give you a name?"

"Yeah." The sheriff nodded. "Tallmountain. Walter Tallmountain."

"You're kidding!"

Lansing looked up, surprised at Gabe's interest. "You know him?"

"No, but . . . just a minute."

Gabe hurried into the dayroom and dug through the stack of newspapers from the previous morning. A moment later he was back in Lansing's office. "Look at this." He pointed to the article on the front page of the *Farmington News*.

Lansing skimmed the article that talked about the Navajo Tribal Council and logging issues. He stopped when he reached the name of Walter Tallmountain. Realizing his deputy might have stumbled onto something, he went back and reread the story in more detail.

When he was finished, Lansing looked up at his subordinate. "I don't know what's going on here, but let's keep this under wraps until I can make some phone calls."

"Yes, sir . . ." Gabe hesitated. "Do you still want me to stay in the office and take complaint calls?"

"No, that's all right. Go ahead and start your rounds. It looks like I might be here for a while." He picked up his phone and pushed the intercom button. "Marilyn, get me the number for the Navajo Tribal Police. I'll hold." He stopped his deputy before he was through the door. "Gabe, good job. You're becoming a damn fine policeman whether you like it or not."

Gabe smiled and nodded, then headed for his patrol Jeep.

11

GABE HANNA'S DAYS OFF ROTATED. ONE WEEK HE might have Monday and Tuesday free, the next week, Wednesday and Thursday. About once a month he'd get a whole weekend to himself. The same went for Jack Rivera, the other full-time deputy.

It was Wednesday, which meant Jack would be back to work the next day. They'd overlap for a day, then Gabe would get Friday and Saturday for his days off.

Gabe was parked on a dirt road next to Highway 15, watching for speeders. That time of year, early spring, and that time of day, early afternoon, there didn't seem to be much traffic. Gabe occupied his time by studying a map of northern New Mexico. Since it was warming up, he thought he might pull his motorcycle out and take a two-day cruise through the mountains. This was all new territory to him and he was interested in seeing what it held.

The radar gun on his dashboard was pointed indifferently toward the north and gave off a monotonous beep every five seconds. Suddenly the radar unit started sounding off as it picked up a target heading south.

Gabe threw the map onto the seat next to him and grabbed the detector. A bright red pickup truck was tearing down the highway toward the deputy. Even without the radar, Gabe could tell the driver was speeding.

The radar gun registered seventy-six miles per hour as the truck whizzed past.

The deputy started his engine, then threw on his lights and siren. Gabe didn't like giving out speeding tickets. He supposed that was because he had gotten so many himself. Highway 15 had a posted speed limit of fifty-five. Gabe usually gave drivers a ten-mile-per-hour leeway. It was open country and a clear, straight road. Sixty-five seemed safe enough for him. But seventy-six miles per hour pushed even Hanna's tolerance.

Once he was on the blacktop, Gabe floored the pedal. By the time he got up to speed, the truck was already a half mile in front of him.

Gabe was going ninety and barely closing when the driver of the truck decided to give up the chase. When the truck began to slow, so did he. He wanted to keep a safe distance, just in case the truck came to an abrupt halt.

The driver of the truck made a miscalculation about his speed. The vehicle was still going too fast when it pulled onto the shoulder. When the brakes were applied, the back end of the truck began to skid sideways, kicking up enough dirt and gravel to create a dust screen.

Gabe could see the driver desperately trying to turn the steering wheel to straighten out. The truck skidded side-ways until the back wheels slammed into a drainage ditch next to the shoulder.

The deputy stopped his Jeep and jumped out. Running through the cloud of dust, he wasn't sure what he would find. He was hoping for nothing more than a stranded truck.

The dust was still stirring when he grabbed the handle to the driver's door. It was locked.

He pounded on the door. "Are you all right?"

At first there was no response.

Gabe pounded again. "Can you unlock the door?"

He hesitated for a moment, wondering if he should try the passenger side. Then he heard a click as the door was unlocked. He pulled the door open.

The driver was too shaken to unlatch the seat belt. Gabe reached across and unsnapped the buckle. Trembling violently, the driver almost fell from the cab into the deputy's arms.

At first Gabe thought the driver was a boy; the hair was close-cropped and Gabe stood almost a head taller.

"Are you all right?" he asked.

The driver nodded. "I think so."

Gabe realized he was holding a woman.

The driver suddenly regained her composure and pulled away. She turned to check the condition of her truck.

"This is just great." She sniffed. "I'll bet I broke an axle."

"Why don't you come over and sit in my Jeep for a moment," the deputy offered.

"Yeah," the woman said, wiping something from her eye. "Okay."

She started toward the Jeep, then stopped. "Let me get my purse. You probably want to see a driver's license or something." She reached inside the truck to retrieve her pocketbook, then followed the deputy to his car.

Gabe held the door open and she slipped into the front seat. Wanting to reassure her that everything was on the up-and-up, Gabe left her door open so she wouldn't feel as if he were trapping her. He walked around to the driver's side.

Picking up the microphone to his radio, he began talking: "Dispatch, this is Patrol Two."

"Patrol Two," Marilyn responded, "go ahead."

"Yeah, Marilyn. I have a single-vehicle accident on Highway 15 approximately ten miles north of town. No injuries. Looks like a 1989 Chevy 4-×-2. It's stuck in a ditch. Could you call Ed Rodriguez and get a tow truck out here?"

"Dispatch copies."

"Patrol Two out." Gabe fixed the microphone in its clip and glanced at the woman sitting next to him. It was his first chance to get a good look at her. She was definitely Native American, high cheekbones, reddish-brown skin. He had no idea what her tribe might be. One day he would learn to tell the difference between a Navajo and a Hopi or a Navajo and a Sioux. But not today.

What he did know, aside from the fact that she was Native American, was that she was beautiful. The short hair, something he wouldn't have expected, accentuated her features. He also noted, though, that she had been crying.

"Are you sure you're all right?"

"I'm fine," she insisted, digging through her pocketbook. A moment later she produced her driver's license. "I know you hear excuses all the time. I just didn't realize how fast I was going. My mind was on other things." She handed the license to Gabe.

The deputy hadn't made up his mind about issuing a ticket. He was sure the woman was suitably shaken by the experience to take it easy in the future. He was about to ask her where she was going in such a hurry when he noticed the name on the laminated card she had handed him: Kimberly Tallmountain. He wasn't sure what he was supposed to say now.

Gabe returned the license. "Are your keys still in the truck?"

Kimberly nodded, surprised at getting her license back.

"We can leave them there. Ed will make sure you get everything." He motioned for her to close her door. He started his engine, then pulled onto the highway.

They rode in silence for a few minutes. Finally, Gabe

ventured to ask, "Walter Tallmountain . . . I take it he was a relative of yours?"

The woman nodded. "My father." She quickly turned her head away from the deputy.

Gabe felt awkward. "We'll go straight to the mortuary, if you'd like."

"Yeah," she agreed, keeping her face hidden. "That will be fine."

To Gabe, the ten-minute drive into town seemed like an hour. He radioed ahead to let Marilyn know he was on his way to the mortuary with Walter Tallmountain's daughter. He also requested that Ed tow the damaged truck to the Phillips 66 station. Gabe would check on the vehicle later.

After the call to dispatch, Gabe and his passenger rode in silence. He wondered if it was possible to feel someone else's pain. He was certain he could feel hers.

When they stopped in front of the mortuary, Kimberly took a deep breath, then opened the door and stepped out. She was surprised that the deputy got out as well. They were strangers and he wasn't obligated to go in with her. She said nothing, but Gabe suspected she appreciated the company.

Kimberly Tallmountain had complete control of herself by the time they reached the mortuary office. She held her head erect and betrayed none of her feelings, acting completely businesslike. She explained who she was to Burt Sellers. She wanted to make a positive identification of the body and, if it was indeed her father, make arrangements for transport back to the reservation.

"Miss Tallmountain," Burt said soothingly. "I know how you must feel, but I don't think your looking at the body is such a good idea."

"And just how am I supposed to know if it's my father?"

"The tribal police told you he was ID'd by his finger-prints. Correct?"

"Yes," the woman replied suspiciously. "So?"

"His other features were"—Sellers picked his words care-fully—"damaged. I'm afraid fingerprints were the only way he could be identified."

"I want to see my father," she demanded.

Sellers gave Gabe a pleading look. All the deputy could do was shrug. "I believe she has a right to see him, if she wants," he said.

Sellers let out a reluctant sigh. "This way, please."

He led them to the refrigeration units in the basement. This was Gabe's first official visit to the Las Palmas "morgue." When he had first arrived in town, Lansing gave him the twenty-five-cent tour of their territory, which in-cluded the mortuary. There had been no reason for Gabe to visit the place since then.

The dim glow of the fluorescent lights gave the room an eerie look. Gabe felt a chill run through his spine. He attributed it to the clammy atmosphere.

Sellers opened the door and pulled out the tray. The man on the slab was cocooned in the body bag once again. Sellers looked at Kimberly to see if she was ready. Setting her jaw, the woman nodded.

He carefully unzipped the bag, then draped the plastic open.

When Kimberly saw what was left of the corpse's head she let out a cry, buried her face in her hands, and quickly turned to Gabe. He put his arms around her and held her tightly. She was trembling violently.

"That can't be my father. . . ." she whimpered. "I don't want it to be my father."

Gabe could only stare at the grotesque mess. He felt abhorrence and fascination at the same time. "Maybe you can recognize the clothes," he suggested softly. He motioned Sellers to cover the dead man's head. The mortician grabbed a towel from a nearby shelf and covered everything above the shoulders.

"You want to take a look?"

Kimberly thought for a moment, then nodded. "I'll try."

Sellers unzipped the bag all the way down to the feet. Kimberly only had to look at the midsection. "That's his belt buckle . . . and his jacket." She turned away from the body. "I don't have to see any more." She pulled away from Gabe and headed for the stairs.

"Thanks, Mr. Sellers," Gabe said. He hurried after the woman, certain that she didn't need to be alone at that moment.

Gabe and Kim emerged onto the main floor of the funeral home. They were surprised to find five men standing around looking somewhat impatient. Three of the men wore highway patrol uniforms. Two were in suits.

"Gabe!" one of the patrolmen said.

The deputy recognized Marty Hernandez. "Officer Hernandez."

"Do you know where Mr. Sellers is?"

"He's downstairs. He should be up in a minute." Gabe was bewildered about the new arrivals. "What's going on?"

"These gentlemen are here to claim the D.B. Sheriff Lansing found yesterday."

"What?" Kim blurted.

"The dead body," one of the men in suits said. "We're taking it down to Santa Fe for forensic analysis."

"What for? It was an automobile accident." Kim turned to Gabe. "That's what the tribal police told me!"

Gabe had no idea what Lansing had passed along to the Navajo Police. He did know Lansing had requested the state crime lab to conduct the autopsy. Before he could say anything the second man in a suit produced a badge.

"I'm Special Agent Hobson with the State Bureau of

Investigation Drug Task Force. We have reason to believe Walter Tallmountain's death is linked to the cocaine trafficking on the Navajo reservation. The SBI is taking over the murder investigation."

"Murder!" Tallmountain's daughter sobbed. She turned to Gabe, tears welling in her eyes. "Drugs . . . What is he talking about?"

"I don't know." Gabe tried to sound as firm as possible. He looked at Hobson. "Have you talked to Sheriff Lansing about any of this?"

"I don't have to, kid," Hobson snorted. "I operate under the governor's authority."

"We were going to stop by the sheriff's office after we retrieved the body," Hernandez interrupted, trying to ward off a confrontation. "It's important we get the remains to the lab as soon as possible."

"That's my father you're talking about," Kim protested. "Don't I have any say-so in this?"

"No, ma'am," Hobson said flatly. "You don't." He turned to the other two uniformed officers. "You can load the body into the meat wagon."

Gabe put his arm around Kim to reassure her. "Detective, I think you can be a little more considerate. That is Miss Tallmountain's father you're talking about."

"Son, when it comes to drug dealers, I could give a damn what their family thinks."

12

"TO BE PERFECTLY BLUNT, SHERIFF," HOBSON CONTIN-
ued, "you have neither the resources nor the expertise to
handle this investigation. And from everything I've heard
so far, Tallmountain wasn't even killed in your county. The
body was simply dumped here."

The meeting in Lansing's office had not been pleasant.
Hobson and his associate, Special Agent Williams, came
in with definite attitudes of superiority. They told Lansing
and his deputy that they were taking over the entire investigation. Everything the San Phillipe Sheriff's Office
had collected up to that point had to be turned over to
the SBI.

"Just what are you basing your assumptions on?" Lansing
asked. "All you have is a dead body. How do you know
that's linked to drugs?"

"For starters, we got a tip," Williams replied, sounding
bored.

"And then this." Hobson pulled a photograph from his
pocket. He turned to Kimberly, who was seated on one
side of the room, listening to the charges in disbelief. "Do
you recognize that?" He handed her the photo.

Kim held the picture with a trembling hand. "It looks
like my father's car."

"It is your father's car." Hobson took back the photo. "We verified the plates and the VIN."

"Where'd you find it?" Her voice was lifeless.

"In south Santa Fe last night. Shot full of holes."

"So what does that mean?" Gabe asked defiantly. He had decided he didn't like Hobson.

"I'll tell you what that means, sonny. Tallmountain was wrapped up in a drug deal that went sour. One of the shots must have torn through a kilo bag of blow. There was enough cocaine dust in that car to fill a dime bag." He turned once more to the young woman. "Do you have any idea where your father was the past few days?"

"He was camping. Up in the mountains just above Spider Woman Reservoir."

"By himself?" Williams interjected.

"Yes. He did it all the time. At least once a month. It was just his way of being close to nature."

"Yeah," Williams mumbled. "A real nature boy, I'll bet."

"So you really don't know where he was or what he was doing," Hobson pressed.

"He was camping," Kim insisted. "Why wouldn't I believe him?"

"We have reliable eyewitnesses that place him in Santa Fe the day before his body turned up here in San Phillipe County," Williams observed.

"That's impossible," Kim protested.

"He had a prison record, missy. Did you know that?" Hobson was doing his best to keep the young woman off balance.

"Yes, I did. When he was twenty years old he got caught with a joint in his pocket." She curled her lip in contempt. "White man's justice. He spent almost two years in jail."

"He broke the law," Hobson replied. "That's what happens when you break the law. And evidently those eighteen months in prison didn't teach him a thing."

"That was over twenty years ago," she protested. "That's the only time he ever got in trouble with the law."

"No," Williams sneered. "That was the only time he got caught." He turned to his partner. "We don't need any more of this. Let's hit the road."

Lansing had been sitting behind his desk during the entire confrontation. Before the detectives left, he wanted to have his say. Standing, he pointed toward the door. "Deputy Hanna, would you please take Miss Tallmountain to the dayroom. I'd like to have a few words with these gentlemen in private."

Gabe nodded and escorted the woman from the room.

Patrolman Hernandez had kept silent during the conversation. He couldn't help but feel nervous. He had a good working relationship with Lansing, but the detectives were his superiors and he couldn't afford to cross them.

Lansing waited for the door to close before he said anything. "I realize you people have your jobs to do. I've worked in big-city law enforcement. I know what a mess it is. But I really don't give a goddamn how important you think your jobs are. I don't give a damn how important you think you are. I sure as hell don't appreciate you treating me or my staff like a bunch of hicks. Before you walk out of this office, I want your cards and your supervisor's name.

"I'll cooperate with you. I don't have a choice. But you already have every piece of evidence we collected. It's in the body bag." Lansing could feel his anger building, but he refused to let it get the best of him. "But I'll tell you right now; in the future, before this office turns anything over to you, I'd better hear a 'please' first and a 'thank you' when you get it."

"Are you finished, Lansing?" Hobson's voice had an edge of contempt.

"For the time being."

"Then let me tell you something. I've been working narcotics for ten years. I've seen thirteen-year-old girls sell their bodies so they can get drugs to feed a habit. I've busted twelve-year-old pushers. There's nothing in the world I hate more than drugs and the people who deal them. If I'm a little callous, if I'm a little abrasive, maybe it's because I've seen too much of this crap on the streets. If you don't like my methods, that's your problem. I've got a job to do. And if I step on some jerkwater sheriff's toes along the way, that's too damned bad."

"Maybe you need a new line of work," Cliff suggested. "You've got a dead man tried and convicted without even looking at the evidence."

"As far as I'm concerned, this case is closed," Hobson snapped. "There's one more drug dealer off the street. I don't really give a damn who shot him."

"Like I said," Lansing repeated, "maybe you need a new line of work."

Hobson stared at Lansing for a moment. Whatever he planned on saying, he kept to himself. He reached into his breast pocket and pulled out his wallet. Extracting a business card, he threw it on the sheriff's desk. "I report to Captain Harding. You can reach him at the number on the card." Without another word, he opened the door and left.

Williams also threw his card on the desk and followed his partner out of the building.

Once they were alone, Hernandez quietly closed the door. "I didn't know you had that kind of a temper, Cliff."

"Yeah? Well, sometimes I surprise myself." He looked the highway patrolman in the eye. "Was I out of line?"

Hernandez shrugged. "It's your jurisdiction. I suppose I would have blown up, too, if I had been in your shoes. The least they could have done was give you a heads-up call. Let you know what was coming down."

"I know they're in your chain of command, so you can't

say much, Marty. But I've been in this business almost twenty years. I know gold-plated jerks when I see them and those two qualify. They think they're important because they wear a badge. Take away the badge and there's nothing there."

"You sure you're just not bitter about them horning in on your territory? It was your investigation."

"Yeah," Lansing admitted, "maybe . . . But that Hobson sure seemed anxious to conclude the case."

"They're shorthanded, just like any other agency. Set aside the fact that they're assholes. They could probably use any help you can give them, even if they won't admit it."

"I'll tell you what, Marty. If I do dig up anything, I'll pass it along to you. You can make sure the SBI gets it. I'm not going to work with those arrogant bastards any more than I have to."

"Fair enough, Cliff." Hernandez opened the door and put on his Smokey the Bear hat. "If you want, I'll pass along anything I hear."

"I'd appreciate that."

Lansing found his deputy and Kimberly Tallmountain sitting across a desk from each other in the dayroom. The sheriff was pleasantly surprised to find that Gabe had an instinctive way of putting people at ease. He had said something that made the young woman smile. There was still pain in her eyes, but she was beginning to cope with the situation.

The smile vanished when Kim looked up at Lansing. "I don't care what those detectives said. My father wasn't a drug dealer."

"I don't doubt that you believe that, Miss Tallmountain," Lansing said. "Unfortunately, the State Bureau of

Investigation is convinced that he was. I'm afraid dead men don't normally get their day in court."

"But you didn't know him. . . . They didn't know him. He didn't drink. He didn't smoke. He was a traditionalist. He spent his whole life standing up for our people. A man like that doesn't deal in drugs."

Lansing sat down in a chair a few feet away. "Did you know your father was shot?"

"Yes. Deputy Hanna told me."

The sheriff leaned forward, resting his elbows on his knees. "Did your father have any enemies?"

"There are a lot of people who did not agree with him. There is a lot of arguing in the tribe right now about timber. My father led the fight to protect our resources. He didn't think there should be any logging done. I suppose you could call the people who opposed him 'enemies.' "

"Do you think they could have killed him?"

Kim seemed shocked at the question. "That is not the Navajo way."

"Miss Tallmountain—"

"I'd prefer 'Kim,' if you don't mind," she interrupted.

"Okay. Kim. Did your father have any enemies outside the tribe?"

She shook her head. "Not that I know of."

The sheriff sighed. "The only facts I have in this case are that your father's dead, someone killed him, and his body ended up in my county. That's not a lot to go on. The SBI has him linked to drugs in Santa Fe. That's something I can't disprove."

"They have his car linked to drugs," Gabe observed.

"Granted," Lansing agreed. "But that's circumstantial evidence at best." He looked at Kim. "Did anyone else have access to your father's car?"

"Yes," she said definitely. "Whoever killed him."

The three sat in contemplative silence for a full minute.

"Isn't there anything we can do, Sheriff?" Gabe finally asked.

"Yeah," Lansing said, standing. "Keep our eyes and ears open. Any evidence we find we'll turn over to the SBI. Let's hope they're better at detective work than they are at public relations."

13

"YOUR FATHER NEVER TALKED ABOUT YOUR NAVAJO heritage?" Kim asked as she huddled next to the space heater.

"No," Gabe said, following that with a grunt. He had finally managed to loosen the last bolt holding the rear spring in place. "I think he was pretty bitter about the reservation. I don't know why he left. He never talked about it." He walked over to warm his hands on the kerosene heater.

Ed Rodriguez had found that the suspension on the left rear of Kimberly's truck had broken when she skidded into the ditch. There was a GM dealership in Los Alamos that had what he needed for repairs, but the parts didn't arrive until late afternoon.

Rodriguez kept the garage portion of his filling station open until six P.M. After that, customers had to wait until seven the next morning before he would get to any repairs.

Kim had been through a bad day and she didn't want to stay in Las Palmas any longer than necessary. When she asked if there was anything Gabe could do he offered to make the repairs himself. Rodriguez had seen Gabe do repair work on the sheriff's Jeep and knew the deputy could handle himself in a garage. He had no problem with turning the station over to Gabe for the evening.

The April nights were still cold and the only heat in the two-stall garage was an ancient 150-Btu kerosene heater that rolled on wheels. It was sufficient for warming one person working on one car. It proved totally inadequate for heating two or more people. As a result, Gabe would have to walk over and warm himself periodically before he could continue his repairs.

"How did he die?" Kim's question was melancholy. She sounded as if she were seeking solace in shared pain.

"I guess he drank himself to death. It got progressively worse the older he got. When I was a kid, eleven, twelve years old, it wasn't so bad. That's when he started teaching me about fixing cars and stuff. But as he got older all the joy seemed to drain out of him. He acted like he missed someone . . . or something."

"I've seen that in others," Kim said. "Other Navajos who moved away from the reservation. It's almost like a sickness, and the only way they get better is when they come back to their home, even if it's just for a short visit. Some believe it's the healing power of the land itself."

"My father didn't have a home to go home to. . . . Somebody took it away from him. . . ." Gabe was becoming uneasy with the subject. He turned back to the truck. "I'd better get this finished."

Sensing Gabe's discomfort, Kim looked for other topics. She asked him how he ended up being a deputy. That was a subject Gabe found easier to discuss. He talked about his unsuccessful academic career, his love of motorcycles, and his eventual migration to San Phillipe County.

"What do you do out on the reservation?" Gabe asked, lifting the new spring into place. "I mean, what is there to do on the reservation?"

"Those are two different questions with two entirely different answers. There's not a lot of industry or jobs out there. Some farming. Some ranching. Mostly, though, people have to go into the towns to find work. As for me, I keep pretty busy. My father was a self-taught ecologist. He knew about farming and ranching, biology and botany, archaeology and geology. I guess I followed in his footsteps. I got my undergraduate degree in biochem and my master's in wildlife management."

Gabe suddenly felt intimidated by the woman seated near him. He had guessed her for twenty at the oldest. She was the most attractive woman he had found since coming to Las Palmas and he had halfway wondered if she could be interested in him. Those thoughts began to dim when she rolled out her diplomas. "You must have started college awfully early."

"Not really. I started when I was eighteen and finished when I was twenty-four. For the last two years I've worked for the tribal council in their conservation office."

Gabe did the math in his head. Two years working for the council put her around twenty-six, three years older than him. He thought in terms of high school. She would have been a senior when he was a freshman. No senior girl with an ounce of respect would ever be caught dating a freshman. No, he decided, there was no chance for a relationship.

"Conservation. You mean like soil conservation and farming? Stuff like that?"

"That's just a small part of it. Yeah, we do advise the farmers. But we also worry about grazing and water use. We deal with protecting endangered plant and animal species. We advise on construction projects and commercial development." Her animated explanation suddenly stopped as she considered her words. " 'We.' I guess I'm going to have to quit saying that."

"Why?"

"I was my father's assistant." She said the last sentence very quietly.

Gabe looked from his work to the woman seated in front of him. Her gaze seemed distant, as if she was trying to remember a time before her pain. With his hands covered with grime, he was afraid to touch her. But he had learned the value of a hug from his mother, who never seemed to run out of them.

Setting down his wrench, he walked over and knelt in front of her. It took a second for her to recognize his presence. When she did, he opened his arms. Tears welled up in her eyes as she leaned forward to rest her head on his chest.

Gabe carefully embraced her, making sure he didn't get any grease on her jacket.

Kim's sobs were deep and soulful. Her tears flowed freely as she surrendered herself to her sorrow.

Gabe lost track of time. He could have held her five minutes. It might have been fifteen. He didn't know. It didn't matter. He could remember when his own father died. He closed his eyes and saw the grief stretch in front of him like a bottomless abyss. His father didn't have to die. He was too young. Only forty-five. But Gabe wouldn't cry. He wouldn't give *them* the satisfaction. Those who drove his father from his home. Those who stole his will to live. He would never forgive them. And he would never let them know how much he hurt.

After a time Kim's sobs were replaced by deep sighs and then quiet breathing. Gabe was almost convinced she was asleep. Then her back stiffened and he felt her pull away.

"I need to wash my face," she said, wiping the tears from her eyes. She stood and hurried to the washroom at the back of the bay.

Gabe felt exhausted from the experience. He knew what she was going through. He got up and finished attaching the new spring.

Kim emerged from the washroom as Gabe was securing the last of the lug nuts on the tire. The streaks of tears had been washed away, but her eyes were still red and she looked tired.

Gabe pressed the DOWN button on the hydraulic control and the lift hissed the truck to ground level. "All done," he announced.

She walked up to him, staring intently into his eyes. "Why did you do that?"

"What?"

"Put your arms around me. Hold me."

The deputy suddenly felt awkward. "I guess because I thought you needed it."

She gently put her hand on his chest, over his heart, and continued to stare into his eyes.

Kim's eyes told him thanks . . . and much more. Gabe couldn't understand what the "much more" was, but he felt a surge of warmth through his entire body.

"You need to come home to your people, Gabriel," she said softly. "You would be welcome."

Those weren't the words he expected to hear, but he wasn't surprised she said them. "I'm afraid I wouldn't belong."

"You belong. . . . Life is a circle. For a man's soul to be at rest, the circle must be complete. Your father's soul is not at rest, nor is yours. I could feel it. It was as overwhelming as my own pain. You have to come home to complete the circle."

Gabe was confused. What had he told her that she could know so much? He said his father didn't have a home. That was all. How could she know the depth of his own sadness, his own sense of loss? He felt himself pulling away from her touch.

"I'd have to think about it." He picked up a rag and began wiping his hands. "As far as I know I don't have any family on the reservation. I wouldn't know where to start."

"You've already started. With me."

"Yeah," Gabe said, smiling weakly. "Guess so."

Kim decided she had pushed the issue as far as it would go. "I'd better get started back."

Gabe looked at the wall clock. "It's almost ten. Isn't it a little late?"

"I have a lot of responsibilities. I can't afford very much time away. Besides, I need to make arrangements for my father's funeral." She picked up her purse and opened it. Extracting a business card, she handed it to Gabe. "I really would like you to come to the reservation. I can show you around. The number on the bottom is my home number."

Gabe took the card and stuffed it in his shirt pocket without looking at it. "Thanks."

She stopped and looked into his eyes again. "No, Gabe. Thank you . . ." She started to say more but stopped, letting her unspoken words linger like frosted breath.

It was a long moment before Gabe broke the impasse by turning away. "Let me get this open so you can get out of here." He began pulling on the cord to raise the garage door.

Kim heaved a sigh and got into her truck. She felt like she had used up all her words. All she could do was wave at Gabe as she backed through the door. A moment later she disappeared into the night.

14

"I THOUGHT YOU WERE GOING TO BE TOO BUSY WITH your murder investigation."

Lansing thought Margarite's voice still had an edge to it, as if she had already decided there would be no camping trip. He wasn't in the mood for arguments or long explanations at the moment. "It's not my murder investigation, as of yesterday."

There was a brief pause at the other end of the line. "What happened?"

"We'll have three days to talk about it when we go fishing. I just wanted to call you early enough so you could get your things ready."

"That'll take me about five minutes. . . . Are you going to pick me up in the morning or should we meet somewhere?"

"To be perfectly honest," Lansing said with a sigh, "I don't want to drag my horse trailer down the pueblo road. Why don't you meet me at the highway around eight? You can follow me in your truck."

"All the way to Raton Pass?"

"I thought we'd try someplace else."

"Like where?" Margarite asked suspiciously.

"Like maybe the San Pedro River north of the reservoir.

It'll cut out half a day of driving and this time of year there shouldn't be anyone around."

Indirectly, Lansing had another reason for choosing the reservoir. Walter Tallmountain supposedly had gone there. That's what his daughter had said. There was always the outside chance he could stumble on some piece of evidence to support her story.

"Can't bring yourself to leave the county, Lansing?"

"We don't have to stay in the county. We can follow the river into Colorado, if you want."

"I guess I can't complain," Margarite admitted. "I thought for sure you were calling to tell me the trip was off."

"Is there anything I need to pick up?"

"Salmon eggs, raw liver, and a couple dozen night crawlers. If one bait doesn't work, maybe the others will."

"What about food?"

"We're going to be eating fish, Lansing," Margarite said, laughing. "That's the whole point of this trip."

"I'm glad you're so sure about that," the sheriff said doubtfully. He made a mental note to include packets of dehydrated meals in the saddle bags. "Anything else?"

"I'll bring what we need for fixing the fish. You just bring an appetite."

"That shouldn't be a problem."

"All right, then, Lansing," Margarite said, having a hard time masking her excitement. "I'll see you in the morning."

"Eight o'clock." Lansing hung up the phone, painfully aware that he didn't like talking on the phone much and that he was awkward with saying good-byes, especially with Margarite.

He glanced at his watch. It was nearly noon and he had wasted the entire morning shuffling paperwork. In a way he envied his deputies. Both were out on patrol. He would have much preferred someone else handling the mundane work while he was cruising in his patrol car.

It looked like it was going to be a beautiful spring. Certainly not the time of year to be stuck inside. Suddenly the prospect of camping outside for the weekend didn't seem so bad after all. His paperwork was done. The State Bureau of Investigation had relieved him of a murder investigation. He had no outstanding projects to worry about. He told himself he should be walking away from the office with a clear conscience.

That wasn't the situation. The Tallmountain case bothered him. As much as he tried to convince himself that he was no longer involved in the investigation, he still wanted to be a part of it.

"Just drop it, Lansing," he said out loud as he picked up his hat. "You're just ticked off that somebody took it away from you. Sour grapes. That's all it is."

He closed his office door and waved at Marilyn as he walked past her counter. "I'm heading over to the diner for lunch."

"Coming back here after you eat?"

"I don't know. I may have Gabe hang around while I patrol for a while. The walls are starting to close in."

"Okay. See you later."

Marty Hernandez found the sheriff planted in a booth toward the back of the diner. "Saw your Jeep outside," the patrolman said as he seated himself. "Thought I might join you."

"Help yourself." Lansing gestured toward his plate of food. "Try the roast beef. It's not bad."

Velma delivered a glass of water to the booth and took the patrolman's order. Hernandez felt a little freer to speak once they were alone.

"I told you I'd keep you informed about the Tallmountain case. . . ." he began.

"Yeah," Lansing said, trying to act disinterested. "So, what's going on?"

"The State Bureau of Investigation managed to get a federal search warrant. They got the FBI and the Navajo Police to go through Tallmountain's place on the reservation. . . ." He paused for a moment. "They found fifty thousand dollars stashed in a shed behind his house. . . ."

"Okay." Lansing made the statement sound like he was waiting for a punch line.

"Nothing more. They just found the money. They're convinced it's drug money." Lansing nodded, but said nothing. "I guess they're bringing Tallmountain's daughter in for questioning. She evidently worked with him and doesn't live very far from his place. They're pretty sure she knew what was going on."

"Did they find any drugs?"

"No. I guess not."

Lansing leaned back. "You said they're pretty sure his daughter knew what was going on. Just what was going on?"

"Tallmountain was buying and selling drugs."

"Who said he was?"

"Hobson, Williams, the State Bureau of Investigation. Even the Tribal Police think there's something to this and they don't generally turn against one of their own."

Lansing wanted to argue about the conclusions the higher authorities were drawing. Tallmountain's death was being wrapped up in a tidy little package very quickly. Since he wasn't officially on the case, he decided to keep his opinions to himself. "Do they have any idea who killed Tallmountain?"

"Not yet. The bureau is filtering through its regular supply of informants. I'm sure something will turn up."

Lansing nodded, not convinced that anything would "turn up." "What's the word on the autopsy?"

"I guess they're going to announce results later on to-day."

"Will you be in Santa Fe?"

"Yeah," Hernandez said, leaning back to give Velma room for his plate of food. "I'm heading that way after lunch."

"How about faxing me a copy of the coroner's report?"

"Sure, but what for?"

"I'd like it for my files. After all, the D.B. showed up in my county. Besides, the paramedics will need a copy for their follow-up reports. You know damned well a bureaucracy can't function without paperwork, even on the county level."

"Yeah." Hernandez chuckled. "I know what you mean."

Lansing quietly returned to his meal, trying to think of more questions to ask about the Tallmountain investigation without sounding nosy. Before he could continue his probe, the two lawmen were interrupted by a big man stomping toward their table.

"All right, Cliff. What are you going to do about it this time?"

The sheriff looked up to see Roger Kellim towering over their table. He wore a Stetson and a sheepskin jacket and carried a sprung steel trap in one hand.

"Now what, Roger?" Lansing asked calmly.

"You know what! Those damned coyotes. I lost two more calves last night and I want to know what you're going to do about it."

"Have you tried traps?"

"What the hell do you think this is, Sheriff?" Kellim snarled. "A bouquet of roses?"

"It's a trap, all right," Lansing admitted.

"I set out a dozen yesterday. Every last one of them was

sprung." Kellim was angry and he wanted to make sure everyone in the diner knew it. "I want to know what you're going to do about this infestation."

Lansing stood to face the rancher. He wasn't about to be intimidated and he refused to get caught up in a shouting match. "How many men do you have working for you?"

"Four. What the hell does that have to do with anything?"

"Counting yourself, that's five. What am I and my two deputies supposed to do that you five can't?"

"Hunt the varmints down! Kill 'em! I can't tie up my men like that. I've got a whole spread to run."

"Well, I can't tie up my deputies like that, either. I've got a whole county to patrol and San Phillipe's a lot bigger than your spread."

Lansing looked around the diner. Both waitresses and all the customers were watching the exchange. Even the cook had emerged from the kitchen to see what was going on. A murmur of support for the sheriff rippled through the crowd. Lansing felt somewhat vindicated.

"Yeah? Well, I'll tell you something, Cliff. I'm not the only one that's suffering. A dozen farms and ranches have been hit by coyotes this spring. Ask anyone in here."

A half dozen heads nodded in agreement. They had heard the same reports or suffered similar losses.

"If you aren't up to doing your job," the rancher continued, "maybe we need a sheriff who is."

"If you want my job, you can have it, Kellim. Election's in two years."

"Yeah? And a recall petition can start this afternoon!" The rancher turned, nearly knocking over one of the tables behind him. Shoving a chair out of his way, Kellim stomped through the diner and out the door.

Every set of eyes in the diner followed Kellim out the

building, then shot back to the sheriff to see his reaction. Lansing calmly sat down and returned to his meal.

Hernandez leaned toward his lunch partner. "Aren't you worried about that guy?"

Lansing shook his head. "I've known Roger since grade school. He's always been a hothead."

"It sounds like he has a legitimate complaint. What are you going to do about the coyotes?"

Lansing looked up and smiled. "Go fishing."

15

HUNTER NIYOL WOKE WITH A START. HE DIDN'T RE-member going to sleep. But there he was in bed, still dressed, the book he had been reading draped across his chest.

Sleep, Hunter thought. Why is so much time lost to sleep? There is so much to do and we waste our lives in sleep.

Hunter was getting old. He never slept more than a few hours each night and what little sleep he did get was fitful. Still, the hours he did sleep he considered time lost forever.

It was still dark outside and Hunter's lamp glowed dimly next to him. The old man knew it was time to get up. His internal alarm clock told him that. In the fog of his first morning thoughts Hunter tried to remember the last words he'd read before falling asleep. He picked up the book to refresh his memory.

"Thus week by week the prisoners of plague put up what fight they could. Some even contrived to fancy they were still behaving as free men and had the power of choice. But actually it would have been truer to say that the plague had swallowed up everything and every-one. No longer were there individual destinies; only a collective destiny. . . ."

Ah, yes, Hunter thought. The collective destiny. He had become lost in the concept of the collective destiny.

He carefully inserted a bookmark at the spot he had been reading and set the book on his nightstand. Then he sat up and stretched. How many times had he read *The Plague*? he wondered. Three, four times maybe. Despite all of Camus's existential trappings, Hunter felt the Frenchman betrayed his innermost conviction: mankind was guided not by individual choice, but by a fate oblivious of our petty desires.

It wasn't the Navajo way, but it wasn't so different, either. Another French existentialist, Sartre, was a little closer. Man may not be able to overthrow evil, but he can—and must—refuse to cooperate with evil. That's where individual choice came in as far as the old man was concerned.

The Navajo way emphasized the collective destiny of the people. Individual choice was the freedom to follow the ancient rules. If a man did that, he would live a long and healthy life, and ultimately contribute successfully to the collective destiny.

Hunter swung his feet over the side of the bed. The stone floor was cold, even through his socks. He hunted for his moccasins and quickly slipped them on.

The two-room adobe hut was usually warm enough in the winter, but Hunter had forgotten to light a fire for the night. He wrapped himself in his blanket and shuffled into the big room. He lit the gas stove in the kitchen corner and a few minutes later he had water brewing for coffee.

Still wrapped in his blanket, Hunter stepped through the door of his shack. The hut sat just below a hill that protected it from the north winds, but it still sat high enough that Hunter could survey the desert valley below. The nearest house was five miles away. Hunter didn't mind. With his wife dead and his children gone he had come to enjoy his solitude. It gave him time to read and ponder the philosophers. Although he firmly believed the Navajo way was the true path to enlightenment, he enjoyed jousting philosophical themes with the other elders during the festivals. The arguments always came full circle: the Navajo way was the best way.

Hunter faced toward the east. There was still no glow announcing the coming day. Stars flickered brightly in the black velvet sky.

In the distance a coyote howled. The lone voice was joined by a second. Then a third. Two more joined in and within a minute an entire chorus of yips and howls echoed through the dark. It had been that way all night. In fact, it had been that way for almost a week, with more coyotes joining in each night.

So many voices, Hunter thought. It had been a long time since he had heard so many coyotes at one time. Twenty years? No. It had been longer than that. Thirty years, at least.

Why were there so many voices? the old man wondered. It was not a good sign. He was sure of that.

Hunter wasn't afraid of the coyotes. At his age, there were few things he feared. Even the Navajo concept of death, a strange amalgam of oblivion governed by evil, didn't frighten him anymore.

But he had to consider the collective destiny of the tribe. The voices were an omen. He was sure of it.

Even though he had enough provisions to last another week, Hunter decided it was a good idea to go into town. He would stop by Walter Tallmountain's office and tell him about the coyotes. Walter was old enough; he would have remembered thirty years earlier. Maybe he would know what it meant.

16

GABE WAS ON THE ROAD BY SEVEN. DAYLIGHT SAVING time had been in effect for almost two weeks, so the sun hadn't poked its head above the San Juan Mountains yet. The approaching morning gradually draped its pale blue mantle over the last stars of night. Only stubborn Venus, low to the horizon but still bright in the sky, refused to yield. Gabe thought he could reach out and touch the goddess. He wondered if the Navajo had a name for the glistening jewel.

The high desert air was crisp and cold. As he bent his body against the wind, Gabe could feel the tears streaming toward his temples. God, how he loved storming down the open road on his motorcycle. With the ambient air hovering at the freezing point, Gabe found the frigid breeze invigorating.

Two days of freedom, he thought. Two days of just him and his hog. He didn't have to be back to work until Sunday.

Fifteen minutes north of Las Palmas, he started wondering if he would ever go back.

Thirty minutes north of town he had to decide which direction to take. To the right was Highway 250. It would take him east, wind through the Colorado mountains for a time, and finally end up in Taos. To the left, Highway

84 would take him past the Apache reservation, past Spider Woman Reservoir, and eventually to Farmington.

Parked at the juncture of the two roads, Gabe reached inside his leather jacket and checked his shirt pocket. Yes, he did remember to bring the business card Kim had given him. He had played a game with himself. If he had forgotten the card, he would go to Taos. But the card was there . . . which meant he could still go to Taos.

Pondering the situation, Gabe pulled a Coke from his bike's storage bin and twisted off the top. After a couple of sips he put the lid back on the bottle and tucked the drink away.

Well, Gabe thought, *if I don't see Taos this trip, I'll see it the next one.*

Gunning his engine, the deputy kicked up dust and gravel from the shoulder as he pulled onto the highway and headed west toward Farmington.

17

FOR THE LIFE OF HIM, LANSING COULDN'T UNDER-
stand why he had been reluctant to take Margarite on a
camping trip. The weather was absolutely delightful and he
couldn't think of anyone with whom he would rather be.

Spider Woman Reservoir sat at the base of the Rocky
Mountains where the high desert made a rapid transition
into steep foothills. The San Pedro River filled the lake
from the north, getting its water from the snowmelt. Spider
Woman Recreation Area was a popular spot in the summer, attracting campers, boaters, and fishermen from Farmington and Santa Fe. Even though it was over an hour's
drive from Las Palmas, it was still in San Phillipe County,
which meant Lansing and his deputies had to patrol it on
a regular basis.

Although the recreation area was open year round,
things usually didn't get busy until after Memorial Day.
They stayed that way through the Labor Day weekend.

In the middle of April only the bravest of souls dared
spend the night. Unpredicted and unwanted snow squalls
could erupt in that region until the beginning of May, so
most visitors limited themselves to day trips only.

Lansing had checked the weather beforehand and decided it was safe to venture into the mountains. Heading

up on a Friday, he was pretty sure they would have the rec area to themselves.

They had parked at the trailhead on the north end of the lake. By ten-thirty the horses were saddled and they were following the bridle path that ran parallel to the San Pedro River.

Doing something stupid like standing mindlessly with a fishing pole in his hand seemed like a small sacrifice, Lansing finally decided. He was outdoors. He would spend the cloudless night under the stars. And he was finally getting to take Cement Head out for a jaunt. Except for occasional one- or two-hour forays over the winter, his horse had been stuck in the barn. They both could use the fresh air.

Margarite was not a master rider. Although she didn't shy away from horses, she wasn't particularly accomplished. Lansing had borrowed an old gelding named Chico from one of his neighbors. Used mostly as a pack animal, Chico had no great aspirations in life. He was content with plodding along at a pace that Margarite found comfortable.

The trail was narrow enough that they had to content themselves with going single file. Lansing took the lead.

"All right, Lansing," Margarite said after they were established on their track. "What happened to your investigation? I know you're ticked about something or you would have told me already."

Lansing glanced over his shoulder. He wasn't sure he was comfortable with someone getting to know him so well. "The State Bureau of Investigation came rolling in Wednesday and said the investigation belonged to them. Something to do with drugs. They seem to think the victim was a pusher. They said he was running cocaine from Santa Fe up to the Navajo reservation."

"From your tone of voice, I take it you don't believe them."

Lansing shrugged. "Not really. The guy's name was Walter Tallmountain. He ran the conservation office for the Navajo Tribe. Evidently he was big-time into ecology and wildlife management. It doesn't make sense to me that someone like that would run drugs."

"There must have been something in his past."

"Yeah," the sheriff grunted. "They busted him for possessing a joint twenty-five years ago. Spent eighteen months in prison for it."

"What else did he do?"

"That was it. Clean record after that. They find his car shot up in Santa Fe. There are traces of cocaine all over the place. And he turns up dead along the side of the road. The SBI adds it all up and decides he was running drugs. Yesterday they searched his place out on the reservation and found fifty grand stashed away." He was silent for a moment. "Maybe they're right. Maybe he was running drugs."

"You still don't believe it."

"I don't know. What makes you think I don't?"

"Because we're still in San Phillipe County. You're staying close to home for some reason."

Lansing looked back at his companion. The smug look on Margarite's face told him she knew she was right and his silence confirmed it. Irritated, Lansing focused his attention on the trail in front of them.

Around noon Margarite called the party to a halt. Below them the river had widened into deep, lethargic pools. She decided this would be a good place to catch some lunch.

Lansing would have preferred another two hours along the trail. The days were still short and he had no interest in pitching camp in the dark. They should make one stop. Set up camp, catch fish for lunch and dinner, and be ready for an early sunset.

"That's all well and good, Lansing," Margarite observed as she got down from Chico. "But what if we pick a spot that has no fish? We'd have nothing to eat. This way we can fish here *and* further up the river. Twice as many chances to catch fish."

Lansing nodded. He decided to keep his stash of dehydrated dinners a secret. He didn't want her to think he didn't appreciate her angling skills.

18

GABE MADE A CASUAL TOUR THROUGH THE MOUN-
tains, stopping at each "scenic view" to enjoy the landscape. It was nearly eleven o'clock before he reached Farmington.

He topped off the tank on his motorcycle at a convenience store on the outskirts of town, then went inside to
pay. Before he reached the counter, Gabe spotted a rack
of road maps. He thought there might be something more
detailed than what he was carrying. Browsing through the
selection, he became aware that the old man behind the
counter was glaring at him.

"What you want, boy?" the old man finally asked. There
was an edge of hostility in the man's voice.

Gabe looked at the proprietor. "I was wondering if you
had a map of the Navajo reservation."

"No, I don't. So's how 'bout payin' for your gas 'n' git!"

The deputy was taken aback. He didn't understand the
man's animosity. "Is there a problem?"

"I'll tell you jus' like I tell the others. I don't like no
Injuns comin' in my place. Jus' pay for your gas 'n' go."

"Hey, man," Gabe protested. "This is a free country. I'm
not hurting anything."

"Yeah, this is a free country, all right. An' this is private
property. So's if I tell you to go, you go!"

Being an army brat, Gabe had grown up with prejudice, but it was usually the subtle kind. People normally ignored you, pretending you didn't exist. In Las Cruces he passed for a Hispanic and blended in with seventy-five percent of the population. This was the first time he could remember someone being openly hostile because he was a Native American.

"Yeah, sure." Gabe pulled five dollars from his wallet and threw them on the counter. "I'll be sure and tell all my friends what a friendly place you have here."

"Just tell your friends to stay away," the old man snarled.

A lot of Pueblos and Apaches came into Las Palmas. Gabe couldn't remember any of them being treated with such open disrespect. There was that possibility, Gabe considered, that it happened when the deputy wasn't around. Maybe the Anglos were only nice because he was present and wore a badge.

Anglos! His entire life, Gabe had never thought in terms of race. The one true melting pot in American society was the military. The racial barriers were almost nonexistent, especially among the kids. When his father was stationed in Germany, the young Gabe was an American, just like all the other children on the post. They were all different from the locals because they spoke a different language. In Georgia he went to a public school and was treated just like any other boy from Fort Benning. He was an outsider, not because he was Navajo but because he was an army brat.

This was the first time he had encountered prejudice because of what he was—a Navajo. The deputy was flushed with anger and resentment. He was angry at the old bigot behind the counter who passed judgment on him because of what he looked like. And for no particular reason at all, he suddenly resented being a Navajo.

A few blocks from the convenience store he pulled into

the parking lot of a strip mall. He had come to Farmington because he wanted to see Kimberly Tallmountain. He knew that. Three hours earlier at the crossroads he knew he wanted to see her again. But in the back of his mind the thought also lingered that he wanted to find his origins. He wanted to know from where he ultimately came.

Parking his bike, he walked over to a pay phone and pulled out Kim's business card. He dialed the office number and waited. It took six rings before anyone picked up on the other end.

"Shiprock Chapter House, Conservation Office," the woman's voice reported.

"Kimberly?" Gabe asked.

"I'm sorry, Miss Tallmountain is in a meeting. Can I take a message?"

Gabe hesitated. He could say he would call back, but he didn't want to spend the entire day hanging around pay phones. "Uh . . . I was wondering if you could give me directions to your office?"

"Certainly, sir. Where are you coming from?"

"I'm on the main highway coming into Farmington."

"Oh, that's not going to be a problem. Just stay on the highway heading west through town. Shiprock is twenty-five miles west of Farmington. When you get to Shiprock, just look for the signs. We're on the north side of the highway. You really can't miss the building. If you get to the big intersection with a stoplight, you've gone too far."

"Okay," Gabe responded. "Thanks a lot."

Gabe had no concept of how big the Navajo reservation really was. Covering over ten thousand square miles, the Navajo lands spilled from Arizona into two adjoining states. When the woman at the other end of the line referred to the "chapter house," he made the assumption that he was going to the central administrative office for the entire Navajo Nation. Nothing could be further from the truth.

The Shiprock Chapter House was a regional lodge house that served those people living in and around the town of Shiprock. There were dozens of other lodge houses sprinkled throughout the reservation. Central administration was located almost a hundred miles away in Window Rock.

Shiprock was located at the intersection of highways 64 and 666. Sixty-four continued west into Arizona. Highway 666 ran south from Colorado and ended in Gallup. All the important buildings in town could be found a block or two off either highway.

North of Highway 64, the three most prominent buildings were the ones containing the Bureau of Indian Affairs, the Shiprock Adult Detention Center, and the chapter house.

Gabe had no problem finding the chapter house. It was a long, low building of fairly recent construction. Sitting only a hundred feet off the highway, it was surrounded by a large gravel parking lot that could accommodate hundreds of cars. Behind the chapter house was a smaller building, equally as new, with a sign declaring it housed Operation Head Start.

The two buildings contrasted sharply with the weathered frame houses that surrounded them.

The chapter house had one large, circular room the size of a gymnasium. Located at the eastern end of the building, it was used for clan meetings and indoor ceremonies. A dozen offices and meeting rooms for conducting official tribal business were clustered at the other end of the building.

"Can I help you?" a woman asked, smiling from her desk. The receptionist was short and round, with straight black hair gathered in a ponytail. She wore a blouse with a bright flowered print that helped accentuate her reddish-brown complexion. Her smile was infectious.

"Yeah." Gabe smiled back. "I was looking for Kimberly Tallmountain."

"Oh, you're the gentleman who called earlier."

Gabe nodded.

"I thought so. I'm pretty good at voices . . . Kim's still in that meeting, but it should be breaking up soon." The receptionist studied the man standing in front of her. "You're new around here, aren't you?"

"Yes. First time I've been here."

"If you'd like, there's a chair against the wall over there. I can get you a cup of coffee."

"Naw, that's all right. I've been sitting all morning. I think I'll stretch my legs."

"You're free to look around, although there's not much to see. If you need anything, my name's Donna."

"Thanks, Donna. My name's Gabe. Gabe Hanna." He wondered if the last name would elicit a response.

Donna only nodded. "Nice to meet you, Gabe."

He excused himself and stepped back into the hallway. The hallway accessed the different offices and meeting rooms and lead eventually to the Great Room. There were numerous pictures and displays along both walls and Gabe found plenty of things to study while he waited.

After ten minutes a door opened at the end of the hall. A dozen men, most dressed in business suits, filed out of the room. Gabe didn't see Kim in the group, so he turned his attention back to the crayon drawings made by the students in Mrs. Wilson's second-grade class.

Gabe couldn't help but feel out of place and he was sure his presence was conspicuous. He ignored the approaching men and hoped they would do the same.

The man in the lead, the man obviously in charge, was

busy giving orders to the individuals closest to him. To make a point, the man stopped a few feet away.

Gabe tried not to be nosy, and shut out the conversation. He hoped they would hurry along so he could look for Kim. It was a moment before he realized no one was talking anymore. He glanced toward the knot of men. The man giving orders was now silent and staring intently at Gabe. The other men were also looking at him.

The important-looking man was dressed in an expensive three-piece suit and string tie. His long black hair was streaked with silver and gathered in the back in a tail. "Excuse me," he said when he made eye contact with Gabe. "You look awfully familiar. Have we met before?"

Gabe felt embarrassed at the sudden attention. "No, sir. I don't think so."

The man approached for a closer look. "The fall festival . . . or maybe the rodeo last September?" he suggested.

"No," Gabe said, shaking his head. "You must have me confused with someone else. This is my first time on the reservation."

"First time?" The man seemed confused. "But you look Navajo."

"I am . . . Well, half . . . on my father's side."

"Your father?" A flicker of realization brightened the older man's face. "Your father. Of course. I can see that now." He took Gabe by the shoulders. "The resemblance is unbelievable! Davy . . . Davy Hania is your father."

Gabe felt uncomfortable in the grasp and tried to pull away. "I'm afraid you've mistaken me for someone else. My father's name was Hanna. David Hanna."

"No," the businessman said firmly. "Your father's name was David Hania. And you look just like him. . . . I should know. He was my brother." He held Gabe at arm's length. "I'm your uncle Edward. Edward Hania."

19

"I—I DON'T UNDERSTAND," GABE STAMMERED.

"God, you look like your father," Hania continued. "You look exactly like he did the day he walked off the reservation. How is he?"

"He's dead," the deputy responded flatly.

"Dead?"

Gabe could see real pain in Hania's eyes. The grip on his shoulders weakened.

"Dead?" The older man's voice was barely a whisper. "When? How?"

"Five years ago." Gabe wanted to feel sorry for Hania, but he couldn't. These were the same people who had driven his father away. "He drank himself to death." Gabe couldn't mask the bitterness in his voice.

Hania was visibly shaken. He released Gabe and steadied himself against the wall. The other men accompanying him rushed to his side but he waved them away. He looked at his nephew. "I'm sorry. I know it's been a long time since I saw your father . . . but I always remembered him as a young man. I . . . I wasn't ready for that kind of news."

The deputy managed an unemotional "yeah." He hadn't been ready for the news when it came, either, even though he had watched his father kill himself a little bit every day for years.

"Is something wrong?" a woman's voice asked.

Gabe looked beyond the group of men to see Kim approaching.

"No, not at all," Hania replied, pulling himself erect. He seemed embarrassed at the show of emotion. "I just received some unfortunate news. My nephew told me my brother was dead."

Kim looked from Hania to Gabe, whom she recognized immediately. "Gabe?" She looked at the businessman. "Gabriel is *your* nephew?"

"He has to be. He's the spitting image of my brother."

"Really, I think we need to sit down and talk about this, Mr. Hania," Gabe insisted. "We're not sure of anything right now."

"Listen, son," Hania interrupted. "I'm pressed for time. I have to be in Gallup by two. But you're right. We do need to sit down and talk. Are you going to be in town long?"

"I suppose. A day or so."

"Good. Come out to my ranch for dinner. Around seven. Anyone within a hundred miles can give you directions."

"Mr. Hania, if you don't mind," the deputy stalled. "I don't have much time in town. I actually came here to see Miss Tallmountain." He didn't want to blurt out that information for everyone to know, but Hania was backing him into a corner.

"Oh," the older man said knowingly. "Well, that's not a problem. Bring her along. She's more than welcome in my home." He took Gabe's hand in his. "Don't disappoint me, son. I need to know about you. I need to know about my brother. You have to come."

Hanna nodded reluctantly. "I'll see what I can do."

"Good," Hania said, confident he had prevailed. "Seven o'clock."

"Yeah. Seven."

Hania turned to Kim. "Again, Kim. My condolences. We can talk more this evening."

Kim nodded but said nothing.

Hania turned and left with the two men he had been talking to earlier. The remaining four dispersed, leaving Gabe and Kim alone in the hallway.

"You came all the way from Las Palmas to see me?"

Gabe shrugged. "You said if I came out to the reservation you'd show me around."

"I figured you would have called first. You caught me at a busy time."

"Oh." Disappointment dripped from that single syllable.

"I guess we can talk about it," Kim suggested. "Have you had lunch yet?"

"No," he said.

"Good." She smiled. "There's a pretty good café here in Shiprock. We can talk there."

"Sounds great," Gabe agreed.

"Let me get my purse. I'll meet you outside."

As Gabe stood outside the chapter house waiting for Kim, a rusty, weather-beaten truck rattled to a stop in the parking lot. An old man dressed in Levi's and a sheepskin jacket nearly as worn as the vehicle emerged from the cab. Making sure his hat was still in place, he slammed the truck door shut and began walking stiffly toward the building.

"Oh, hello there," the oldster said when he spotted Gabe.

"Hi."

The old man stopped a few feet short of Gabe. The faintest flicker of recognition passed over the old one's eyes when he got a better look at him. Before he could say anything, Kim emerged from the building.

"Hunter. What brings you down from the hills?"

"Ah, Yazhi. Normally, it would be just so I could see your smile." Hunter grinned. "I'm afraid it is business this time. Is your father around?"

"No." The young woman averted her eyes. "I guess you haven't heard. My father is dead."

"Walter is dead?" The words came out stiffly, as if the old man was trying to comprehend their meaning. "Oh, no. This cannot be."

"I'm afraid it's the truth, Hunter."

Hunter opened his arms for the young woman. "My Yazhi. My little one. I am so sorry."

Kim welcomed the embrace. Hunter Niyol had been like a grandfather to her. "I thought someone would have gotten word to you," Kim apologized, fighting back the tears.

"Few people come my way," Hunter said, patting her back tenderly. "But I am here now." He waited a respectful moment, then asked, "How did it happen?"

"Someone shot him." She gave the old man a quick hug, then pulled away. "I'm sorry. It's not easy to talk about. I have to make funeral arrangements today. His body is being brought in from Santa Fe tomorrow."

"Santa Fe?" Hunter seemed confused.

"It's a long story," Gabe said, trying to help.

"Oh." Kim realized the two men were strangers to each other. "Hunter Niyol, I'd like you to meet Gabriel Hanna. He's a deputy over in San Phillipe County. Gabe, this is Hunter Niyol, one of my father's oldest friends."

The two men shook hands.

"Hanna?" Niyol asked doubtfully. "I don't know any Hannas . . . but I think I know you from somewhere."

"Yeah," Gabe admitted quietly. "I've heard a few people say that."

"Hunter, we're going over to the café. Please come have lunch with us."

"I will come," he replied. "There is much we have to talk about."

20

BY ONE IN THE AFTERNOON THE CHILLY MOUNTAIN
air had warmed nicely. Lansing had removed his jacket and
had even rolled up the sleeves on his flannel shirt.

Despite the pleasant surroundings, he was bored. He had
been casting his bait into the water for an hour now, getting a tug and each time dragging in an empty hook.

"Go easy on those fish eggs," Margarite warned. She was
fishing ten yards farther up the river. "At the rate you're
going we won't have enough to last us the rest of today."

"Yeah, yeah," Lansing grumbled. He slipped two eggs
onto the tiny hook and cast into the water again. In less
than thirty seconds he had a tug on his line. Determined
to snag his quarry this time, Lansing jerked on the pole
with all his might.

The hook, sinker, and bobber came flying out of the
water. He ducked as the rig flew past his head and tangled
in a bush behind him.

"Son of a bitch," he swore under his breath.

"Did you get him?" Margarite asked, responding to the
commotion.

"Almost!" the sheriff lied.

As Lansing fought to untangle his line, Margarite walked
up carrying a stringer with four nice trout dangling from
it. "See, I told you this looked like a good spot."

Lansing didn't appreciate the smirk on her face.

"Remember our deal," Margarite reminded him. "I have to clean all of your fish and you have to clean mine." She offered the stringer to her partner. "I think all this fishing's made me hungry."

"I just had a thought," Lansing said, picking up his own empty stringer and handing it to her. "Why don't I clean those fish and fix us lunch while you fill up another stringer?"

"That's what I like about you, Lansing. Unlike most men, you can be reasoned with." She laughed and gave him a peck on the cheek. "Call me when it's time to eat!" She turned and hurried back to her fishing spot.

Lansing retrieved an aluminum skillet and a can of Sterno from Cement Head's pack. He normally didn't like cooking with Sterno. It gave off a low heat and it took forever for something to cook, especially in the mountains. On the other hand, it was quicker than building a fire and waiting for the hot coals to develop.

Using three rocks from the riverbank, he made a tripod to set the skillet on and set the Sterno can in the center. Lighting the waxy jelly in the can, he set the pan over the low heat. By the time he had the fish cleaned, the skillet would be hot enough for cooking.

The spot on the trail Margarite had chosen for their stop was wide enough to give Lansing room to cook. Additionally, he was only ten feet from the river, which was where he had to clean the fish.

The bank next to the river was not very steep, which made cleaning the fish relatively easy. Despite the convenience, though, Lansing was sure his Stetson was going to fall into the water. To preclude such a catastrophe, he set his hat on a small boulder close to where the horses were tied.

Lansing didn't mind cleaning the fish. It was a lot easier

than dressing out a deer. In one quick motion with his knife he beheaded and gutted the fish, tossing the unwanted remnants into the water. Leaving the tail and back fin in place, he quickly scaled the rest of the body. Once the fish was rinsed in the river, he set it on a rock next to him and started on the next. The entire process took less than a minute for each fish.

He found the icy water numbing. After the third fish he had to stop to try to return the circulation to his fingers. As he vigorously rubbed his hands together and blew into his cupped palms he heard Cement Head's protests.

Lansing knew his horse wasn't the smartest thing on four legs, but he wasn't skittish or high strung, either. The animal kicked up a commotion only if something bothered him, and that usually took a lot.

As they were in the mountains, Lansing's first thought was that a bear or lion might be close. Possibly a rattlesnake was finding its way toward a warm rock for sunning.

He hurried up the bank to investigate. Chico stood oblivious of whatever was going on. Cement Head was whinnying and pulling at his reins, clearly upset over something.

Lansing looked around trying to figure out what was bothering his horse. Nothing seemed out of the ordinary. He gently caressed the animal's neck. "That's all right, boy. Nothing's wrong. You smell a skunk or something?"

Cement Head calmed down, but he continued to shake his head back and forth as if he were trying to point at something.

Lansing looked around again. This time he realized something was different. His Stetson was missing.

"Margarite?"

"Yes?" she called from the bank.

"You didn't take my hat, did you?"

"No," she responded. She reeled in her line and started up the bank. "You lose your hat?"

Lansing looked up and down the trail. "I didn't lose it. I think somebody took it."

Margarite approached along the path. "You didn't drop it somewhere?"

"No. I left it right here on this rock."

They both heard the sound of feet shuffling through dry leaves.

"Shhh!" he instructed.

The sound came again, somewhere above them.

Lansing squinted his eyes and surveyed the sun-dappled forest above them. Forty feet higher, almost hidden by a tree, stood a coyote. The coyote was motionless, watching the humans below. From it's mouth dangled the sheriff's hat.

"Well, for crying out loud," Lansing complained.

"What?" Margarite hadn't spotted the culprit.

"Up there behind that tree." He pointed. "A damned coyote has my hat."

Margarite giggled when she finally saw the animal.

"It's not funny," Lansing said, pulling his rifle from the saddle holster on Cement Head. "That hat cost me sixty bucks."

"What are you doing?"

"I'm going to get my hat back." Lansing raised the rifle so he could take aim.

"Are you going to kill him?" Margarite sounded worried.

"Nobody's going to miss a coyote."

Lansing had no particular animosity toward coyotes. He certainly didn't feel what Roger Kellim and the other ranchers did. Coyotes were all part of the natural order and Lansing had a deep respect for the natural order. That is, just as long as the natural order of things didn't interfere with him. He drew the line at some varmint stealing a sixty-dollar Stetson.

As he drew a bead on the coyote the animal remained motionless. Lansing could see the yellow eyes staring at him. There was no sign of fear. If anything, the gunman felt, his mark sensed what was going on.

Lansing lowered his rifle. *This is stupid*, he thought. *Just shoot the damned thing.*

But Lansing had never been in a staring match with a coyote before and the animal looking down at him had a spark of awareness. To the human, the beast even looked intelligent.

"Why do you have to shoot him?" Margarite protested.

"I don't!" Lansing growled, shoving his rifle back into its holster. He picked up a rock and threw it at the coyote. "Give me my goddamn hat!" he yelled.

The coyote ducked as the rock sailed past him. Refusing to give up his prize, the animal turned and scampered up the mountain, stopping thirty feet higher. He then turned and stared at the humans, as if daring them to follow.

"Cripes!" Lansing complained under his breath. Picking up another rock, he started up the side of the slope after his hat.

Margarite, grateful he had put the gun away, joined in the chase.

"Well, this is certainly something different!" she said with a laugh.

"Yeah, and I'll bet there are two more coyotes back by the river stealing our fish," Lansing observed, pulling himself along with a sapling.

The coyote watched as his pursuers approached. When it appeared the man was close enough to throw another rock, the critter trotted farther up the mountain. Once he was confident he was out of reach, he turned to watch the chase.

A hundred feet above the river, Lansing stopped to catch his breath. Margarite stumbled into him as she took a seat on a fallen tree.

"Is your hat really worth all this?" She giggled.

"Yes, it is," he insisted. "What the hell does a coyote need with my hat, anyway?"

"Maybe he was jealous because it looked so good on you."

Lansing wasn't amused by Margarite's sarcastic flattery. He stood and searched the mountain above him. The animal had suddenly disappeared.

"Do you see him anywhere?"

Margarite stood to get a better look. "Looks like he's gone."

"I'm not giving up yet," Lansing said defiantly. He cupped his hands around his mouth to amplify his voice. "All right, you son of a bitch!" he shouted. "Drop it now! I'm coming after you!"

Before he had taken five more steps up the slope a rifle shot rang out. The sheriff could hear the bullet whiz past his head. Before he could react a second shot echoed down the mountain.

Lansing dove for the ground. "Get down!" he ordered as a third shot sounded. Rolling to one side, he found protection behind a pine tree. He listened intently, but no more sounds came from the mountain above them.

"Lansing?" Margarite whimpered from behind him.

"What?" he asked, peeking around the trunk to see if he could see their assailant.

"I hate to bother you, but . . . I think I've been shot!"

MARGARITE WAS ON THE GROUND, HIDDEN BY THE log she had been sitting on a moment earlier. Keeping the pine tree between himself and the top of the mountain, Lansing scooted down to the log, then rolled over the top.

Margarite had her hand pressed against her left shoulder. Blood oozed between her fingers.

"Let me see," Lansing ordered, pulling her hand from the wound. She had been hit in the upper chest, just below the shoulder joint. He leaned her forward. There was no blood on her back, so the bullet had not passed through.

"How bad is it?" she asked, wincing.

"The bullet's still inside and you're bleeding pretty good. But I don't think they hit an artery."

"That's good to know, but I need to keep pressure on this." She winced as she pressed her hand against the wound. "Somehow slow the bleeding."

"We need to get out of here." The sheriff peeked over the log to see if anyone was coming after them. There was no sign of movement. "Come on."

Lansing tried to support her with her right arm over his shoulder. That lasted only a few steps.

"This isn't working," Margarite said groaning. The effort almost made her pass out from pain. "We need to try something else."

Margarite's shirt was becoming soaked with blood. Lansing knew he couldn't fool around with trying to make her comfortable. He picked her up in his arms and carried her as if she were a child.

The slope was steep. He tried walking down in a zigzag pattern. Three times he slipped, sliding ten or more feet on his backside before he could regain his footing. When they finally reached the trail next to the river, Lansing felt he had wasted an hour, and the horses were still a hundred feet away.

He carefully laid Margarite on the ground so he could check the bleeding. As he did, she forced her eyes open.

"How ya doing?" he asked.

"I've been better," she admitted. "I'm thirsty."

"Stay right here. I'll get a canteen."

Lansing ran to where the horses were standing. He untied the reins of both animals. He looped Chico's leather strap around the horse's saddle horn. Knowing he wouldn't have time to guide the old gelding back to the truck, he hoped Chico was smart enough to follow.

He then swung himself into Cement Head's saddle and hurried back to Margarite. Lansing held her head as she tried to gulp the water he was offering. Once she had her fill, he pulled the first aid kit from his saddle bag. There wasn't much to the kit. A few Band-Aids, a roll of gauze, and some tape.

Lansing took the entire roll of gauze and placed it over the seeping wound. Tearing off strips of tape, he secured the bandage as tightly as he could.

Margarite was just barely conscious when he lifted her into the saddle. "Are we going now?" she asked.

"Yes, we are," Lansing said, climbing onto the saddle behind her.

"Did you get the fishing poles?"

"Yes," he lied. "They're all broken down and ready to go."

"Good," she said as her head nodded. "Don't want anyone to steal them."

Lansing turned Cement Head so that they were pointed toward the trailhead. Giving the animal a kick in the sides, they started off at a medium trot.

Lansing wasn't especially familiar with the trail. He kept looking for some landmark to tell him how much farther they had to go. Cement Head was sure footed enough that Lansing could concentrate on keeping himself and Margarite in the saddle.

The farther they went, the more limp Margarite became. The more limp Margarite got, the faster he urged his horse.

Lansing had completely lost track of time. He knew he was going in the right direction, but still he suffered the persistent doubt that he wasn't. Before he decided it was time to panic, he spotted the northern end of the lake a quarter of a mile in front of him. And just as he was about to spur Cement Head into a gallop, a rifle shot rang out.

Lansing reined in his horse. The shot was too far away to be intended for them.

A second shot rang out. Two seconds later, a third.

All three shots came from the direction of the trailhead.

Lansing didn't like the thought of riding into trouble, but he had no choice. Margarite needed medical attention. At Lansing's urging, Cement Head broke into a swift trot.

Above the clop of the horse's hooves, Lansing could hear the rev of an engine just ahead, followed by the grind of tires on gravel.

A cloud of dust lingered in the air over the parking area as the trio emerged from the trail. The departing vehicle was already out of sight.

When they had arrived that morning, a black Ford Bronco and a small Nissan truck had already been parked at the trailhead. Lansing had assumed they belonged to day trippers out to avoid the weekend crowds. The Bronco was now gone. The sheriff was confident the Ford belonged to their assailant.

He was even more convinced of it when he reached the vehicles. The Nissan, Margarite's truck, and his own truck each had a tire shot out to prevent pursuit.

Cursing under his breath, Lansing slid from his saddle, then gently lifted Margarite. She was limp and lifeless. He laid her in the bed of her truck, then ran for his own.

Flicking on his radio, he began calling: "Dispatch. San Phillipe Dispatch. This is Sheriff Lansing. Can you read me?" He clicked off his microphone to listen for a response. There was none.

Lansing was afraid of that. Nestled in the mountains as they were, his radio signal was blocked. He tried again.

"San Phillipe Dispatch. San Phillipe Dispatch. This is Sheriff Lansing. This is an emergency. How copy?"

He stopped once again to listen. A crackle came over his speaker, but nothing more.

"Damn, damn, damn," he swore, slamming the mike back into its cradle.

It was nearly fifteen miles to the main highway and another two to the closest phone. He refused to look at his watch. He didn't want to know how much time he was wasting.

Throwing the hood to his truck open, he grabbed the jack and set to the task of changing his flat tire. He knew that would devour at least ten minutes, but he had no choice.

When the frame was lifted, Lansing pulled the flat tire and rolled it out of his way. The spare, stored under the back axle, slipped on easily. Once the lug nuts were tight, he uncoupled the horse trailer and set the tongue clear.

Picking up Margarite, he noticed her breathing was shallow . . . almost imperceptible.

"Don't die on me, Margarite," he whispered to her as he set her in his truck cab. "Please, don't die on me."

With his reins tied to the rear of the trailer, Cement Head had watched Lansing's frantic efforts with a detached interest. He became more concerned when it appeared his master was leaving without him. He whinnied in protest.

"You're on your own for now," Lansing snapped. "I'll be back for you as soon as I can."

The sheriff slammed the door and started his engine. A moment later, he was gone.

Lansing did his best to cradle Margarite's head in his lap as he negotiated the winding gravel road that traced the shore of the lake. He was grateful there was no other traffic as he cut corners, trying to save time.

Keeping an eye on his speedometer, he guessed he was averaging forty miles an hour. In his mind, that would take too long. He accelerated a little, but had to back off when he nearly lost control on a hairpin turn.

"Hang on, Margarite," he repeated over and over again. "Hang on. We're going to be there before you know it."

Margarite's olive-copper complexion was almost gray and Lansing couldn't tell if she was still breathing. He refused to despair. They were nearly to the highway. He had gotten her that far. He'd see to it she made it to a hospital in time.

"See, I told you!" he said, as he slowed at the recreation area entrance to turn onto the highway.

Two miles west of the entrance was Willard's Grocery, a combination food store, bait shop, and filling station. Lansing covered the distance in just over a minute, screeching to a halt at the front door.

He ran inside.

"Sheriff!" May Willard exclaimed. "What happened to you?"

Lansing was covered with dirt, sweat, and blood. "I need your phone, May. Now!"

Without hesitating, she handed her phone across the counter. Lansing punched in 911. The emergency operator for San Phillipe County worked out of the Las Palmas Fire and Rescue Center. Two rings passed before the dispatcher picked up on the other end.

"Operator, this is Sheriff Lansing. I need for you to call the Life-Flight unit in Farmington. There's been a shooting. I'm at Willard's Grocery on Route 84, two miles west of Spider Woman Rec Area. I need a helicopter here immediately."

"Yes, Sheriff. Do you want to hold while I make the call?"

"Yeah." He looked at May. "There's a woman in the cab of my truck. Dr. Margarite Carerra. Please go check on her. She's been hurt."

"Sure thing, Sheriff." May hurried around her counter and out the door.

Lansing tapped the countertop impatiently. Farmington was less than an hour away by highway. It would be even shorter by air. He tried to guess how soon the helicopter could be there.

"Sheriff, you still there?"

"Yes, I am."

"Life-Flight's in the air. Estimated time en route, fifteen minutes."

"Thanks."

"Do you need any further assistance?"

"Yes. Call my office and tell them I'm blocking off part of Route 84 for the emergency unit. I'll call them when it's open again."

"Yes, sir."

As Lansing hung up the phone, May came rushing back into the store. Her face was white. "She's in real bad shape, Sheriff. I don't know what to do."

"Is she still alive?"

May nodded. "I think so."

"Do you have any road flares?"

"Yes. Along the back wall, next to the automotive."

"Get a blanket and cover her," he barked. "And stay with her."

May hurried to retrieve a blanket as Lansing grabbed a box of flares. As much as he wanted to, he knew he didn't have time to be with Margarite. He needed to block off the highway to give the helicopter a landing zone.

To make sure motorists got the right idea, Lansing set off six flares, blocking the highway from the east. Running a hundred feet in the other direction, he set off another wall of flares. The road was completely blocked in front of the station.

Lansing ran to his truck. May was just covering the motionless Margarite.

"Let me see her," Lansing said. May moved out of the way. He knelt on the floor of the cab and gently took Margarite's hand. "It's going to be all right, Doc. There's a helicopter on the way. You're going to be okay. Just hold on."

Margarite's hand was cold and there was only the slightest hint that she was still breathing. As if to tell Lansing she was doing her best, she gave his hand a frail squeeze. It was all the response she could muster.

A couple of motorists, perturbed at the imposition of the roadblock, came grumbling over to the grocery story. May, a normally placid woman in her late sixties, sternly explained the situation, advising them that this inconvenience was minor compared to what the woman in the truck was suffering. After her words, there were plenty of volunteers to assist with anything that needed to be done.

Lansing was almost oblivious of the sound of the helicopter when it arrived. He stayed with Margarite from the time the paramedics arrived at the truck until the metal stretcher was secured in the aircraft.

As much as he wanted to go with them, there was not enough room. He could only watch helplessly as the helicopter lifted off and turned in the direction of Farmington.

"It's just as well," he said to himself, his teeth clenched in rage. "Because now I'm going to find the son of a bitch who did this."

22

GABE FOUND THE ATMOSPHERE IN THE SHIPROCK café strained. The dozen or so people scattered in the booths stared at Kimberly, as if they resented her being there. The waitress, an Anglo with bleached hair, was friendly enough to explain. She leaned over the table and talked in low tones.

"When word got out your father had been killed, everyone felt sorry. He was a good man and everybody liked him. Then the police said he was selling drugs to schoolkids . . . and they found all that money. Well, Kim, you know how it is. Small town. Small minds. Since your dad's not around to defend himself, it's real easy to convict him."

"That's why no one's talking to me?"

The waitress nodded. "That and they think you probably knew about it."

"There wasn't anything to know," Kim said defiantly. "He wasn't selling drugs!"

"Hey, hey, honey. You don't have to convince me," the waitress protested. "My second husband got thirty years in the federal pen for running drugs. I know the type and Walter Tallmountain doesn't fit the mold. I don't care what the police say."

The waitress looked around the room. The other customers kept sneaking glances in their direction. No one seemed to approve of her conversation. "How 'bout I bag your sandwiches so you don't have to stay here and put up with those stares?"

"No." Kim was definite in her decision. "My father didn't do anything wrong and I have nothing to hide."

"Suit yourself, honey."

Despite Kimberly's defiance, she, Gabe, and Hunter ate in silence. The deputy was grateful when they finally left.

As they walked back to the chapter house, Kim turned to the old man. "Hunter, George Akima said he would sing at the funeral tomorrow. He doesn't think my father did anything wrong, either. Will you sit with me at the ceremony?"

Hunter nodded. "I will sit with you."

"George said he would sing 'Dsichl Biyin' to bless the journey."

"The Mountain Song is a good choice. Walter would have chosen that one himself."

Gabe was mystified by the conversation. To his mind, a funeral meant a sermon over a grave. Maybe a song meant the same thing.

Kim looked at Gabe. "Will you be here?"

"I don't know. I don't have any clothes to wear. What time are you talking about?"

"Early afternoon."

"His spirit is very restless by now," Hunter observed. "He has been dead these four days and yet his soul has not started the journey."

"Why not?" Gabe hoped he didn't sound too ignorant.

"You were not raised in the traditional ways?" He was not surprised. Few young people were raised that way.

Gabe shook his head.

"Did your parents at least tell you about the old ways?"

"Only my father was Navajo . . . and he never spoke about his people."

Hunter's face clouded with concern. "It is not healthy that a man reject his heritage. It leads to illness and sickness of mind. . . ." He gave Gabe a sidelong glance as they walked along. "Why have you come to the reservation?"

"To see how Kimberly was getting along."

Hunter nodded, but he suspected there was more behind Gabe's visit than a woman. "When a man dies, it takes four days for his spirit to travel to the place of the dead. But his spirit cannot make the journey unless the body has been properly buried. Then it can be at rest. It is important that the dead be buried as soon as possible after death."

"What happens if a man isn't properly buried?"

"His spirit becomes a ghost, an agent of evil. He will walk the nights, live in the dark shadows and haunt the living with his presence."

"You don't really believe that stuff, do you? I mean ghosts and spirits walking around at night."

The old man shrugged. "I have never seen one, if that's what you mean. I've never seen a single atom, either, but scientists say everything is built with them. Should my faith only be built on things I see?" He paused for a moment, then asked, "Have you ever been around a decaying body?"

Gabe shook his head.

"It stinks, it bloats, it is disease ridden. It is a very unhealthy thing. Whether there is a spirit involved or not, a dead body should be buried as soon as possible, especially in a hot, dry climate like ours. Religion notwithstanding, there is a practical reason for disposing of the dead."

"Can we talk about something else?" Kim asked.

They had reached the entrance to the chapter house and Gabe opened the door for the other two.

"Yes. We should," Hunter agreed, following Kim inside. "I need to talk with you about why I came to town."

"Should I leave you two for now?" Gabe asked. He didn't want to interfere in personal matters.

"It would not hurt for you to listen to what I say," Hunter said. "You do not know much about your own people. The more you hear, the more you will learn."

"I have a little time," Kim said. "We can talk in my office."

"Did your father ever talk about the Season of the Voices? It was a long time ago, before you were born."

Kim shook her head as she rested her elbows on her desk. "I don't remember anything like that."

"It was the time of the coyotes," Hunter prompted. "When their howls were so thick at night a man couldn't sleep."

"I remember him talking about the coyotes. It was in the spring, I believe."

"Yes." Hunter nodded. "In the spring. Thirty years ago. I still kept a flock of sheep then. It wasn't a large flock. Maybe a hundred. But I lost nearly half of them to the coyotes that year."

"I remember my father saying a lot of people on the reservation suffered that year. Sheep, cattle, pets . . . The coyotes were even digging up gardens. There didn't seem to be anything anyone could do."

"Yes, yes. That was the time." Hunter paused. "That's why I needed to talk to your father. I heard them on the mountain all last night. The voices are back. Coyote has returned."

23

GABE LOOKED AT THE OLD MAN DOUBTFULLY. " 'COYote has returned'? You mean, as in 'one' coyote has come back here?"

Hunter shook his head. "Not as in 'one' coyote. I can't even say it is 'the' coyote. It is just 'Coyote.' "

Gabe looked at Kim. The conservationist looked as though she had her own doubts.

"What is . . . Coyote?" Gabe directed the question to Kim.

"In the Navajo legends, Coyote was the first animal. He was created the same time the Great Spirit created First Man and First Woman. First Man and First Woman were the *diyin dine'e* who helped create everything else."

"I'm confused," Gabe confessed. "What are 'dying dinnies'?"

"*Di-yin Din-a-a*," Kim said slowly, emphasizing the separate syllables. "They are the Holy People of our religion. They are spirits . . . gods. . . . It's hard to explain to someone not raised in the old ways."

"How were you raised, Gabriel," Hunter interrupted, "in your religion?"

"Catholic."

"So when you were raised, you were taught there was one true God."

"Yes."

"But you were also taught that below God are a host of holy beings you can pray to that can intercede on your behalf: the Virgin Mary, Saint Benedict, Saint Peter . . ." Gabe nodded. "And beyond that is the hierarchy of angels and archangels, cherubim and seraphim, all made by the Creator to do His work."

"Yeah, I remember all that from catechism."

"In the Navajo religion, we are also taught that there is a single Great Spirit, the Creator. In our creation stories, there are a host of holy beings that helped make the world. Your Christianity has its saints and angels. We have our *diyin dine'e*. Does this parallel make sense?"

"Yes." Hanna nodded thoughtfully. "Yes, it does."

"I cannot teach you much about the Navajo way or our beliefs. It would take many years and I am not a Holy Man. But maybe I've given you a frame of reference. . . . Maybe now we can speak of Coyote."

"Okay," Gabe agreed, hoping he could put his disbelief aside for a while.

"As Kimberly said, Coyote was the first creature. He is the source of all that is wise and all that is foolish. In some stories, he named all the other creatures as they emerged from the *Sipapu*, the lower worlds. The Hopi believe he even helped create the first humans. Those that know the Coyote stories know he created death, although he himself can never die."

Gabe began to feel as though he had been suckered. The old man had started off with an eloquent comparison of religions and now seemed to be sinking into a morass of mythology. He hoped Hunter would get to the point.

"Coyote, because he has been since the beginning, is very powerful. He has the power of the *yenaldlooshi* and can change his shape if he chooses. He can become a man. He can become a woman. He can become any creature he wants. Because he has this power, he likes to play tricks on people. It is because of his pranks that he is also known as the Trickster."

"Hunter, I grew up with all the Coyote stories," Kim interrupted. "Every child on the reservation has. I still don't know what you're getting at."

"Before the human beings and all the other creatures emerged onto the fifth world of creation, this world, spirits walked the land. They now only live in the underworld, but their power is still great, which is why we pray to them. Of all the spirits, though, only Coyote chooses to walk the fifth world with men. When he does, his cousins walk in his shadow; they feel his power and they use it.

"A single, four-legged coyote can do little more than filch a newborn lamb from a flock. With the spirit of Coyote, that same animal can take down a ram. Two can kill a steer. Four coyotes once drove an entire herd of wild horses over a cliff.

"Coyote can do other things. When he changes shape he can open windows and doors. He can enter a man's house and unplug everything electrical or turn everything on. He likes to play tricks like that. He will open an irrigation gate and flood a field. Or drive the pigs from a sty into a newly planted garden. Old Joseph New Horse even said Coyote drove his truck into a ditch, though I think Old Joseph had been drinking and did it himself. He just didn't want his wife to know. These are the powers of Coyote."

Hunter was finished speaking. He leaned back in his seat and crossed his arms, waiting for a response.

Part of Gabe wanted to corroborate the old man's feport. There had been dozens of complaints about coyotes in San Phillipe County. But he also knew he wasn't an expert on the animal. In fact, the only wild coyote he had ever seen peed on his Jeep. That hardly made him an authority. He decided to keep his thoughts to himself and let Kim talk.

"Why did you need to talk to my father about this? He was the reservation conservation officer. Shouldn't you be talking to the Holy Men?"

"Maybe." Hunter nodded. "The elders would remember thirty years ago. But I wanted to talk to your father about how the voices stopped."

"What do you mean?"

"The coyotes were all crazy and aggressive and then suddenly they weren't. They went back to being just coyotes. No more livestock were killed. No more barns were broken into. No more houses raided. I will talk to the Holy Men. They will remember. But they will also say it was their prayers that sent Coyote away."

"So what's wrong with that?" Gabe asked. It sounded to him like the perfect solution, if there was, indeed, a problem.

"Coyote is very vain. He would not stop unless he proved his power. Somehow he proved how powerful he was thirty years ago, and then he went away. I thought maybe Walter remembered what happened."

"I guess I can't help," Kim said, frowning. "I'm sorry."

Hunter stood. "There is nothing you should apologize for. I will talk to the Holy Men and see what they think. Then I will go home. But don't worry, Yazhi. I will be back tomorrow."

"Thank you, Hunter."

The old man left, leaving Gabe and Kim alone. Gabe thought Hunter's tale was silly but he didn't want to offend Kim by saying so. Instead, he asked, "What did you think of his story?"

Kim shrugged. "I love that old man and I would never say anything to hurt his feelings. But he lives alone up in the hills. All he has is his imagination to keep him company."

"So you don't believe any of this about Coyote?"

She gave Gabe a half smile. "You think because I was raised on the reservation I have to believe in all the superstitions?"

"No. That's not what I meant . . . I mean, this is all new stuff to me. I wouldn't know what it means to be Navajo any more than what it means to be Chinese. I don't know what I'm supposed to believe in. And if I don't believe in something, have I offended everyone else on the reservation?"

"I don't think you have to worry about that." She smiled. "There's a lot more to being Navajo than simply following the old religion. There are Catholics and Baptists and Lutherans on the reservation. Some people practice the old ways and still go to church every Sunday . . . I'm glad you decided to come here to find out for yourself."

"Yeah," Gabe said, returning the smile. "Me too." He was also glad they were finally alone. He wasn't sure if anything would happen between them, but this gave him the opportunity to find out. His expectations quickly fizzled.

"I hate to do this to you," Kim apologized. "But I have to make arrangements for the funeral tomorrow."

"Oh, I don't mind keeping you company."

"No, that's not what I meant. I'd prefer to make these arrangements alone. I have to see a lot of people and, well . . ."

"I'd just be in the way," Gabe completed her thought. "That's okay. I understand . . . What about tonight?"

"What about tonight?"

"Mr. Hania had asked us out to dinner at his ranch."

Kim bit her lower lip. "I don't know how much company I would be. . . ." She pulled a piece of paper from her desk drawer and drew a map. "This will show you how to get to my place. I should be there after five. Give me a call or stop by. I'll let you know about dinner then."

"Okay." Gabe folded the map and stuck it in his pocket. He took a step toward the door. "You sure you wouldn't like some company this afternoon?"

"I'm sure." Kim nodded. "But thanks, anyway."

"See you later then." Gabe half waved.

"Yeah. Later."

24

LANSING TIED CEMENT HEAD'S REINS TO A LOW BUSH
and looked around. The Sterno can had burned out. The
sheriff silently cursed himself for leaving a fire burning in
the forest like that. He knew better, but he'd been over-
come by events.

The fishing poles were still leaning against the rock. The
fish were gone. They might have been taken by coyotes,
or a raccoon, even birds. The rocky bank didn't leave a
clue.

Lansing checked to make sure his pistol was secure in
its holster, then took a flashlight out of the saddle bag. It
was already late afternoon. He was sure it would be dark
by the time he got back from his climb.

After Margarite had been whisked away in the helicopter, Lansing contacted his office. He needed someone to
drive up and retrieve Margarite's truck from the rec area.
He left instructions to have it parked at Willard's Grocery.

Cement Head gave Lansing a severe scolding when he
got back. Lansing knew the animal was thirsty and he apologized as he lead his horse down to the river. That's where
he found Chico. The old gelding had made himself comfortable in the shade of a pine tree and was contentedly
grazing on young spring shoots.

As much as he wanted to drive to Farmington, Lansing

knew there was nothing he could do for Margarite. Instead, his policeman instincts kicked in. If he was going to find out who did the shooting, he needed to get on the trail while it was still warm.

The first stop would be the scene of the crime. Someone on that mountain didn't want to be seen . . . or didn't want something found. The assailant left in a hurry. The sheriff could only hope they left evidence behind.

A hundred feet above the river he found the log he and Margarite had hidden behind. Searching the slope above him, Lansing could see little in the darkening shadows. He continued his climb, wondering how much farther he would have to go.

After another hundred feet he emerged onto a flat clearing. A hiking trail, tracing the top of a ridge line, appeared to his right. The clearing seemed to be a favorite spot for campers. Brush had been cleaned away to make room for a tent and a blackened circle of stones had been arranged for a fire.

Lansing sniffed the air. The fire had been used recently. He went closer to inspect.

Whoever had used the hearth last had burned more than wood. There were burnt pieces of cloth and metal tubes hanging outside the stone circle. Lansing picked up one of the tubes. It was blackened, and melted nylon clung to the metal. To Lansing, it looked like it could be a support for a backpack.

He examined a piece of cloth. It was heavy nylon, the type used for a sleeping bag. Another piece was cotton and had a plaid pattern to it. Lansing suspected it was the lining to the sleeping bag.

Using a stick, he poked through the ashes. They were still warm and wisps of smoke drifted up from the burnt remains. He spread them around so that they would cool faster, but couldn't find anything of significance.

Lansing stood and looked around. He considered what he would take, as a minimum, on a backpacking trip. Sleeping bag, backpack . . . he had found those. Cooking pot, knife, flashlight, canteen.

He began circling the perimeter of the campsite. If he were trying to conceal evidence, and it wouldn't burn, he would bury it. What if he were in a hurry? What if he didn't have a shovel? No problem. This was mostly a pine forest and the ground was covered with fallen needles. Scoop out a clear spot, then cover it with handfuls of more needles.

All he had to do was find a spot where the needles had been disturbed.

He began a systematic inspection of the area closest to the clearing. If he didn't find anything close, he would expand his search.

As he worked his way around the edge of the clearing he found where the trail continued deeper into the mountains. Ten feet down the trail, he saw a shape that looked out of place. Maybe this was it. Coming closer, Lansing could only laugh. The strange tan mound was his Stetson, the hat stolen by the coyote earlier in the day.

He stifled his chuckle. If it hadn't been for the damned coyote running off with his hat, none of this would have happened. He brushed off the hat and put it on.

Going back to his search, Lansing finally found the pile of needles he wanted. They were next to the trail leading down the mountain. Lansing couldn't understand why he didn't look in that area first. Kicking off the needles, he found the canteen and the cooking pot. There was no flashlight or knife.

It was getting dark. Lansing gathered up his evidence and started down the mountain. He found it a lot easier than when he was carrying Margarite.

Margarite . . . He tried pushing the thought of her out of

his mind. She was in good hands. There wasn't a thing he could do for her now and worrying wouldn't help. He knew he would call the hospital as soon as he reached a phone.

As he and Cement Head picked their way along the darkening trail, Lansing tried to decipher the evidence he had found.

Someone had been camping on the mountain. They were trying to hide the fact that they were there, so they burned their equipment. Lansing and Margarite had stumbled into him and the camper tried to shoot them.

That didn't make sense. Whoever the camper was drove a Ford Bronco. He, or she, Lansing considered, didn't want to be followed, so they shot out his tires. They shot out everyone's tires.

Maybe the shooter wasn't trying to hide the fact that he was camping at that spot. Maybe he was trying to hide the fact someone else had camped there. It was important enough that they would try to kill an innocent victim who was in the wrong place at the wrong time.

When Lansing picked Spider Woman Rec Area, he only remotely thought he would find something to back up Kim's story about her father. He was almost positive he had found the evidence he wanted. However, in light of everything that had happened, he also regretted the moment he ever heard Walter Tallmountain's name.

25

GABE FOUND HIMSELF STANDING ALONE AT THE FRONT door of Edward Hania's hacienda. The main house was built in the pueblo style: exposed beams extended beyond the whitewashed adobe walls. Arched portals supported a flat roof. He suspected the thick stone and masonry walls kept the house warm in the winter and cool in the summer.

When he left the chapter house, Gabe wasn't sure how he would occupy his time. He had expected to spend his afternoon with Kim doing whatever she needed to do. He considered touring the reservation, but he felt like an intruder . . . like he didn't belong. He would have felt less so with Kim as a guide, but that didn't turn out to be one of his options.

In a way, he wished he could have gone with Hunter Niyol. The old man, despite his quirky view of the world, seemed to know a great deal. Now that he had broken the ice, Gabe would have welcomed a formal introduction to the tribe elders. He certainly didn't have enough gumption to do it on his own.

Gabe, despite his skepticism, was intrigued with Hunter's story about nature gone berserk. He wondered if it had really happened. The deputy didn't have the luxury of a congress of elders whose memories he could prod.

As bad a student as he had been, Gabe had learned

something in school. When no one was around who knew the answer, you could always go to the library. (That's where he learned to replace his first set of disk brakes.)

The Farmington Public Library wasn't very large, but Gabe didn't need many references. In fact, all he wanted to look at were the newspaper microfilms from thirty years earlier. If the coyote activity had been as rampant as Hunter had reported, surely something had shown up in the paper.

He requested microfilms covering the months of March through June. The *Farmington News* was not a big paper, so it didn't take long to filter through the first month of news. There was nothing about coyotes. Hanna was beginning to think everything Hunter had said was only the product of senility.

But then he found one paragraph article buried on page eight of April seventh. A rancher had reported six lambs and three ewes slaughtered overnight. He suspected it was the work of a mountain lion, although he could only find coyote tracks in the vicinity of the flock. The San Juan County Animal Control Office said it would investigate.

On the eighth of April, two stories appeared. In one case, sheep had been attacked again. In the other, two calves had been killed. There were four stories about coyotes on April ninth. Five on the tenth.

THE COYOTE PLAGUE was the front page story on April eleventh. A dozen more farms and ranches reported coyote attacks in San Juan County alone. Stories about aggressive coyotes were being told from as far west as Flagstaff and east to Taos.

Every day for the next week the Coyote Plague was front page news. Trapping wasn't working. Poisoning didn't help. Professional hunters, tracking the animals by helicopter and shooting them from the air, couldn't stop them. The paper showed a photograph of three hundred coyote carcasses, nearly fifty animals killed per day over a week's time.

On April eighteenth, eleven days after the first published report, the coyote stories stopped. The next day the Animal Control Officer for San Juan expressed guarded optimism that the plague was at an end. By the first of May, ranchers and politicians alike declared total victory.

So, Gabe thought, Hunter's story about the coyotes was true. None of the articles really explained why there were so many coyotes or why they acted so aggressively. One biologist from the University of Arizona said the large influx of animals was due to an oversupply of food. The coyotes had exceptionally large litters the year before because the natural habitat could support large litters.

A second biologist from the University of New Mexico took the opposite view. There was an undersupply of food in the natural habitat the previous year. As a result, coyotes were breeding to become more aggressive.

No one could account for why the behavior suddenly stopped. There hadn't even been a tapering-off period.

Just to make sure, Gabe rolled through a few more days of microfilm. The only article that caught his attention was on May third. There was a photograph of a very young Edward Hania standing in the middle of a dozen cars. The article announced the opening of Navajo Motors, a used-car lot wholly owned and operated by a tribe member.

He read the article, not so much because he was interested in Hania, but because he wanted to see if his father was mentioned. He wasn't.

Gabe rewound the spool and returned the microfilm to the library counter. He had completely lost track of time. It was after five. Before leaving the library he used the pay phone in the lobby. He wanted to see if Kimberly had made a decision about dinner.

The phone rang six times before her answering machine

picked up. Gabe didn't feel much like leaving a message. He decided he would ride out to her place. She lived five miles south of Shiprock. He figured it would take him about thirty minutes to get there. She would be home by then.

Kim lived in a small frame house a mile off the highway. Two mailboxes marked the turnoff. Both boxes had the name Tallmountain stenciled on the side.

Kim's house was white with green trim. Two tall cottonwood trees sheltered the house on the south side, helping keep it cool in the summer. A hundred yards beyond her house was another group of buildings. One building was stone and adobe with a flat roof. Behind it was a small wooden barn and a strange, circular building made of adobe. To Gabe, it looked like a truncated silo. He would learn later it was the family hogan.

All three buildings, though old, looked well maintained.

Kim's truck was nowhere to be seen. Knowing it was a waste of time, Gabe knocked on the door to her house anyway. There was no answer. He didn't expect any better luck at the adobe house, but still he rode down to check. No one was there either.

He went back and sat on the front step of the frame house. He was sure Kim would show up soon.

After waiting an hour, Gabe gave up. It was nearly seven o'clock and he still needed to get directions to Edward Hania's place. He wanted to let Kimberly know he had been there, but he didn't have a pen or paper for a note. Picking up a handful of pebbles, he spelled the letters G-A-B-E on her front step. He hoped she saw them before it got too dark.

"Gabe! I'm glad you decided you could make it," Hania said, holding the door open for his visitor. "Is Kimberly with you?"

"No. I guess she got tied up with other things."

Gabe was impressed with the interior of the ranch house. The walls were clean, white stucco. The high ceilings were supported by exposed beams and the floor was red tile. He didn't know much about furniture, but Hania's looked Spanish to him.

Hania escorted Gabe through the spacious entry into the den area. Three other men, drinks in hand, were already waiting.

"Gentlemen," Hania said, smiling, "I would like you to meet a long-lost relative of mine. This is my nephew, Gabriel Hania."

Gabe felt uncomfortable being called Hania. He didn't know for sure that Hania was his last name. If it was, he wasn't sure he wanted it.

"Gabriel," the older man continued, "I'd like you to meet my friend and personal lawyer, Thad Berkeley. This is Samuel Elverson, with Rocky Mountain Resources. And his associate, Beck Lundquist."

Gabe shook hands with each man as they were introduced.

"Thad, get my nephew here a drink. What'll you have, son?"

"A Coke, please."

"Make it a Coke, Thad."

Hania indicated they should all sit.

"It really is unfortunate Miss Tallmountain couldn't make it here tonight," Hania said. "She's a very pleasant young woman."

"She has her hands full trying to make funeral arrangements for her father."

"Yes." Hania shook his head. "What a terrible thing to have happen." The other men nodded but said nothing.

Gabe thanked Berkeley when his drink was delivered. "Mr. Hania," Gabe started, "I don't want to sound ungrateful about the invitation this evening, but I have to be honest with you. I don't know that you're my uncle. I don't know that I have any relatives out here on the reservation. For all I know my father was an orphan."

"Your father was no orphan, son. I could tell you had your doubts this afternoon, so I went to the trouble of digging this out." Hania picked up a photo album from the coffee table in front of him. He handed it to Gabe. "Go ahead and browse through there. See what you think."

Gabe opened the book and began thumbing through the pages. The first photographs were in black-and-white. They showed a Navajo man and woman standing in front of an adobe hut. There were pictures of the couple with two boys. Judging from their sizes, Gabe guessed the boys were about five years apart in age.

The pictures showed the boys from early childhood through their teens. The photos changed from black-and-white to color. More formal photos—probably school pictures, Gabe thought—were mingled with the family pictures.

Gabe turned to the next page. He was startled at what he saw. It was like looking into a mirror. It was David Hania's high school graduation photo . . . or would have been if he had finished school. The deputy was shocked at the resemblance.

"You see, Gabriel. You understand my reaction when I saw you this afternoon. That picture was taken just a few months before Davy left. That's the way I remembered him. When I saw you today, I knew you had to be his son. . . . You are my nephew and David Hania was your father."

26

GABE WANTED TO BELIEVE HE HAD FOUND HIS FAther's family. All his life other kids had grandparents to visit on holidays and vacations. Their parents always talked about going "home" on trips. Gabe never had that luxury. He had no reference point to mark his beginnings. He had always been jealous of that. He had also been haunted by *why*.

"My dad spelled our name H-A-N-N-A. I can see how someone else might have misspelled it, changing an *I* to an *N*. But that's the way he wanted it spelled." Gabe looked Hania directly in the eye. "Why did he feel like he had to change his name? And why did he leave the reservation?"

Hania cleared his throat. He didn't seem anxious to talk about the subject. "I don't think we need to dig up old family stories tonight. Thad and the others wouldn't be interested. . . ."

"The only reason I came here tonight was to talk about my father," Gabe said pointedly. "Because if we don't talk about him, you and I don't have anything in common."

"All right." Hania nodded. "I'll tell you about your father. I'll start it off by saying I loved Davy very much. I was his big brother. As the oldest, I was the one who had responsibility heaped on him. I was the one who watched the flocks all day while my father worked in town. I worked and Davy played.

"As we got older, Davy was always getting into scrapes and I was always bailing him out. It wasn't that Davy was a bad kid. Fact was, everyone liked him. But he was a joker. A real practical joker." Hania chuckled. "His nickname was Coyote . . . Coyote the joker. Coyote the trickster."

Coyote, Gabe thought. He had heard that word more times in one day than in his entire life.

"I remember when your father was seventeen. He had souped up an old '53 Pontiac. He was really proud of that old junker. When he got it tuned just the way he wanted he put out the word: he was going to stage a drag down Apache Street on the north side of Farmington. Midnight on Saturday. And not a single cop was going to touch him.

"Though Davy had never been arrested for anything, he wasn't popular with the local cops. They were going to make sure some punk Navajo kid didn't make fools of them. When that Saturday rolled around, two city police cars, the sheriff, and one of his deputies were spread out along the strip. Back then, Apache Street, from one end of the city limits to the other, ran about two miles. They were ready. They were going to nail his red hide to the wall if he got one mile over the speed limit.

"To make sure they didn't miss anything, they showed up thirty minutes early. Davy figured that's what they would do. He showed up the same time they did. He drove down Apache minding the speed limit, waving at all the officers when he drove past. He wanted to make sure they were good and steamed. Then he headed about a half mile past the city limits so he could get a running start.

"Well, a bunch of the Anglo boys didn't care much for Davy. They didn't like his smart-aleck attitude. Who did he think he was, pulling off a stunt like that? Besides, they knew they had better cars than he did. Three boys from

the city high school showed up in their cars to challenge
him. If he could make that run, so could they.

"Farmington can be a rough little town and Davy knew
he had to back up his brag. I don't know where he got the
money, but he flashed a wad of bills and bet them he could
beat them to the other end of town from where they were
parked. Now those boys had a real motivation. The drag
was on.

"All four cars lined up, engines revving. It sounded like
the Indy 500. I swear, every kid in town showed up to see
what would happen. One of the Anglos' girlfriends yelled
'go' and they were off.

"First quarter mile Davy had those boys. All they saw of
him was the smoke from his tires. It looked like they would
never catch him. Then, a hundred yards short of the city
limits, something exploded under Davy's hood and smoke
started pouring out.

"Those city kids had him. As Davy's car slowed down
they came whipping past a-hoopin' and a-hollerin', laughing their heads off.

"Of course, with all those cop cars waiting, those city
boys never made it all the way through town. Davy did.
He never went over the speed limit. He won the bet. Of
course, those Anglo boys never paid off. . . . I don't think
they ever found out he faked his engine blowing up. He
never told them about the M-80 and the smoke bomb under his hood. If those Anglos had seen him slow down on
purpose, they would have figured something was up."

Hania glanced at Gabe. "Davy said he would stage a drag
race and he did. He never once said he'd be in it. That's
the kind of pranks your father would pull."

Gabe couldn't help but be impressed and a little proud.
He wondered why his father never told him stories like
that. Hanna could tell his uncle was proud of the story he

had just told. "If my father was so well liked, why did he leave the reservation?"

"His last prank got out of hand. Several of the clans had been saving up for the new chapter house at Shiprock. It was the mid-sixties and money was pretty tight, but they had managed to scrape together five thousand dollars. It was enough to secure a building loan. The money was being kept at the old house. The day before they were to take it to the bank someone stole it. Every last penny."

Hania's face clouded in a frown. "A dozen people saw Davy walk out of the building with the deposit bag. In plain daylight. When the tribal police picked him up, he denied all the charges. Said he hadn't even been to Shiprock that day.

"The elders were fair. They told him if he would return the money no more questions would be asked. He said he was innocent. He said he couldn't return money he didn't have. I talked to him. I begged him. But he wouldn't change his story.

"The elders and the council didn't want to deal with the white authorities. They know how Navajos are treated in jail. They gave Davy three options: return the money, go to the white man's jail, or join the white man's army. That was common back in those days. If a young man got in trouble, the army was always offered as an option.

"Davy said he had no money he could return, so he chose the army. That was the last I ever heard of him . . . until today."

"If my father had never been in trouble with the law before, why did they think he stole the money?"

"Because he was seen. People saw him with their own eyes. Coyote was always playing tricks. People thought, Ah, this is a good trick. We were frightened our money was gone. Now it is time to return the money. I thought that.

But he never would return the money. So he was sent away."

"Do you think he took the money?"

"Yes. Why else would he have left? Why did he never return?"

"What if he didn't take the money? If he had stayed, you would have sent him to jail."

"Not me. The elders. The council. They would have sent him. I argued on his behalf. . . ."

"But you didn't believe him."

Before Hania could respond, the door chimes sounded. "Excuse me," he said, standing. "I'll be right back."

Gabe felt uncomfortable being left alone with the three white men. Maybe family stories were better left for more private occasions, he thought. It didn't matter now. Everyone knew.

Gabe's uncle returned to the room followed by Kim.

"I'm sorry I'm late," she apologized. "Things were a bit more complicated today than I expected."

"There is no reason to apologize," Edward said. "We were just getting ready to move to the dining room. Gentlemen, this way."

27

"YES. THIS IS CLIFF LANSING. I'M THE SHERIFF OVER IN San Phillipe. I'm calling about a shooting victim that your Life-Flight brought in this afternoon."

"Yes, Sheriff. Do you have a name?"

"Yeah. Carerra. Dr. Margarite Carerra."

"One moment, please . . ."

Lansing took the cup of coffee May Willard offered. It was dark outside by the time he had reached the grocery. He was still covered with dirt and Margarite's blood. He wanted to be by her side, but he had to know how she was doing. It would be another hour before he reached the hospital.

"Sheriff Lansing?"

"Yes, I'm still here."

"The patient is in the intensive care unit. Would you like me to transfer you?"

"Yes, I would."

"One moment . . ."

There was a subdued ring over the line followed by a click. "Intensive care. Mrs. Clay."

"Yes, ma'am. This is Sheriff Lansing, San Phillipe County. I'm calling about one of your patients, Margarite Carerra. She was brought in this afternoon."

"I'm sorry, sir. I'm not allowed to give any information over the phone."

Lansing was tired and he was worried. He didn't feel like dealing with any bureaucratic bull. "Listen, ma'am. This is an official police investigation. Unless you want to face a charge of obstruction of justice, you'd better answer some questions."

"I'm sorry, sir," she said stiffly. "I'm not at liberty to give out patient information. If you want to talk to the physician on duty, I can put him on."

"That would be just fine," the sheriff snapped.

"Dr. Morton. Can I help you?"

"Yes, Doctor. This is Sheriff Lansing. I was with Margarite Carerra this afternoon when she was shot. I'm the one who got her to the Life-Flight helicopter. All I'm trying to do is find out how she is."

"One moment. Let me check her chart. . . . It's right here." There was a pause on the other end while Morton reviewed the paperwork. "I just came on duty, so I haven't had a chance to familiarize myself with the new patients. Just looking at the chart . . . I'm afraid it doesn't look good. She was unconscious when they brought her in. . . . Looks like they had to administer three pints of whole blood to get her stabilized before they could take out the bullet. . . ."

"How is she doing now?" Lansing pressed. "Is she resting comfortably?"

"Right now, Sheriff, she's in a coma. You have to remember, she lost a lot of blood. There's a possibility the brain suffered from oxygen deprivation. . . . Hello? Sheriff, are you still there?"

"Yeah," Lansing said hoarsely. "I'm still here."

"Until she recovers consciousness, we really won't know how much damage there is."

"How long will that take?"

"It could be a day. It could be a week. She may never

come out of the coma. We'll just have to wait and see. . . .
I notice in these records there's no personal information
like family, residence, things like that."

"I can bring that information in," Lansing said. "I'll be
stopping by later."

"Is there anything else I can do for you?"

"No. You've done plenty, Doc. Thanks."

Lansing felt numb as he hung up the phone.

"How is she?" May asked.

"Not well," he admitted, shaking his head as he walked
out the door. "Not well."

The night air helped revive Lansing a little. There was
no point in sitting next to Margarite all night, he decided.
Not if she was in a coma. Besides, sitting in a hospital room
would not find the person who shot her.

Pulling onto the highway, Lansing pointed his truck toward Las Palmas. He was towing his horse trailer again.
Cement Head and Chico still needed to be taken back and
he needed to get cleaned up. Maybe a couple of hours of
sleep wouldn't hurt him, either, he thought. He knew he
couldn't sleep long. There was too much to do and not
enough time to do it.

28

GAYLE HANIA, EDWARD'S WIFE, WAS BUSY LOADING
the table with food when the host and his guests entered
the dining room. Hania made a short round of introductions. When he came to Gabe, he made it a point to emphasize Gabriel was their nephew.

Gabe found his aunt to be particularly demure. She
acted, and seemed to be treated, more like a servant than
a spouse. Hania asked his guests to be seated, then instructed Gayle to bring the rest of the food.

Hania sat at the head of the table and the others took
the chairs he indicated. Gayle continued to bustle about,
refusing Kim's offer of help. Once her preparations were
complete, the hostess took a seat conveniently close to the
kitchen.

Gabe was impressed with the meal: roast pheasant, wild
rice, baby yams, and chilled asparagus in vinaigrette. He
suspected this wasn't the normal meal served on the reservation. But he was rapidly becoming aware his uncle
wasn't the typical Navajo, either.

The discussion over dinner started with mundane obser-
vances of the weather, what a nice spring it had been, how
hot the summer was going to be, if there was going to be
a drought. When the climate card had been played to its
fullest, Hania changed the subject.

"I hope you didn't have any problems making arrangements for tomorrow, Kimberly. I know how painful setting up a funeral can be."

"There were a few minor inconveniences," the young woman admitted. "I had to borrow some money so I could pay for the funeral. It seems all of my family's assets have been frozen by the State of New Mexico pending its investigation. If the state in its infinite wisdom decides my father was a drug dealer, everything he owned will be forfeited to the government. Probably everything I own will go too."

"I am terribly sorry to hear this," Hania said, shaking his head. "I wish you had come to me. I know your father and I had our differences of opinion, but I deeply respected Walter. I would be glad to do anything to help . . . especially with the funeral expenses. Observing the old ways is important, particularly during a tragedy like this."

"Thank you, Mr. Hania, but I've already taken care of the funeral." Kim poked at the food on her plate as she considered her next words. "I do have to admit, Mr. Hania . . ."

"Edward. Please," the older man insisted.

"I . . . That would show too much disrespect, sir. I would feel more comfortable with addressing you properly."

Hania nodded. "If you prefer."

"So much has happened over the past few days, I'm afraid I haven't been able to keep up with my job. I do know you and my father had your differences. I also know my father held your business successes in high regard. He appreciated the work and employment you've brought to the reservation."

"Thank you," Hania said, smiling.

"It is because of your mutual respect that I came here tonight. I was told this afternoon that the council is considering a vote on the logging proposal as early as Tuesday."

"Yes, that was mentioned when I was in Gallup, but no firm date was set."

"With all the accusations being made against my father, a lot of people have turned against him. He wanted to make a presentation before the final vote. I'll have to do that now, but I'm afraid I won't get a fair hearing."

"I think you're being overly sensitive," Berkeley interjected. "I'm sure the council will determine the issues on their own merits, personalities notwithstanding."

"I'm sure they would if this were a perfect world," Kim rebutted. "But we all know what kind of world this really is, Mr. Berkeley."

"We don't need to make this contentious, Kimberly," Hania said. "Bad for the digestion." He took a sip of water before continuing. "You said you came here tonight because of the respect your father and I held for each other. What's the point you're trying to make?"

"If I ask for the council to delay the vote, I don't think anyone will listen to me."

"Why do you need the vote delayed?" Berkeley pressed. "Your father made his position clear weeks ago."

"My father was expecting another report to arrive in the next few days. He said it would shed new light on the issue."

"What kind of report?" Hania asked.

"I'm not sure, but we were completing studies on the long-term affects of deforestation. It probably had something to with that. We all know there is very little timber left on the reservation. Our computer model shows that even a twenty-five percent reduction in the number of trees could doom the rest of the forests. Within a generation soil erosion would destroy what is left. Clear-cutting, like you've proposed, would turn most of the reservation into another Death Valley."

"You're being way too dramatic about this entire business, Miss Tallmountain." This was the first time Elverson had spoken since dinner began. "Clear-cutting also means reforestation. For every one tree removed, three are planted. Soil loss is minimal. Rocky Mountain Resources has been in business for nearly fifty years. We could hardly do that if we weren't renewing our resources as we went along."

"How do you renew the top two thousand feet of a mountain when you've scraped it away in strip-mining? How do you renew a stream that's been polluted with mercury and heavy metals from your slag heaps?"

Elverson was unflustered. He was used to attacks from what he called the "ecologically enhanced." "RMR has always met . . . even surpassed state and federal guidelines. Our strip mines are not scars on the earth. We return topsoil and replant native vegetation. Mercury, sulfur, heavy metals . . . these are all naturally occurring elements. We don't dump that stuff out there. Much of it would have been leeched from the soils even if there hadn't been mining."

"That's RMR's contention," Kim fired back.

"That's what RMR's studies have proven."

Although he was enjoying the battle, Hania decided it was time to separate the combatants. They would get their chance again. "We understand RMR's position, Sam. That's why the council has looked at your offer so favorably. But, Kim, I still don't understand why you need a delay in the vote."

"Like I said. We . . . My father and I were expecting a report. It may have come in already. I just haven't had time to look through our offices. I need some time. The council won't listen to a request from me for a delay. But they will listen to you."

Gabe, who had only a superficial understanding of the issues, glanced around the table to see what kind of response Kim's request would get. The two men from RMR, Elverson and Lundquist, gave each other sideways glances through slitted eyes. Lundquist, a blond Nordic type with a lantern jaw, appeared impassive. Elverson had the slightest twist of a smirk at the corner of his mouth. Berkeley looked like he was trying to squelch a laugh.

Kim didn't notice the reactions. She was locked in a stare with Hania. The businessman's face was inscrutable and Gabe couldn't tell what his uncle's true feelings were.

"You know you're jeopardizing millions of dollars in earnings for the Navajo Nation, Miss Tallmountain," Elverson warned. "RMR is already negotiating for other potential sites. I'm afraid we can't wait much longer."

"Why would a delay hurt anything?" Gabe blurted. "I mean, the trees are going to be there whether you cut them down in a month or a year."

Hania gave his nephew a disapproving scowl but didn't say anything.

"It's not the trees that may disappear, Mr. Hania," Elverson countered. "Just our offer."

"That's Hanna," Gabe corrected, avoiding his uncle's glare. "I read that you wanted to log here on the reservation because logging in other forests was being curtailed. That made the Navajo timber valuable. If it's valuable this year, wouldn't it be even more valuable a year from now?"

Elverson shook his head. "What do you do for a living, Mr. Hanna?"

"I'm a deputy sheriff."

"Well"—Elverson smirked—"it's evident you don't

know a thing about business." He turned his attention back to Kim. "As I was saying, Miss Tallmountain, a delay in the council vote may force us to take our business elsewhere. That's the bottom line . . . and I don't think you want to be held responsible if that becomes our decision."

"My father was murdered. Whoever killed him is also out to destroy his good name and reputation. Right now there are not a lot of people who think very highly of me, so I really don't care what they might think tomorrow. But I do care about my people and their land. My father would have laid down his life to protect it and I will do the same." She turned back to her host. "Out of respect for my father, will you ask the council to delay their vote on the timber issue?"

Hania sat silent for a very long moment. Even Gayle, who had started clearing the table to avoid the confrontation, stopped her activity. Hania took a deep breath. "As an honorable man, and out of respect for your father, I will *consider* asking the council to delay their vote."

"I see." Kim nodded. She wiped her mouth with her napkin and stood. "I know you're a very busy man, so I won't tie up any more of your evening. Thank you for the dinner, Mr. Hania . . . Mrs. Hania . . . and thank you, sir, for the *consideration*." She turned and started for the door.

Gabe jumped up. "Kimberly . . ."

"Sit down, Gabriel," Hania ordered.

It had been a long time since Gabe had been talked to like a child. He decided he didn't like it. "If you'll excuse me, Uncle, I'm going to talk to her."

"Gabriel!"

The word was spoken as a warning. Gabe couldn't help but wonder what the hell his uncle Edward thought he could threaten. He ignored his elder and followed Kimberly through the house, catching her at the front door.

"Kim, is there anything I can do?" he asked, touching her shoulder.

"No, Gabe. Just leave me alone. Go back to your family."

"They're relatives. Not family. There's a big difference."

"Whatever." She brushed his hand away. "I did what I came to do. I begged Edward Hania for help . . . and got a slap in the face for trying. It's time for me to go."

"Where?"

"Home. Where do you think I would go?"

"Stupid question, I guess. Would you mind if I followed you there?"

"Why?"

"To make sure you make it there safely . . . After that, maybe we could talk."

"What would *we* have to talk about?"

"I don't understand a lot about this logging issue. It sounds to me like you could use someone on your side. Maybe if I knew a little more I could help."

Kim began to soften a bit. "Yeah. Maybe. What else would we talk about?"

"Coyotes." Gabe smiled. "I did a little checking this afternoon. That old man, Hunter, wasn't blowing smoke. Something did happen thirty years ago. Something about coyotes."

"Oh?" Kimberly sounded genuinely interested now. "I guess your coming over isn't such a bad idea. I can put on a pot of coffee. How does that sound?"

"Great!" the deputy lied. "I'll be right with you. I have to thank the Hanias for dinner."

"Sure. If you don't mind, I'll wait outside."

Gabe found the four men in a huddle around Hania's chair when he returned to the dining room. The three white men cleared away from Hania when Gabe entered.

"Gabe, I apologize," Hania said, standing. "I had no right to order you around like that. Here. Sit down. We're about to have dessert."

"Thanks just the same, Uncle Edward." The words sounded strange to Gabe and they had an unfamiliar feel in his mouth. "I think I'll be running along myself."

"Oh?" Hania sounded genuinely disappointed. "I thought there was a chance you would spend the night. Your aunt Gayle has already fixed a room for you."

"She shouldn't have gone to that trouble. You two don't have to worry about me. I can take care of myself."

"I had hoped we could talk about your father. . . ."

"Maybe next time, Uncle Edward."

Hania searched his nephew's face. "Will there be a next time, Gabriel?"

"Yes, sir. I'm sure there will."

Hania pulled a business card from his wallet and handed it to Gabe. "Here's my Farmington office address and phone number. If you ever need anything . . . anything at all . . . please call me. And get in touch the next time you're in town."

Gabe tucked the card in his pocket. "Thanks. I will."

Gayle stayed hidden in the kitchen as Edward walked his nephew to the front door.

"Tell me one thing, Gabriel," Hania asked as they shook hands. "How did Davy die?"

"Too much smoking. Too much drinking. Bad heart, bad liver, bad kidneys. He did everything he possibly could to kill himself . . . and succeeded."

"But why? He was so young."

"Yeah. Forty-five. A son's love wasn't enough to keep him alive. He needed something else. Something I couldn't give him."

"What was that, do you think?"

"His home. He wanted to come home . . . and I found out tonight why he couldn't."

Gabe opened the door and stepped into the chilly evening air. He could feel his uncle's stare as he followed Kim's truck down the driveway, into the moonlit night.

29

"HISTORICALLY, THE NAVAJO SETTLED INTO NORTH-ern Arizona and New Mexico relatively late. Between four and five hundred years ago. After the Old Ones disappeared."

"Who were the old ones?" Gabe asked, admitting to himself he liked the aroma of the coffee brewing on the stove.

They were sitting at the kitchen table in Kimberly's tiny house. The L-shaped kitchen and the living room made up most of the dwelling. The bed and bathroom took up the rest. The living room looked more like a library to Gabe. Shelves were stacked with books, computer printouts, and maps. A long table that served as Kim's desk was cluttered with notebooks and stacks of paper. A small space had been cleared away to make room for a laptop computer.

"The Anasazi. The people who built the villages and Pueblo Bonita in Chaco Canyon. They also built the great cliff dwellings."

"Yeah, I've heard of them. There's a part of San Phillipe County called the Anasazi Strip. They found some ancient ruins there last year. I guess the Zuni tribe now owns that property."

"Yes." Kim nodded. "That's the same group. As a cul-ture, they simply disappeared around A.D. thirteen hundred. My father and I, along with the Forestry Service, have been doing a lot of research about the ecology of this region. For two thousand years this part of the country has been desert, but somehow the Anasazi managed to build a flourishing culture, taking advantage of every drop of rain that fell.

"We believe an extended drought drove the Anasazi from Pueblo Bonita and into the mountain canyons where there was still enough topsoil to hold water and raise crops. Unfortunately, it didn't take them long to deplete those resources as well. Maybe a hundred years. Once the land was played out, they had to move on. Some people think they died out. I don't. All the tribes here in the Southwest are direct descendants."

"You said the Navajo came here later."

"Yes, but we also integrated with the people who were here. We brought great skills as hunters and warriors. The descendants of the Old Ones taught us farming and building. Through intermarriage and hundreds of years of peaceful coexistence we have become part of this land. The blood of the Anasazi flows through our veins. This land is our heritage."

The coffeepot on the stove began to sputter and Kimberly stood. "Do you take anything in your coffee?"

"Yeah. Milk and sugar, I guess."

Kim returned a moment later with two steaming mugs. "Whitener and sugar are on the table." She handed him a spoon so he could serve himself.

"So what does all this have to do with timber rights?"

"People have lived in this desert for ten thousand years. Maybe longer. Most of that existence was based on hunting and gathering, with some subsistence farming. When farming became the chief source of food, men destroyed the land. At least that's what my father had concluded. The nutrients in the soil were depleted. The natural accumulation and storage of water in the aquifer was disrupted and semiarable land was turned into desert. The only thing that keeps this region from turning into barren rock and sand is the green belt: a stretch of forested land between the mountains and the desert.

"A hundred thousand acres of timber can hold millions of gallons of water. That water is released slowly into the air and into the ground again when leaves fall and plants decay. It's a delicate balance. Without those forests, what little rain we get would evaporate or soak into the ground before it could be used."

Gabe couldn't help but be fascinated by Kim's passion for her work. He was also embarrassed by his own ignorance of the subject. He tried to console himself that he was at least making an effort to learn.

"My father believed . . . I believe, cutting what little timber we have left will tip the balance of nature. What happened to the Anasazi will happen to us. The Old Ones didn't understand conservation. We do. They destroyed their environment through ignorance. We're getting ready to do the same thing, not through ignorance, but through greed. And it doesn't have to happen. That's going to be the great tragedy."

Gabe nodded thoughtfully. "The whole tribe doesn't see it that way, though."

"No," Kim admitted. "Some people, like your uncle, think there's nothing more important than economic development. They maintain the land has been here for thousands of years and that it will take care of itself. Spontaneously regenerate, I suppose.

"Then there are many traditionalists who agree the land should not be harmed. It should be left untouched for future generations. But they opposed my father's ideas. They claim we Native Americans have always had deep respect for the land. Our ancestors could never have ruined the land through overuse. To them, Walter Tallmountain was a heretic. I guess I am, too."

Kim took a sip of her coffee and stared into the mug. "The unfortunate thing is, even though many in the tribe agree the trees shouldn't be cut, they'd go along with the logging just to prove my father wrong. Doesn't make any sense, but that's the way politics go."

"Is there any way you can prove that cutting down the trees will ruin the land?"

"I have twenty years of data from the sub-Sahara. I have the archaeological studies done on Easter Island. I have films and photographs of Haiti. I can show what it looked like thirty years ago and what it looks like today now that the forests have been depleted."

"You said earlier you were waiting for some kind of report."

"Yeah. My dad said it would arrive the end of this week or the first part of next. But I don't know of any new facts that would change a thing. If the report shows up late, it will be a moot point. Your uncle is going to push through the vote and whatever is in the report won't matter."

Gabe winced every time Kim said "your uncle." He felt he was being blamed for his relative's actions. He wondered if there was some way he could steer the conversation away from the timber issue.

Kimberly must have felt his discomfort. As she stood to get more coffee she asked, "What was that you said about coyotes?"

"Yeah," Gabe said, relieved. "You wouldn't believe what I found out at the library."

30

IT WAS ONLY AN HOUR PAST DAWN WHEN LANSING reached the hospital in Farmington. He didn't know how long he stood next to the bed holding Margarite's hand. He kept telling himself if he held it long enough and wished hard enough, she would open her eyes. The only movement, though, was the slight heave of her chest as she breathed.

He had never noticed how small her hands were compared to his own. He also knew, despite their size, they were strong hands, competent hands, healing hands. Whenever Margarite talked about her job as a doctor she referred to it as "healing"—"Well, Lansing. It's time for me to go. I have to get back to my healing." To Margarite, being a doctor was a spiritual experience, as metaphysical as it was physical.

And now . . . ?

Lansing kicked himself mentally for going to Spider Woman Reservoir. Why didn't they head out for Raton Pass like they had planned?

"Because your ego was bruised." Lansing whispered to himself. "Because you had some sort of 'investigation' you thought you had to pursue. Because you couldn't put down the badge for a weekend."

The anger started boiling inside. The *what ifs* were a

waste of time. Whatever decisions he had made in the past didn't matter now. Margarite was lying in a hospital bed clinging to life and it was his job to find out who put her there.

He gave Margarite a soft kiss on her forehead, then gently laid her hand on the white linen. "Don't go anywhere," he whispered. "I'll be back soon."

It had been a short night for Lansing. The horses were bedded down by eleven. By midnight, after he cleaned up, he was in his office filling out the incident report. It was a sketchy summary of the shooting and the items he found at the campsite on the mountain. Maybe he would flesh out the details later.

Larry Peters was manning the dispatch desk when he arrived. The deputy knew Lansing was taking a few days off, but he wasn't surprised to see him. San Phillipe County covered a lot of territory, but news still traveled fast. Margarite's shooting and the Life-Flight to Farmington was big gossip.

"I'm sorry about Dr. Carerra," Peters said in his meticulous manner. "Is she going to be all right?"

Lansing shrugged. "I don't know. I hope so." He looked over the deputy's shoulder at the duty board. Deputies Rivera and Cortez were on for Saturday. Deputy Hanna would also be on Sunday. The sheriff wasn't going to be missed.

"Larry, as far as the rest of the county is concerned, I'm still not available. I think you and the rest of the boys can handle things. I'm going to Farmington for a few days. If anyone needs to get in touch, they can leave a message for me through the San Juan Sheriff's Office."

"Yes, sir . . ." As an afterthought, Peters grabbed a large envelope from his desk drawer. "I don't know if you want to see this or not. Marilyn left a note. Patrolman Hernandez dropped this off sometime today."

"Yeah. I'll take that."

Lansing planned on heading for bed once he finished his incident report. Before he did, he wanted to see what Marty had left for him.

Hernandez had faxed the autopsy report on Walter Tall-mountain on Thursday, but Lansing had found the narration lacking. Essentially, Tallmountain had bled to death as a result of gunshot wounds. That made sense to Lansing. Margarite had pointed out there was very little blood on the highway.

There was no firm estimate on approximate time of death. The coroner had been working on a body that had been dead at least two days. During that time the body had been chilled at the mortuary, so the normal decaying process had been interrupted. Time of death was placed between noon on Monday and 5:00 A.M. on Tuesday, a seventeen-hour window.

Tallmountain had been hit in the back by two .44-caliber bullets. Spiraling on the slugs indicated the bullets were fired from a rifle. Lack of powder burns indicated he was not shot at close range.

Lansing thought the report had been hurried and it raised even more questions in the sheriff's mind. After he had read the initial autopsy, he faxed a series of questions to Hernandez. He hoped the package Peters had handed him were the responses.

Lansing opened the manila envelope and dumped out the contents. There were a half dozen photos, a dozen photocopies of preliminary reports written by Agents Hobson and Williams, and a cover letter from Hernandez.

Cliff,
This is everything I could dig up. The SBI was not too happy with me when I came in to ask questions.

They seem to be in a big hurry to close this thing. They still maintain it's an open-and-shut case. One of their secretaries let me photocopy the files on the sly. (Hope we don't get into too much trouble.)

After reading your questions, then looking at their findings, I'm starting to think you're onto something. The circumstantial evidence falls into place too conveniently and the links to Tallmountain are beginning to look contrived. To save you time, your questions along with the answers are summarized on the next page.

Talk to you after your fishing trip.

Marty

Lansing hurriedly flipped to the next page.

1. Q: How long did it take for W. T. to bleed to death after he was shot?
   A: Depending on amount of physical exertion—1 to 3 hours.
2. Q: W. T.'s car was dusted with cocaine powder, indicating a bag might have been torn open during a struggle. Was there cocaine residue on W. T.'s body or clothing?
   A: No.
3. Q: Was there any indication in the hematology exam that W. T. used illegal drugs?
   A: No.
4. Q: What caliber weapon was used to shoot up W. T.'s car?
   A: 9mm.
5. Q: Was W. T.'s blood found in his car, and if so, where?
   A: Yes. Backseat. (See photos #1 and 2.)
6. Q: Was any camping gear found in W. T.'s car? If so, what kind of gear?

A: No camping gear was found. (See Contents list,
photocopy #5.)

7. Q: Are there any leads as to possible perpetrators?
A: No firm leads. Interviews on photocopies 7 through
12.

As much as he wanted to read all the reports, Lansing
had to stifle a yawn. It was pushing two in the morning
and he wanted to be on the road by six. He stuffed the
photos and reports back into the envelope and folded the
clasp. He'd read them over the weekend when he had time.
That is, if he had time.

After the hospital, Lansing's first stop was the San Juan
County Sheriff's Office in Aztec, thirty minutes away. It
was more than a social visit, even though he had known
Bud Spence for ten years. Lansing had decided, since he
was going to be poking around on official business, he
would wear his uniform. He was giving Spence a courtesy
call. He wanted the sheriff to know he was in San Juan
and was going to be asking a few questions. He wanted to
make sure Spence didn't have any problems with him being
there.

"No, I'm sorry, Sheriff Lansing," the duty officer said.
"Sheriff Spence hasn't stopped in this morning. Would you
like us to raise him on the radio?"

"Yeah, if you don't mind. I really do need to talk to
him."

"One moment." The duty officer picked up his phone
and spoke to the dispatcher in the next room. The conversation was brief.

"Sheriff Lansing," the duty officer said after hanging up
his phone. "Dispatch said he stopped into Rock's Café for
coffee. You can catch him there." He noticed the questioning look on Lansing's face. "I'm sorry. It's back in Far-

mington. Just stay on 550. You'll see the café when Main turns onto Broadway."

"Thanks." Lansing nodded, putting his Stetson on as he pushed the outside door. "If I miss him, tell him I'll stop by later." He could have kicked himself. If he had called first, he wouldn't have wasted an hour driving to Aztec and back.

Charles "Bud" Spence was a big man. At the age of sixty, he still looked like he pumped iron two hours a day. He had softened a little around the midsection, but his forearms were massive. Spence's grip reminded Lansing of the first time he lassoed a steer with the rope wrapped around his hand. He thought he'd never see his fingers again.

"What the hell brings you here, Cliffy?" Spence grinned. "I hope you're not bringing me any prisoners because your dinky jail is overflowing." Spence pointed at an empty chair across the table, then signaled for the waitress to come over.

"No. Nothing like that." Lansing didn't take offense about his "dinky jail." It was a running joke at the State Sheriff's Association meetings. He was grateful he didn't need a bigger one. "Would you believe me if I told you I came all this way because I missed your smiling face?"

"Hell, no." Spence laughed. He turned to the waitress. "A coffee for Sheriff Lansing and I'd like a refill." He looked at Lansing. "A sweet roll?"

Lansing shook his head. "I had breakfast early."

"Just the coffee, Dana . . . So what does drag you out of the mountains? You're wearing your uniform, so I know this isn't anything social."

"I just wanted to let you know I was going to be in San Juan for a couple of days. Official business. There was a shooting at the reservoir yesterday. I thought there might be someone around here who could give me some help."

"I heard about the Life-Flight getting dispatched," Spence said, nodding. "What happened?"

Lansing gave a brief description of the incident. He didn't go into great detail about his relationship with Margarite, but his expression must have betrayed his feelings. Spence picked up on his concern immediately.

"I can tell she means a lot to you, Cliffy. Could be tough to do a good investigation if it's personal. How 'bout letting my office help? We know the people around here."

"I'll keep that offer in mind, Bud. But there's only one person I need to speak to at the moment. Maybe she can point me in the direction I need to go."

"Who's that?"

"A Navajo woman. Kimberly Tallmountain."

"Tallmountain . . . Geez. If I hear that name one more time this week I'm going to puke."

"Why? What's been going on?"

"I understand they found this body over in your county. Turns out it's Walter Tallmountain." Lansing nodded. "The next day the SBI comes storming into my offices wanting to have all the files on the man. Trouble is, we don't have any files. He's a fine, upstanding citizen. At least, we don't have anything on him.

"Then they start stirring things up. They demand search warrants. They have authorization from the DEA to do any damned thing they want. We get dragged out to the reservation. I have to smooth things over with Lieutenant Hawk. He's with the reservation police. The SBI never told him what they were up to. Now a lot of Navajo feelings have been hurt. It's been a mess."

"Who came in from the SBI?"

"Some numb-nuts by the name of Hobson. A real arrogant little snot . . ." Spence stopped his tirade and eyed his fellow peace officer. "You think your shooting yesterday is tied in to this drug case?"

Lansing wanted to keep his suspicions about the Tall-mountain investigation quiet. At least for a little while. But he knew he couldn't do everything himself. Judging from Spence's attitude toward Hobson, Lansing suspected he might have a ready ally. "Before I say anything else, I need to talk to Kimberly Tallmountain, but yes, I do think the cases are connected."

"I don't know what you're being so secretive about, but I'll make you a deal. You fill me in later and I'll give you directions to Tallmountain's place. I'll even get you in touch with Noah Hawk. I don't want anybody ruffling any more Navajo feathers."

"It's a deal."

Spence took a sip of his coffee. "I know this is off the subject, but I just thought I'd ask. Have you had a lot of trouble with coyotes lately?"

31

IT WAS FOUR IN THE MORNING WHEN GABE AND KIM finally quit talking. The discussions about timber rights and coyotes kept Kim's mind occupied for most of the night. Eventually, the fact that she was going to be burying her father the next day overwhelmed her.

The change was abrupt. One moment she was carrying on an animated conversation. Then, as if someone snapped their fingers, her face went blank.

"Kim? Is something wrong?" Gabe touched her arm and she jerked as if he had just wakened her.

"What? What did you say?"

"Is something wrong?"

"No." The response was curt. She stood and gathered up their coffee mugs. "If you don't mind, Gabe, I think I'd better get some rest." She gestured toward the cluttered sofa a few feet away. "Would you like me to make you a bed?"

Kim had neglected to turn on the gas heater and Gabe noticed the small frame house was chilly.

"No. That won't be necessary. Maybe a blanket."

She set the mugs into the sink. "I'll get you one from the bedroom. Go ahead and put that stuff on the floor."

Gabe started clearing the papers and books from the sofa. A moment later Kim emerged from the bedroom with a heavy Navajo blanket and a pillow. She set them on the back of the couch.

"Can I get you anything else?"

"No." Gabe shook his head. "This is fine."

Kim turned toward the bedroom but hesitated at the door. "Gabe," she said, without turning around, "I'm glad you came over tonight."

"Yeah. Me too."

Kim hesitated a second longer as if there was more to be spoken. Instead, she simply said, "Good night."

"Good night, Kim."

Hanna was a novice coffee drinker. He had spent his adulthood avoiding the black liquid because he simply didn't like the taste. He'd had three full mugs that night. He had no idea that the caffeine would impact him so strongly.

When he turned off the lights he assumed he would doze off immediately. That wasn't the case. The first thing he noticed was that his eyes wouldn't stay shut. He forced himself to yawn, but it had no effect.

He thought if he concentrated on a single sound the monotony would lull him to sleep. When he shifted his attention to his hearing, he became acutely aware of every sound available.

There was the steady click-click-click of the wall clock. Below that was the hum of the compressor on the refrigerator. An irregular, muffled sound came from Kim's bedroom. It took Gabe a second to realize it was sobbing, deep and sorrowful. He wanted to knock on her door and see if he could help, but he suspected she didn't want that. Her sudden termination of their conversation and her retreat to the bedroom told him she needed to be alone with her grief.

Gabe fought back the memories of his own loss. Instead he listened intently to the noises beyond the little house.

Hunter Niyol was right. There were voices. Gabe hadn't noticed it before but there were dozens of voices in the night.

A single coyote howl splitting the serenity of the frosty April darkness would have been distinctive. In the distance, though, the voices blended. There were three and four howls carrying on at the same time. When they finished, a half dozen other voices would reply. Nearby, a chorus of yelps and howls echoed in response.

Gabe listened to the symphony for an hour. These were not random sounds. There was point and counterpoint to the singing. To the deputy, the voices had a pattern. They were talking to one another.

He closed his eyes and tried to interpret their language. It seemed plausible that he could. Just at the moment he thought he had broken the code his body jerked him awake. He had dozed. He was sure of that. But he was aware that his hearing was sharper.

Gabe swore he could hear the soft padding of coyote feet just outside the window. There was a snort of disapproval as some animal caught the scent of man in the area. Sharp nails clawed against the front door.

He wasn't afraid. He understood the voices. He knew the coyotes would do him no harm.

He tossed the blanket aside and quietly crept barefoot to the door. Carefully turning the knob so it wouldn't make a sound, he threw the door open.

There was no coyote at the door.

There was no coyote in the yard.

The nearly full moon in the cloudless sky gave the landscape a dull glow. Wearing only his shirt and jeans, Gabe forgot about the cold as he stepped from the house. There was something out there.

He was only slightly aware of the pebbles and rocks as he walked from the house to the road. The dirt rut stretched to the highway a mile away. The deputy studied the path for any movement.

His concentration was interrupted by a snort.

Gabe wheeled around.

Thirty feet away sat a coyote. Something limp hung from the animal's mouth. In the dim light, Gabe couldn't tell if it was a rabbit or a chicken or a snake.

The coyote cocked his head to one side as he studied the human. Gabe didn't make any sudden moves. He didn't want to scare the animal away.

After almost three minutes of the two sizing each other up, their joint scrutiny was interrupted by a howl coming from a nearby hill. Both of them looked in the direction of the sound, then back to each other.

The coyote dropped what he had in his mouth and looked at Gabe. Neither moved. As if to emphasize the point, the coyote leaned forward and nudged the object with its nose, toward him. The animal gave Gabe one more look, then stood and trotted off in the direction of the last howl.

Gabe walked over to the object and picked it up. It was a man's belt with a sheath. A heavy bowie knife was stuffed in the sheath. Suddenly he became acutely aware of the fact that his feet were cold.

Gabe woke with a start. He had pulled the blanket around his neck, leaving his bare feet exposed. He quickly covered them.

"Whew," he mumbled. "What a dream."

It was still dark outside and a moment later he was dozing again. His fitful sleep was a kaleidoscope of images: He was in his patrol car at night when he caught sight of a coyote in his headlights. He hit the animal. When he went back to check the animal it was lying still in the road. He rolled the carcass over. It had his father's face.

He shook off the image only to see his father driving

down the streets of Farmington in a beat-up old car. His father waved at him, then disappeared into the darkness. Gabe tried to call to him but no words came out of his mouth.

A moment later his father reappeared. He was running down the street toward Gabe, being chased by the same car he had been driving. There was a look of terror in his father's face. He was holding out his hand. He wanted Gabe to grab it. To save him. Before Gabe could reach him, the car ran over his father. Gabe looked up in time to see his uncle behind the wheel, laughing.

With shaking hands, Gabe rolled the body of his father faceup. But it was no longer his father. It was the lifeless carcass of a dead coyote.

"No!" Gabe screamed. "No, no, no!"

His own screams woke him. He was still in Kim's small house, still on the sofa. But it was daylight now.

He sat up quickly, wondering if he had disturbed Kim. He looked toward the bedroom. The door stood wide open. Beyond the door he could see the bed had already been made.

"Kim?" he called out, standing. He noticed his feet were gritty, dirty, as if he had been walking in sand. He quickly brushed them off. "Kim!" he said again. There was no response.

He looked in the bedroom and bathroom. They were empty.

On the kitchen table he found a note.

Dear Gabe,
    You were sleeping so peacefully I didn't want to disturb you. I have to run to Farmington for some last-minute arrangements. If you want to attend the

ceremony, meet me at the chapter house. I'll be there at noon.

There's coffee on the stove.

Kim

Gabe shuddered at the thought of drinking any more coffee. He looked at the wall clock. It was already nine-thirty.

He sat down at the kitchen table and yawned. He supposed he would go to the funeral. There was a clean long-sleeved shirt in his storage compartment. He could pick up a tie somewhere.

As he began to slip on his socks and boots he wondered how his feet got so dirty. Then he remembered his dreams. But those were only dreams. He hadn't gone outside. He remembered that he had pulled the blanket too high.

Out of curiosity, he finished putting on his boots and hurried outside. Standing in the spot he remembered from his dream, he looked down the road toward the highway, then toward where the coyote had been sitting. Nothing seemed unusual.

He walked over to where the coyote had dropped the belt. Still nothing.

"Just a dream, Hanna. Just a dream."

He opened the saddle compartment of his cycle to retrieve the clean shirt. Sitting on top of his travel gear was the belt from his dream, complete with sheath and knife. His hands shook as he picked up the items and examined them.

"This is too weird!" he mumbled.

Looking around to make sure no one saw him, he stuffed the belt and knife underneath the other items in the compartment. He knew he wanted to talk to someone about this. He just didn't know who, or for that matter, what he would say without sounding nuts.

He hurried back into the house to clean up and change. All he could think about was getting the hell away from there.

"This is just too weird," he kept mumbling. "This is just too weird."

32

GABE HAD MORE THAN TWO HOURS TO KILL BEFORE HE had to be at the chapter house. His motorcycle needed gas and he wanted something to eat. The closest restaurant was the café in Shiprock, but after the reception he and Kim had gotten the day before, he decided he'd find someplace else.

He had plenty of time. He'd head in the direction of Farmington. One of the little towns along the way would have a place he could stop.

Cruising down the highway, Gabe tried to appreciate the clear morning air. He kept trying to remind himself how free he felt when the world consisted of only himself, his bike, and the road. It didn't work. He ended up thinking about the belt and knife he had found. Bits and pieces of his dreams flashed in front of him.

He managed to bring himself back to reality when he glanced at his gas gauge. The needle was bouncing against EMPTY. About the same moment his stomach gave a warning growl. He knew it was time to get serious about stopping somewhere.

Melba's on the east side of Kirtland looked like a promising diner. His motorcycle, however, needed immediate attention. There was a gas station a half mile farther up the road. He decided he would fill up first, then grab a bite.

The station wasn't very busy. When Gabe filled his tank the only other vehicle in the area was a pickup truck parked next to the door to the cashier/convenience mart. Two white men hovered around the tailgate. Some sort of cage sat in the bed of the truck. One of the men, dressed like a rancher, kept poking a sharp stick through the cyclone-fence mesh. When he did, the cage's occupant let out a yelp.

As Gabe walked up to pay for his gas he got a better look at the action. The piece of wood the rancher held was more than just a stick. It was a pool cue whittled down to a sharp point. The point had been hardened with fire.

"Yeah," the man with the stick said. "Caught him when he tried to steal chickens from one of my tenants. You know Rodriguez." His listener nodded. "His place. We tied a pullet down in the back of the trap. This stupid animal walked in like we were serving him breakfast or something."

The rancher gave the cage another poke. Over the man's shoulder, Gabe could see a coyote cowering in the far corner, whimpering. The animal was bleeding in several places where the cue stick had penetrated the hide.

"Worthless piece of crap!" The man poked at the animal again but the coyote managed to fend off the point by biting the cue. "Let go of that!" the rancher growled. He shook the stick violently. The coyote managed to hold on for a few shakes, then lost his grip.

"You like playing pool, huh?" The man's mouth curled into a sneer. "Well, how 'bout some more?"

"That's enough!"

The rancher turned around angrily. "What? You say somethin', boy?"

Gabe stood facing him, his fists clenched at the sides of his body. "Yeah. I said that's enough!"

"This is none of your business, boy. Go peddle your papers back on the reservation where you belong."

The man turned back to the cage and was about to jab the coyote one more time when Gabe grabbed his arm. The man yanked the stick from the cage and wheeled around, swinging the cue at the intruder's head.

Gabe was twenty years younger than the coyote's tormentor. He easily ducked the swing.

"I don't want any trouble," Gabe insisted.

"Too bad, Navajo. You got it."

The man took another swing at Gabe. They were both about the same height, but the rancher outweighed him by thirty pounds. The deputy knew if that cue stick connected, he would be in a world of hurt.

The man the rancher had been talking to ran into the convenience mart. Through the window, Gabe could see he was telling the cashier to call someone.

The combatants circled each other cautiously. The rancher poked the stick once or twice, then reared back and took another swing.

The deputy jumped back. As the pool cue swooshed past, Gabe grabbed the end. There was a short tug of war until the rancher realized the sharp end was pointed at the Navajo's chest. Suddenly the man quit pulling and began pushing.

Gabe let the rancher's momentum work against him. As the bigger man pushed, Gabe stepped aside and pulled. The rancher found himself off balance and there was nothing he could do to stop from crashing into the side of the truck. The man crumpled to his knees, holding his head and groaning.

Satisfied for the moment that his assailant wasn't going to jump up swinging again, Gabe walked around to the back of the truck. The coyote, crouched at the far end of the cage, watched him warily. Gabe thought he could sense more curiosity than fear from the animal.

The coyote looked his rescuer in the eyes and cocked

his head to one side as if he were asking, "All right. What are you going to do now?"

Gabe shook his head. He knew, left to the mercy of the rancher, the best the coyote could hope for was a quick bullet to the head. The deputy was sure there would be a prelude of pain and torture before that happened.

He was quickly learning that the prevalent philosophy of the region was "Who's going to miss one more coyote?" Gabe decided if that question was true, the opposite was equally valid. "What does it matter if there's one more coyote running loose?"

Without any second thoughts, Gabe unlatched the cage door and swung it open.

The coyote looked from the open door to Gabe, then back to the door. The animal didn't have any second thoughts either. He was through the opening in two quick bounds. Leaping from the tailgate, the coyote scampered between the gas pump islands and onto the busy highway.

The sound of screeching tires and honking horns shattered the calm morning as drivers avoided hitting the fleeing animal. Cars and trucks on both sides of the four-lane highway skidded and squealed to stops. Miraculously, none of the vehicles slammed into each other, nor did they hit the frightened coyote.

For his part, the coyote stopped suddenly when he reached the other side of the road. He turned and stared at Gabe, as if to reassure his deliverer that everything would be okay now. When the animal seemed satisfied he had communicated that message, he turned and trotted nonchalantly off toward the hills.

Gabe was so wrapped up with watching the coyote he barely heard the words: "You son of a bitch!"

What followed was blinding pain at the base of his skull, then darkness.

33

SHERIFF SPENCE PULLED A COUNTY MAP FROM HIS glove compartment when he and Lansing reached his patrol car. Spence always found it easier to give directions when he had a map available. As the two studied the best way to get to Walter Tallmountain's place, the sheriff's radio crackled into action. Spence slid into his car to answer.

"Spence here."

"Yeah, Sheriff. Deputy Collins. I'm at Kerry's Arco on Highway 84. There's been a minor incident here. Chub Willet got into it with some Navajo. They were fighting over a coyote Chub said he trapped."

"So what's the problem?" Bud asked.

"Willet says he wants to press charges. He said the Indian jumped him, beat him up, and let the coyote go."

"What'd the Navajo say?"

"Not much. He was knocked out cold when I got here. When he woke up all I could get out of him was he was a deputy sheriff from San Phillipe County."

Lansing had only casually been listening to the conversation. The mention of his county immediately got his attention. "What's the deputy's name?" he interrupted.

"Yeah, Collins. You got a name on that deputy?"

"His ID says Hanna. Gabriel Hanna."

"Yep, that's one of mine." Lansing frowned.

"You said the deputy got knocked out. How's he doing now?"

"He's on his feet, Sheriff. Looks like he's going to be all right."

"Good. I want you to have that deputy and Willet follow you in to the Farmington Police Station. I've got the deputy's boss here with me now. We'll see if we can sort things out."

"Ten-four. I'll meet you there."

Spence hung up his microphone and looked at Lansing. "What are you doing with a damned Navajo as a deputy?"

"We're an equal opportunity employer. We'll take anybody we can get."

"Has he been with you long?"

"Three, four months. He's a hard worker. I don't have any complaints."

"How'd you get him off the reservation?"

"I didn't," Cliff said, folding up the map. "As far as I know, he's never lived on the reservation."

"One of those city Indians, huh?"

"Not even that." He handed the map to Spence. "It's a long story."

"You keep wrapping things up in mysteries, Cliffy. Come on. Follow me down to the station and we'll see what this is all about."

The two sheriffs were standing in the police parking lot when the San Juan deputy's car pulled in followed by a pickup truck and a motorcycle. Lansing didn't have any trouble recognizing his deputy. Gabe was riding without his helmet.

"Where's your head gear, Deputy?" Lansing demanded, forgoing any pleasantries. He wasn't very happy that one of his men was in trouble in another county.

"I tried wearing it, Sheriff," Gabe said sheepishly as he walked up. "It didn't work very well with this bump on the back of my head."

"Let me see." Lansing reached around and felt Hanna's neck. He found a protrusion the size of a walnut. He checked his fingers for blood but no skin had been broken. "What the hell happened?"

"I coldcocked the son of a bitch," the rancher named Willet bragged, slamming his truck door as if for emphasis.

"What did you use," Lansing snapped, "a baseball bat?"

"It was a pool cue," the rancher said defensively. "After he jumped me."

"I didn't jump him, Sheriff," Gabe asserted.

"The hell you didn't! And I'll tell you what, Bud. For two cents I'd do it again."

"All right," Spence interrupted. "What did happen?"

"I was minding my own business," Willet began, "showing off this coyote I trapped. All of a sudden this punk jumps me, knocks me to the ground, and turns my coyote loose. I want him arrested for assault and theft of property. Letting that coyote go is the same thing as stealing it."

"How'd he get the bump on the head?" Spence asked.

"When he turned the coyote loose his back was to me. I figured he was going to try and beat on me some more, so I picked up the cue stick and whopped him a good one."

"What? You were parked in a pool hall?" Lansing asked sarcastically.

"No. I just happened to have one with me."

Sheriff Spence suppressed a chuckle. He turned to Gabe. "All right, Deputy. What's your side of the story?"

Gabe explained how he was simply trying to stop Willet from torturing the animal. He had been jabbing the poor animal with a sharpened pool stick. The rancher became unhinged and started swinging first. Gabe said he never hit him. Willet ran into the side of his own truck. The deputy did admit he let the animal go, but only to save it from any more cruelty.

"Is that right, Chub? You were torturing the animal?"

"He's full of it, Sheriff. Why would I do something like that?"

"Where's that pool cue you two keep talking about?"

Willet reached in the back of his truck and produced the stick. He handed it to Spence.

"What's the point for, Chub?" the sheriff asked, examining the fire-hardened tip.

"I use it for a walking stick. Sometimes you run into snakes."

"Maybe so." Spence nodded. "Course, you know we have cruelty to dumb animal laws in this county."

"Yeah. So?"

"Might have to have this cue tested. See if there's any coyote blood on it."

"You taking the Navajo's side?"

"I'm not taking anybody's side, Chub. I just want to get to the truth of the matter. I could arrest him for assault, if you want. Of course, I'll have to talk to witnesses, keep this stick for evidence, maybe impound the truck."

"My truck?"

"Then if it turns out the deputy was telling the truth, I'll have to arrest you for filing a false police report. Then there's the cruelty to the animal charge. Also, Deputy Hanna can turn around and sue you for causing his false imprisonment."

"Just—just—just a minute, Bud," Willet stammered. "I don't think we have to go to all that trouble."

"You want me to arrest him for assault, don't you?"

"No, no. We don't have to go that far. But he did turn that coyote loose. He admitted to that. A coyote hide's worth twenty-five bucks."

Spence turned to Gabe. "Deputy, you have twenty-five dollars on you?"

"Yes, sir."

"Good. Pay the man."

Gabe pulled out his wallet and removed a twenty and five ones, then handed the money to Willet.

"Can I have my pool cue back?"

Spence studied the fire-hardened tip. "You know, cruelty to animals is a serious charge in this county, Chub. Serious enough I just may have to investigate. I mean, the deputy wouldn't have turned the animal loose unless it had been mistreated."

The rancher nodded. "I see your game, Sheriff. How 'bout I just give the Navajo his money back and we call it even?"

"It's up to you, Chub."

With a sour look on his face, Willet stuffed the money into Gabe's jacket. "All right. Now can I have the cue stick back?"

"Sure." With very little effort, Spence held the cue stick in front of him with both hands and broke it over his knee. "There you go." He smiled, handing the two pieces to the rancher. "Have a nice day."

34

AFTER THE FUROR WITH WILLET SUBSIDED, LANSING
and his deputy expressed surprise at finding the other in
Farmington. Lansing didn't keep tabs on what his men did
on their off days. Gabe usually talked about his trips to Las
Cruces to visit his mother. Lansing assumed that's where
his deputy had gone this time around.

Gabe was sure his boss would be up in the mountains
fishing.

The sheriff suggested they should take a trip to the hospital to have Gabe's head X-rayed, but he insisted he was
fine. At the moment he was more interested in eating.
Besides, he had to be somewhere at noon. When Lansing
found out Gabe's appointment was to attend Walter Tallmountain's funeral, he decided the two had better sit down
and talk.

"I'll tell you what, Gabe," Lansing observed as the waitress set down the deputy's plate of food. "I can understand
your interest in Kimberly Tallmountain. She's a very attractive young lady. But I don't think it's the smartest thing
in the world for a deputy to get involved with someone
who's under investigation."

"You mean the drug business?"

The sheriff nodded. "Yes, I do."

"I don't think she's involved with drugs. I don't think her father was either."

"It doesn't matter what you or I think. The SBI is still conducting an investigation and she's still a suspect. It's inappropriate for you as a law officer to become personally involved with her."

"Sheriff, when I came to work for you, you made it clear that my free time was my own. I'm here on my days off. This has nothing to do with my job. Besides, my relationship with her is strictly as a friend. And, to tell you the truth, she needs all the friends she can find right now. It sounds like her own tribe has her tried and convicted already."

Gabe pushed the food around on his plate. The more he thought about Kim, the more his appetite dwindled. The last time he had heard her voice she was sobbing in her bedroom.

"I thought you said you were hungry?"

"Yeah." Gabe filled his fork and stuffed the food into his mouth. He looked around the room as he chewed, not particularly interested in making eye contact with the sheriff.

"You're right," Lansing finally admitted. "Your time off is your own time. As long as you're not doing anything illegal like setting coyotes free, I guess I'll keep my mouth shut."

Lansing's comment elicited a small smile from Gabe. "Thanks, Sheriff." His appetite started creeping back. "By the way, what happened to your fishing trip?"

It was the second time that morning that Lansing had to describe the incident at Spider Woman Rec Area. He found that telling the story again and again didn't make it any easier, especially when asked how Margarite was doing. He wanted to give a positive prognosis, but knew he couldn't.

"I can understand why you want to be here in Farmington," Gabe admitted.

"There's more to it than being close to Dr. Carerra. I'm trying to find out who shot her."

"Here? In Farmington?"

Lansing had always been very careful to keep his personal feelings separate from his official duties. When he had the confrontation with Hobson in his office, he made sure Gabe was out of the room. He would have done that with any of his deputies. He wanted to make sure his personal views didn't affect how they performed their duties.

The official line was the SBI was investigating a drug case. Lansing didn't like it. He thought they were doing a shoddy job. But that was his interpretation. He didn't want his opinion interfering with his deputies toeing the official line. As of yet, Lansing hadn't even offered his opinion to Bud Spence. The official line was still the drug case.

Lansing knew he had to talk to Kimberly Tallmountain. All morning long he was wondering how he could approach her. Gabe's intimacy could offer him access. But to get Gabe's full cooperation, the sheriff knew he had to reveal his own personal convictions about the case.

"I need to talk to Miss Tallmountain."

"Kim?" Gabe was surprised. "Why? She didn't have anything to do with Dr. Carerra getting shot."

"I know that. After the Life-Flight helicopter took off, I went back to the rec area. About a hundred feet above the spot where Margarite was shot I found a clearing. Someone had tried to destroy camping gear in a fire. They were trying to hide the fact that either they or some other person had been there."

"So what does that have to do with Kim?"

"She said her father had gone to Spider Woman Reservoir. I gathered up all the evidence I could find in the clearing. I need her to look at it. See if she can identify it. I need to find out if it belonged to her father."

Gabe looked at his superior for a long moment before saying anything. "You don't think he was dealing drugs either."

"Right now I don't know what I think. I'm at least trying to keep an open mind. That's what an objective investigator is supposed to do." From twenty years of experience, Lansing knew if an investigator had already formed an opinion, he would only find pieces of evidence that supported his conclusions.

"If what I found belonged to Walter Tallmountain, someone was awfully desperate to destroy the evidence."

"What if it isn't his?"

"The only other clue I have is a black Ford Bronco. That whittles my suspects down to about twenty-five million car owners." The sheriff glanced at his watch. "How long will it take us to get to Shiprock?"

"Thirty minutes."

"You need to hurry up and finish. Lieutenant Hawk of the tribal police is going to meet me at the chapter house. He and I can talk while you attend the funeral. I know this isn't a very good time, but after the service I really would like to talk to Miss Tallmountain."

"I'll see what I can do," Gabe said. "But if she doesn't feel like talking . . . You know what I mean."

Lansing nodded. "How's your head doing?"

"Couple of aspirin, I'll be okay." Gabe touched the back of his head gingerly. "I think I can even get my helmet on now."

"Good," the sheriff said, standing. "I'll pay for your breakfast. Grab your chopper. You can lead the way."

───────────── ❊ **35**

A DOZEN CARS AND TRUCKS WERE PARKED IN FRONT of the Shiprock Chapter House when Gabe and Lansing arrived. Three Navajo men stood at the main doors talking and smoking cigarettes. Their conversation ended abruptly when they saw Lansing emerge from his truck wearing his uniform. They quickly conferred among themselves, then approached the intruding white man.

"You want something, mister?" the self-appointed spokesman asked. The spokesman was not threatening, but his tone of voice made it clear this was his turf.

"Certainly not trouble," Lansing said calmly. "I was supposed to meet Lieutenant Hawk here."

"He's not around." The Navajo looked at Gabe. "You with him?"

"Sort of . . . I'm mainly here for the Tallmountain funeral."

"You're too late for that. They buried him this morning."

"No," Gabe corrected. "His daughter told me to meet her here for the ceremony."

"Oh, you mean the singing." The Navajo nodded. "The one with Hosteen Akima."

"Yeah, I guess."

"That's at Peña Hogan." He looked at his watch. "You'd better hurry. They'll be starting any time now."

"Where's Peña Hogan?"

Turning, the spokesman pointed toward a ridge north of town. "It's up there. Take 666 four miles north of the cross-roads. You'll see a dirt road. Just follow the road to the top of the ridge. It's the only thing up there."

"Thanks." Gabe looked at Lansing.

"Go ahead." The sheriff nodded. "I'm going to wait around here for the lieutenant."

The hogan was a round structure of wood, clay, and adobe. It reminded Gabe of the building behind Tallmountain's house. A rectangular doorway facing east was the only access to the interior.

The building was foreign to Hanna. He couldn't understand why a ceremony of any type would be conducted in such a humble structure when the chapter house was available. Having never seen a hogan before, he didn't realize the one he was entering was much bigger than most.

The interior gathered light from four small windows and from the doorway. Nearly thirty feet in diameter, it was much bigger than Gabe had initially thought. Though he had to duck as he passed through the door, once inside, the ceiling was high enough for him to stand.

Opposite the doorway at the far end of the hogan sat an old man. Gabe suspected this was the "singer." Next to him was a younger man with a drum. There were no furnishings and the only decoration was an elaborate sand painting on the floor in front of the singer.

To the left of the sand painting, on the south side of the room, sat four men, among them Hunter Niyol. On the north side of the room was Kim and an older woman. Everyone had their eyes closed and seemed to be in silent prayer.

Since there was more room on the north side, Gabe decided to sit next to Kim. As he approached, the older woman opened her eyes. She seemed genuinely upset at Hanna's presence. She grabbed his arm and pointed toward the opposite side of the room.

"You sit there!" she ordered.

Completely ignorant of the customs, Gabe did as he was told.

He managed to find room next to Hunter. He was hoping the old man could explain the proceedings.

"Hunter?" Gabe whispered.

"Shhh!" the old man commanded. "It is almost time."

As Gabe waited patiently for the ceremony to begin, one more person entered the hogan. It was his uncle, Edward Hania. Hania nodded to Gabe, then took a seat on the earthen floor along with the other men. As soon as he did, the singer began his chant joined by the hollow rhythm of the drum.

"You must be Sheriff Lansing," Hawk said as he closed the door to his Jeep. Both men wore the khaki-tan uniforms familiar to many law enforcement agencies.

Lansing guessed he and his counterpart were close to the same age. He extended his hand. "The name's Cliff."

The two men shook hands. "Noah. Noah Hawk."

"I appreciate your meeting me on such short notice."

"No problem," Hawk admitted. "I don't get many days off around here, so I'm usually available. Sheriff Spence said you were investigating a shooting over in San Phillipe County. What brings you out here to the reservation?"

"I'm here mostly to talk to Kimberly Tallmountain."

"More drug business, I suppose." Hawk's disposition had suddenly changed from friendly to antagonistic. "I think Miss Tallmountain has suffered enough this week. Why don't you whites just leave her alone? Especially today. She's burying her father."

"I don't think you understand—"

"I understand plenty. Unless you have some sort of court order, you're out of your jurisdiction. Why don't you get in your truck and get off my reservation!"

Lansing studied the Navajo officer. He was pretty sure Special Agents Hobson and Williams had done an outstanding job of alienating the lieutenant. Lansing wasn't fond of their tactics himself. He could understand Hawk's animosity toward outside agencies.

"I don't know if it makes any difference," Lansing offered, "but I don't think Walter Tallmountain was running drugs."

"Oh, yeah?" The lieutenant sounded unconvinced. "Why not?"

"He doesn't fit the profile. Conservationist, family man, respected member of the tribe. Someone like that has too much self-esteem to run drugs."

"He spent almost two years in prison for possession. Don't you know? Once a rotten Indian, always a rotten Indian."

"I don't know that any more than you do."

"They found his car full of cocaine. They found fifty grand stashed on his property. You white men have him tried and convicted."

"That's all circumstantial evidence. There's just as much evidence that says he wasn't dealing."

"Yeah?" Hawk asked suspiciously. "Like what?"

Lansing walked over to his truck and pulled out the manila envelope Marty Hernandez had left him. "Can we sit down somewhere and talk?"

Lieutenant Hawk looked the sheriff over for a moment "Why not? We can use one of the chapter offices."

By Navajo standards, the ceremony was brief. The "*Dsichl Biyin*" took less than an hour. Gabe had no way of knowing. Eventually he would come to learn that some religious ceremonies, such as the Blessing Way, took nine days. For the moment he was satisfied that he had made it through this one. He was glad he had been there for Kim.

Kim thanked George Akima for singing at the ceremony. Then the few attendees stopped to give her their condolences. There were none of the tears from the night before. Kim stood strong and dignified, keeping her pain to herself.

Gabe hung back, letting the tribe members have their turns first. He hoped that he could walk with her alone when the others left. While he stood to one side, his uncle came up to him.

"I imagine this was your first Navajo funeral," Hania said.

"Yes." Gabe found his uncle's kindly attitude disarming. "I heard they already buried the body. I was kind of surprised."

"It's the Navajo way of doing things. The belief is the soul cannot begin its journey until the body has been properly interred. The ceremonies come later, after the soul is at peace."

"I see," Gabe said, nodding, although he really didn't. "I hope you're not offended, but I was surprised you came."

Hania smiled. "Walter and I may have had our differences, but like I told Kimberly last night, I respected him very much. I also thought that, as a council member, my presence was required."

The thought that his uncle sounded like a politician crossed Gabe's mind, but he kept his mouth shut.

"Gabriel, I know this is out of the blue, but have you given any thought to moving to the reservation?"

"No, sir. To be perfectly honest, I haven't." Except for Kim, he hadn't found a single thing to attract him to the reservation.

Hania looked over his shoulder. Others were still standing around Kim, so it appeared he would have Gabe to himself for a few more minutes. "Walk with me, Gabe. We need to talk in private." The older man led his nephew toward the far end of the hogan away from curious ears.

"I have two daughters, your cousins, that are both grown and married. Unfortunately their husbands don't seem to be very business minded. I've built a respectable business over the last thirty years that will eventually go to my grandchildren." He smiled with some pride. "I have two grandsons. Fine-looking boys. They're both still toddlers, though. A little young to be running anything . . ." He paused for a moment to gather his thoughts. "I know I'm not going to live forever. One day I might like to retire and do a little traveling. Of course, I can't do that unless someone is watching the store, so to speak. Hopefully, it will be someone in my own family." He glanced at Gabe to see if he was getting his point across.

"You want me to come work for you?"

"I stayed up all last night thinking about it. I always promised myself if there was some way I could help Davy, I would. It's a little late for that. But maybe I can do for you what I never could do for my brother."

"Uncle Edward, I'm flattered at the offer, but I have a job. A good job that I like. Besides, I don't know anything about running a business."

Hania smiled. "Son, I wouldn't expect you to know how to run a business. At least not now. But you could learn the ropes. Maybe pick up some college courses. A little extra education never hurt anyone. Of course, I'd gladly pay for it. I can write it off as a business expense."

Gabe shuddered at the thought of going back to school. He and book learning had never gotten along. Then he thought about Kim. She had a master's degree. He had a high school diploma. How could a beautiful, educated woman like her be interested in someone who barely escaped from twelfth grade? That thought was chased by another. Was she interested in him at all? That first night in the garage he had held her, but it was only as one human being comforting another. They had stayed up all night talking, but there was no indication she was attracted to him. After all, he did spend the night on the sofa. He had known her only a few days. They had never kissed. Why the hell was he even thinking that way?

"Gabe, you're awfully quiet there."

The deputy had to bring himself back to the present. He was so lost in his own thoughts, he had forgotten he was in the middle of a conversation. "I'm sorry. I was thinking about what you said."

"It's a reasonable offer, son. It's also an opportunity for you to come home to your family . . . to come home to your people, where you belong. And I guarantee, you'll be making twice what you're making as a sheriff's deputy."

Money wasn't overly important in Gabe's life. Not at the moment. But he hadn't found anyone he wanted to impress yet . . . except for, maybe, Kim.

"I know it's a good offer, Uncle Edward. Probably the best job offer I've ever had. It's just that . . . Well, I guess I wasn't expecting it. I don't know what to say."

"You can start off with 'yes' and we can go from there."

Gabe thought for a moment. "If it's all right, I'd like a little time to think about it."

The older man nodded. "I suppose I can understand that. . . ." He glanced toward the front of the hogan. Kim stood talking with old Hunter Niyol. The other attendees had left. "There's no rush, Gabriel. The offer was kind of spur-of-the-moment on my part. . . . We'll talk later. I need to give my condolences to Kimberly."

Hania left his nephew standing alone as he hurried to talk with Kim.

Gabe stuffed his hands into his jeans' pockets and kicked a stone. He had come to the decision the evening before that he didn't like his uncle. He still blamed Hania for the death of his father.

But his uncle was offering him more than a job. He was offering Gabe a "home." Home, as in family. Home, as in a position in the tribe. Gabe's yearning to belong was almost an ache in his soul. And he couldn't understand why he wanted to belong to the same nation of people who had ostracized his father. It didn't make any sense. All it did was compound his pain.

Numbed by his own confusion, Gabe glanced up to see Kim shove an envelope into Hania's hand, then slap him. The councilman called after her as she ran toward her truck, but she ignored him.

Hania looked up to see Gabe staring at him. The older man quickly averted his eyes as he stuffed the envelope into his pocket. Without saying a word he turned and started toward his own car.

Gabe broke into a run, trying to catch up with Kim. He forgot about his own muddled feelings. All that mattered to him now was Kim.

36

"KIM! WAIT!" GABE SHOUTED.

Hunter Niyol was already seated on the passenger side of her truck as Kim slammed her door. She didn't even look at Gabe as she started her engine, then sped off.

Gabe scrambled to his motorcycle and followed her. He tried several times to wave her over, but she ignored him. The chase was not long. Kim turned south at the highway, then east at the crossroads. A quarter mile past the light she turned into the chapter house parking lot.

Gabe parked his cycle behind her truck. Ripping off his helmet, he ran to her door. "Kim, we need to talk."

Kim pushed him away with her door. "Did your uncle send you after me so you could change my mind?"

The look on Kimberly's face reflected absolute rage. Her question was squeezed through clenched teeth.

"Yazhi," Hunter interrupted as he climbed through the opposite door. "I will wait for you inside."

"You don't have to leave, Hunter," Kim insisted. The old man ignored her as he shuffled toward the building.

"Kim, I don't know what you're talking about," Gabe said. "My uncle didn't send me."

"I saw you two talking together. It's a little game you and he are playing. If he can't buy me off, you're going to weasel your way in. Pretending like you're my friend."

"I am your friend," Gabe protested. "What are you talking about?"

"Twenty-five thousand dollars to shut me up. To walk away from my father's work."

"Uncle Edward . . ." Gabe caught himself. "Mr. Hania offered you twenty-five thousand dollars? For what?"

"He told me the council vote will be Tuesday and there's nothing I can do to stop it. He said there have already been enough bad feelings stirred up. My making one more presentation would only confuse the issue. Then he offered me the money. Pay off my debts. Forget about the vote. I was going to lose anyway."

"He offered you a bribe?"

"Yeah, you can call it that. Since his ploy didn't work, what had you planned to do? You fooled me last night. I was convinced you were interested in my work. I thought you wanted to help. What was your next step? Seduce me? Tell me you love me? Is that what you and your uncle decided after I left this morning?"

At that moment, Gabe could have easily told her he was falling in love with her. He also knew it was the last thing he dared to say to her. "I've seen Edward Hania three times in my life and each time you were with me. You know the man better than I do. . . . I swear on my father's grave I don't know a thing about his plans and I sure as hell am not part of them."

Kim tried to stare the deputy down, make him break, but she couldn't. His soft, soulful eyes answered her stare. He wouldn't blink and he wouldn't look away. "Why do I want to believe you?" Her voice had softened slightly, but there was still an edge to it.

"Because I'm not lying to you. . . . I don't think I could ever lie to you."

Kim turned away at his words. "I'm not in the mood for your kindness. I'm angry. I hurt and I'm angry."

Gabe put a gentle hand on her shoulder, but she immediately shrugged it off. "Please, don't," she begged softly. "Let me be angry. Let me hate you. . . . Let me hate you and your uncle and all the other bastards in the world."

Gabe remembered the anger when his father died. When the need to cry passed, Gabe got angry. At first he was angry at his father. Then he got angry at the army for letting his father's alcoholism go as far as it did. Then he got angry at the entire Navajo Nation for driving his father away. It was hard to be angry at a faceless mob. His anger had a face now. It was Edward Hania.

Kim was through crying. Now it was her turn to be angry. She had to blame someone . . . someone with a face, someone she could visualize.

Gabe stooped and picked up a handful of pebbles. He tossed one toward the far end of the gravel parking lot as he walked over to lean against the side of the truck. "When my father died, I got into a fistfight with my best friend. For no reason. After the funeral we had a few dozen drinks and he said something that set me off. I told him I hated his guts and just started swinging. He was bigger than me. Had me by a good twenty pounds. If he had wanted to, he could have put me through a wall with a single punch. Instead he covered his face and just let me pound away until I was worn out. He knew I was angry. He knew I had to strike out at something. He let me get it out of my system." He threw another pebble. "I saw him the next day. His forearms were covered with bruises . . . but we were still best friends."

He looked to see if Kim was listening. Her head was turned away, but somehow he felt she was hearing every word. "I understand the need to be angry. I know why you have to hate someone right this moment. If it helps, I'll even volunteer. But that doesn't mean we can't still be friends."

It was a long moment before Kim finally looked at him. Her eyes were no longer filled with hate. "How did you end up in my life?"

Gabe smiled. "You were speeding."

"Miss Tallmountain, I'd like to have a few words with you."

37

GABE IMMEDIATELY RECOGNIZED THE VOICE. IT WAS
Sheriff Lansing's. Lansing, Hunter Niyol, and a uniformed
Navajo policeman were emerging from the chapter house.

"Isn't that your sheriff?" Kim asked.

Gabe nodded. "You and I haven't had much of a chance
to talk this morning. I was supposed to tell you he was
here."

"This is about my father, isn't it?"

"Yes . . . and no."

Lansing approached the two. "Miss Tallmountain, I
know this isn't the best time in the world, but I really need
to talk to you."

"If this is about my father and drugs, you can talk to the
State Bureau of Investigation. I told them everything there
was to tell."

"Kimberly," Lieutenant Hawk interrupted, "I think you
do need to talk to the sheriff. The SBI seems satisfied with
letting someone frame your father. Sheriff Lansing is trying
to find his killer."

Kim thought hard. "He never took much when he camped.
Whatever he could fit in his backpack. Tent, sleeping bag,
canteen, a pot to cook in. He never carried a gun or rifle,

just his bowie knife. And packets of dried food in case he
didn't snare something. He always traveled light."

The group had adjourned to one of the meeting rooms
in the chapter house. Lansing and Hawk sat across the
table from Kim. Gabe and Hunter sat to one side, listening.
Gabe had not been privy to all of his sheriff's discoveries
and felt a little useless. All he could do was remain atten-
tive.

"Would you happen to know what his equipment looked
like?" the sheriff asked.

"Sure. I always made him sit down and have a decent
meal before he went camping. I'd cook him something at
his house while he packed his gear at the kitchen table."

"Okay," Lansing continued. "What kind of tent did he
have?"

"One of those small nylon dome tents. Blue. It was supported by hollow bamboo sticks connected by bungee
cords."

"What about his sleeping bag?"

"Pretty standard. It was a Coleman. This time of year
he took his medium weight. It was green with a red plaid
lining." Kimberly anticipated the next questions. "He took
a one and a half quart aluminum cooking pot and a half
gallon aluminum canteen. His bowie knife he carried in a
leather sheath. He wore that on a separate belt."

Gabe perked up at the description. It sounded very familiar. However, he didn't want to say anything that would
interrupt the interrogation.

Lansing got up and went to the hallway. A moment later
he reappeared with a paper bag. He dumped the contents
on the table. There were charred pieces of metal and cloth
along with a cooking pot and a canteen.

"Judging from your descriptions, I think I found where
your father last camped."

Tears welled up in Kim's eyes as she carefully touched

the separate items. She turned over the burnt remains of the sleeping bag. "Yes," she said firmly. "These belonged to my father." She looked up at the sheriff. "Where did you find them?"

"At Spider Woman, above the reservoir in the mountains. He had gone there just like you said."

"Then this proves he had nothing to do with drugs!"

"Not necessarily," Lansing said, shaking his head. "All it proves is that he was at Spider Woman Reservoir. A clever prosecutor would say he set up the camp as an alibi. I'm sure that's what the SBI would say."

"Then we don't have anything?"

"Oh, we have plenty. Someone wanted to make sure no one found out about the camp. That's why they went back and tried to destroy everything. Unfortunately, some innocent campers stumbled onto them."

Lansing gave a brief description of the shooting the previous afternoon. He kept his emotions to himself, being as matter-of-fact as he could. He then showed the evidence Patrolman Hernandez had left for him.

"I'm still trying to piece things together," the sheriff admitted. "But these are the facts as we know them. You said your father left to go camping Monday morning. We know he was shot and bled to death. The coroner said he died between noon Monday and five the next morning. At some point after he was shot he was in the backseat of his car. . . ."

"Do you think it's necessary that Kim sits through this?" Gabe asked.

"Yes. I do," the sheriff said flatly. "She knew her father. She might know some little fact or quirk about him that an outsider wouldn't know."

"It's all right, Gabe," Kim reassured him. "I want to be involved." She looked at Lansing. "Go ahead."

"We know he was not in the car when someone planted

the cocaine dust. Otherwise his clothes would have been covered with residue."

"Why would his murderer have overlooked something like that?" Gabe asked.

"I don't think he did," the sheriff remarked. "The coroner said it took one to two hours for Tallmountain to die from the time he was shot. My guess is he escaped. He was being transported in his own car. He had already been shot and was riding in the backseat. That's why all the blood was there. Whoever shot him might have thought he was already dead. That's why they weren't keeping an eye on him.

"He opened up the rear door and jumped or rolled out. He managed to hide in the sagebrush until the killer left."

"Maybe they pushed him out on the highway," Lieutenant Hawk suggested. "You said that's where the trucker found him."

"That's a possibility," Lansing agreed. "I thought about that. But if that was the case, why didn't they just leave the body where they shot him?

"I even considered the idea that he was the victim of a carjacking. The carjackers killed him, took his car, and later got involved with a drug deal. But that wouldn't explain why someone would go back and destroy his camping gear. And I guarantee, whoever went back to that camping site did not want to be seen. Otherwise Dr. Carerra wouldn't have been shot."

"But who would want to kill my father?"

"That's exactly what I wanted to ask you, Miss Tallmountain," Lansing said grimly. "Who would want to kill your father?"

"You know, that's funny." There was no humor in Lieutenant Hawk's voice. "The SBI never once asked that question."

Lansing tucked that bit of information away in the back

of his mind. He continued to press Kim. "Did your father have any enemies? Anyone who ever made threats against him?"

Kim strained to remember. "I know some of his ideas weren't popular, but no one ever threatened him. In fact, I thought everyone liked him." She continued to think, shaking her head. "I can't think of anyone."

Lansing thought for a moment. "The other day you said your father often went camping alone. Did he always go up to Spider Woman Reservoir? I mean, would other people assume that that's where he went?"

"No, not at all. In fact, he said he wanted to go to Spider Woman because he hadn't been there in almost a year."

"Who else besides yourself knew he was going there?"

"No one that I can think of."

"Did anyone stop by and see your father just before he went camping?"

Kim thought for just a second. "Yes. Thad Berkeley. Sunday afternoon. My father must have said he was leaving, because Berkeley was there again Tuesday when I got home from work. He thought my father might have gotten back from camping."

"Who's Thad Berkeley?"

"He's a lawyer," Hawk said. "He works for one of our tribal councilmen, Edward Hania."

"Why would he want to talk with Walter Tallmountain?"

"Politics, probably," the lieutenant continued. "There's been a lot of in-fighting in the tribe about timber cutting. Councilman Hania has been leading the charge to allow logging. Walter Tallmountain had been his biggest opponent."

"Now I am," Kim said defiantly.

"Is the issue big enough that someone would be killed over it?"

"If one person was going to see a lot of money, I suppose so," Hawk admitted. "But all the proceeds would end up going to the tribe. The tribal council is supposed to vote on the issue in the next month."

"Tuesday," Kim said flatly. "They've moved up the vote to Tuesday. I asked Edward Hania if he could get the vote delayed, but he refused. I can see why. The vote will go his way. My father is dead. Almost as bad is the fact that his reputation has been ruined. Everyone thinks he was dealing drugs. No councilman would vote on his side now."

"What about the money they found in your father's shed?" Lansing queried. "Where did that come from?"

"I don't know, Sheriff. But I know my father didn't put it there."

Lansing shook his head. "I don't know where we go from here. I guess I need to see this Berkeley fellow. He seems to be the last person to talk to Walter Tallmountain before he was killed."

"Sounds like a waste of time to me," Hawk observed. "If he knew anything about the murder, why did he come around looking for Walter on Tuesday?"

"I guess I'll have to ask him that." Lansing turned to Kim. "Thanks for all your help, Miss Tallmountain."

"No. Thank you, Sheriff Lansing. You're just about the first person who's listened to me about my father."

38

IT WAS MID-AFTERNOON WHEN THE MEETING BROKE up. Hawk and Lansing promised each other they would share any information they found. If necessary, they would pass messages through Sheriff Spence's office.

Lansing had a dozen questions plaguing him and he wanted time alone to sort things out. It had been a long time since breakfast. A late lunch seemed in order. After that he would check into the Super Six Motel, then go to the hospital. Concentrating on his work kept his mind off Margarite. But when he let his thoughts drift, they always returned to the hospital room.

Lansing stood, holding the handle to his truck, immersed in thoughts about Margarite, when Gabe approached. He was only half aware of the deputy's presence.

"Sheriff Lansing, I was wondering something."

"Huh? You say something, Gabe?"

"Yes, sir. I was wondering if you were going back to Las Palmas today."

"No. I'm going to hang around Farmington for a few days. Make sure everything's all right with Dr. Carerra."

"And work on this case?"

Lansing nodded. "Probably. Why?"

"I have some sick days accrued. I'd like to take them if I can. Hang around Shiprock a few days."

"Is there some particular reason?"

"Well, there's a chance you might need some help. And I'm worried about Kimberly. I'd like to make sure she's safe."

"Why would you think she's in danger?"

"Someone killed her father. None of us think it had anything to do with drugs. That only leaves his work. She's doing the same work he did. Couldn't that make her a target?"

Lansing nodded thoughtfully. "It could . . . if it does concern her work." He looked at his young deputy. "You sure you don't have one or two ulterior motives?"

"Would you believe me if I told you no?"

The sheriff shook his head. "Not in the least."

After giving the proposal a long consideration, Lansing sighed. "I'll call the office and see if Danny Cortez wants to pick up a couple of days of overtime. You can have the days off if he can cover. Call me at the Super Six Motel in about an hour."

"Thanks, Sheriff." Gabe hesitated before leaving. "Your attitude toward Kim seems a little different than it was this morning."

"I had a long talk with Lieutenant Hawk. He filled me in on what kind of man Tallmountain really was. He was an odd bird in his own way, going off and communing with nature . . . things like that. He didn't make much of a salary working for the Navajo Tribe and only kept enough of his pay to make ends meet. The rest he usually donated back to the tribe. A man like that doesn't run drugs. And there's nothing to indicate his daughter did either.

"I already had doubts about the SBI charges. I'm more convinced now than ever that someone's railroading this investigation. It's going to be up to us to find out who and why."

"Anything you need, Sheriff, you can count on me." Gabe started for his motorcycle.

"By the way, where the hell can I reach you?" Lansing asked.

"Kimberly Tallmountain's . . . I hope."

"Do you need any help?" Gabe asked.

Kim stood at the kitchen sink peeling potatoes. The small house was already filled with the aroma of onions wilting in a pot alongside the roast. "No, I'm almost finished. The carrots are already scraped. I'll throw everything in the same pot and cook the roast and vegetables at the same time."

Lansing had given Gabe his blessing to stay in Shiprock for a few days. It took a little effort, but Hanna finally convinced Kim she could use a bodyguard . . . at least until the tribal council voted on the timber issue. He told her, if it made her more comfortable, he could sleep outside. Kimberly assured him she wasn't worried. She kept a baseball bat close to her bed.

The toilet flushed in the back of the house and Hunter Niyol emerged, still zipping his jeans.

"Something smells good," the old man announced.

"You're just happy you don't have to cook for yourself," Kim kidded.

"I am a very good cook," Hunter said. He sat at the kitchen table next to the glass of tea Kim had poured for him. "It's the company at meals that I miss."

Gabe was glad Kim had invited both him and Hunter to dinner. The more he learned about Navajo culture, the more he wanted to know. Hunter seemed like a valuable source for furthering his education. His first questions were about the funeral.

"Everything we do in the traditional ways is a form of worship," Niyol explained. "The hogan is always built with a single door. That doorway always faces to the east to show our respect for the Sun God, the giver of light. The interior is divided in half. The women live and work on the north side. The men on the south. It is in recognition of the fact that, although men and women live together, their responsibilities and duties are different. That is why you could not sit with the women during the ceremony. It would have shown them disrespect.

"George Akima sang 'Dsichl Biyin,' the Mountain Song. It is an ancient song most often used in the healing ceremony. But it was appropriate for this funeral. In it the singer describes the journey to the Chief of Mountains and beyond it. It is a journey to the Holy Place where there is Life unending. It is also a journey home. Walter would have liked it very much.

"It is not the oldest song. There were older songs that were sung by the ancient ones before the coming of the Navajos. But those songs are lost because the ancient ones disappeared. It is said they grew wicked, so sandstorms and whirlwinds were sent to destroy them and their villages."

"That's one interpretation," Kim said quietly, smiling. "Hunter doesn't always agree with scientific methodology."

"Science is new. The legends are old," Hunter observed. "Every time an educated man comes along with a new science he reinterprets history. Once all the peoples of the New World were thought to have come from the Lost Tribes of Israel. Or we were descendants from Atlantis.

"The white man found the Clovis point and said the red man had been in the Americas for only ten thousand years. Then they found a cave in Pennsylvania and dated the red man back thirty centuries. In South America, they say we have been here forty thousand years. Every time a scientist turns over a rock, science adjusts its interpretation to whatever's popular.

"Our legends say we have been here since the beginning

of time. Through hundreds of years our stories never changed. It is better to put faith in a constant story than in a mound of theories that shifts like a dune in the desert, hostage to whatever scientific wind is blowing."

Hunter constantly surprised the deputy. One moment the old man seemed like a rock embedded firmly in a foundation of traditions. The next moment he was citing current scientific dogma or quoting some arcane Western philosopher to support his arguments. Maybe, Gabe thought, that's why he trusted the old man's opinion. Hunter had examined his beliefs in the context of a larger world and had decided they were sound.

It was nearly dark outside when Kim announced that dinner was ready. Hunter's philosophizing ceased while he concentrated on the home-cooked meal his hostess had prepared. Gabe realized he, too, missed the simple elegance of a meal cooked by someone who knew their way around the kitchen. He rued the thought of going back to an existence of Dixie Queen hamburgers or cold ravioli eaten directly from the can. Neither man could heap enough praise on the chef.

Kim tried to return the compliment by saying she couldn't think of anyone else she'd rather cook for. At least not now. All three tried to ignore the fact that she would never cook for her father again.

When the meal was finished, Hunter pulled out a corncob pipe and lit a bowlful of sweet-smelling tobacco. Gabe helped with the dishes while Kim stored the few leftovers in her refrigerator.

"I really should be thinking about heading home," Hunter admitted. "I don't sleep much these days, but after that meal it would be very easy to doze all evening in an easy chair."

"Would you like some coffee before you leave?" Kim asked.

"Coffee would be good."

"Gabe, would you care for any?"

The deputy thought about the parade of nightmares from the previous evening. "I think I can pass."

Kim prepared a pot of coffee as Gabe dried his hands and returned to his seat.

"I was curious about the coyotes you were talking about yesterday, Hunter. So I went to the library and looked up some old newspapers. There were lots of stories about coyotes thirty years ago. Just like you said."

"Oh? You didn't believe me?"

Gabe tried to find a face-saving way of saying "no," but couldn't. "I guess not."

Hunter puffed on his pipe. "I suppose if some old fool tried to pawn off stories like that on me, I'd be a little skeptical myself. What did you find out?"

"There were lots of incidents being reported about coyotes. And the stories weren't confined to just Farmington. There were reports ranging from Flagstaff to as far east as Taos. It was like you described: herds of livestock being attacked, pets getting killed . . . even homes broken into. The paper carried stories for a little over a week, then the reports stopped. It was as if the coyotes just up and left."

Hunter sat with his arms crossed, deep in thought. The only movement was his lips parting occasionally to let a small cloud of smoke escape. He offered no comment.

"Hunter," Gabe finally said, "I have to know more about Coyote."

"You what?" Hunter was truly surprised at the demand.

"You have to tell me more about Coyote."

Hunter studied the young law officer carefully. "Why?"

Gabe started off with the stories Hania had told about his father. He described how Davy Hania had earned the nickname Coyote when he was still a boy. Then he began talking about the previous night . . . how he had lain awake listening to the voices, how he could almost tell what they were saying. He told about his dream where he had hit a coyote. When he turned the coyote over, it had his father's face. Then he told about the dream where Hania ran over his father. But his father had a coyote's face.

"Dreams can be very powerful." Hunter nodded. "But sometimes they are nothing more than our subconscious mind reviewing all the things we had experienced that day."

"He's right," Kim agreed. "Yesterday was the first time you had ever heard about Coyote. It was also the first time you ever knew you had an uncle. Your uncle tells you your father's nickname was Coyote. It makes sense that everything got jumbled up in your dreams."

Those weren't the reactions Gabe wanted to hear. Anything Navajo was foreign to him, but one of the first things he was introduced to was the mystic concept of Coyote. David Hanna had taught him that if something couldn't be torn apart and put back together, it wasn't worth knowing about. Gabe wanted to believe in something more than the pragmatic world to which he had been exiled.

"Just a minute," he said. "I'll be right back." Gabe got up and went outside. He returned a minute later with something wrapped in one of his shirts. He laid the object on the table.

"I didn't tell you about all the dreams I had last night." He recounted hearing scratching at the door and going outside barefoot. There was a coyote in the road with something in its mouth. The coyote dropped the object and indicated Gabe should pick it up by pushing it toward him.

"Just as I picked up the object I woke up. I was still over there, on the sofa. I thought it was a dream. But this morning when I woke up my feet were covered with sand. Kim, you had already left by then. I went outside to find whatever it was the coyote dropped, but there wasn't anything there. Then I opened the storage on my bike and found this."

He unwrapped the shirt to reveal the belt and knife.

"Those are my father's," Kim exclaimed. "Where did you get them?" She picked up the objects for a better look.

"I just told you."

"I can't believe some coyote gave them to you. My father must have dropped them before he left. You must have found them in the grass."

"A coyote had the belt and knife in my dream. This morning I found them in my motorcycle."

Kim couldn't buy any of his story. "I'm sorry, Gabe. I don't believe in ghosts or spirits or coyotes that can change their shape. The only way those things could get in your motorcycle was that you put them there. You must have been walking in your sleep. You said your feet were dirty."

"May I see those?" Hunter asked.

Kim handed him the knife and belt.

"Do you really think your father dropped his knife belt?" the old man asked as he examined the leather closely. "That would be like him forgetting his tent."

"He might have," Kim argued. "He might have been in a hurry. He might have had other things on his mind. We all forget things once in a while." She watched as Hunter turned the belt over, studying different parts intently. "What are you looking at?"

Hunter looked up and smiled. "Teeth marks."

39

"I DON'T KNOW," LANSING SAID. "SOME OF THIS MAKES sense. Some of it doesn't. There is no way that Walter Tallmountain was involved with drugs. But that seems to be the center of everything. The drugs, I mean.

"I know drugs are the scourge of our society. I understand the SBI's attitude. They're hell-bent-to-leather to get another drug pusher off the streets. In their shoes I guess I'd be the same way. But I can't buy the drug angle with Tallmountain.

"We know someone shot him. We know he bled in the backseat of his car. He wasn't in his car when the drug deal went down, because there would have been cocaine on his clothing. But there wasn't.

"He was definitely in the mountains. I found his campsite and his daughter ID'd the things I found. How did he end up in San Phillipe County and his car in Santa Fe? He didn't drive it there. Someone else did.

"I know I mentioned this. . . . I figured he was shot, put in the backseat of his car, and he regained consciousness. He opened the door and dove out.

"But why did someone shoot him in the first place? His daughter said he didn't have any enemies. I thought the logging issue was an angle, but Lieutenant Hawk said no single person on the reservation was going to make any money off the deal. . . ."

Lansing mulled over his last few observations.

"Let's back up a little bit. The drug angle. Someone wants me, as a law enforcement officer, to believe Tallmountain dealt in drugs. Someone shot him in Santa Fe, then drove an hour and a half north to dump the body. . . . That doesn't make any sense. But that's what the SBI believes. . . . Why?"

Lansing realized he was getting tired. He rubbed his eyes in an effort to wake himself a little.

"Where do the drugs fit in?"

He concentrated on that question.

"Let's say your next-door neighbor was a schoolteacher. . . . Let's say he was a cop! Fine, upstanding citizen of the community. People trusted him. They trusted his opinion. They believed in what he stood for. All of a sudden, you find out he's pushing drugs. . . .

"He'd be a scum. He violated the trust you put in him. Anything he ever said . . . anything he ever stood for . . . even the good things, would be suspect. Miss Tallmountain . . ." He tried to remember the conversation. "What was it she said? It had to do with that tribal council vote. Her father's reputation had been ruined? I think that was it. Her father's reputation was ruined now and no councilman would vote on his side. . . ."

Lansing suddenly jumped up from his seat. "Dammit, that's got to be it! Kill him. Make it look like it was in the middle of a drug deal. Everything he ever stood for would go out the window. . . ."

He ran the fingers of both hands through his hair, then he pushed his palms against his temples. He was exhausted and there was the slightest hint of a headache.

"I hope you don't mind, but I think I'm going to sit down and close my eyes for a few minutes."

Lansing scooted the chair closer to the bed and took Margarite's hand in his.

"You know, Doctor, you can be a real good listener sometimes. I just wish you could hear me."

He kissed her forehead, then sat down, still holding her hand.

40

INITIALLY, HUNTER WAS RELUCTANT TO DISCUSS THE Coyote stories. Navajo tradition limited the telling of Coyote's exploits to the winter months. However, since he was not a Holy Man and because the voices had come again, he reasoned he could be excused for bending the rules a little.

"Coyote's greatest power over men is that he understands their vices," Hunter began as he repacked the tobacco in his pipe. "Maybe that is because Coyote has the same vices.

"If a man is greedy, Coyote can use that greed against him to make that man look foolish. It is said there was a young man who owned five horses. He was greedy and wanted more horses to make him look important in the village. But he was also lazy and refused to catch them for himself. Coyote came to him in the form of a tribal elder. Coyote told the man a horse's ears were like the ears of corn. If the man cut them off and planted them, each ear would grow into a new horse. The lazy man did as Coyote suggested. However, when he cut off his horses' ears the animals either bled to death or ran away. The lazy man did not care. He would plant the ears and have ten new horses. Of course, the ears did not grow into horses and the greedy man now did not have any."

"I was hoping you were going to tell me something a little more factual." Gabe was disappointed. He wanted to hear eyewitness accounts of Coyote's exploits. He wanted to know how Coyote actually behaved in the real world.

"The best way to understand Coyote is to listen to the stories about him. They are the key."

Hunter then told the story about when Coyote taught the deer how to dance. He explained it showed Coyote's own capacity for greed and laziness. The next story was about how Coyote stole Ram's horns because Coyote thought the curved horns would look better on himself. Ram eventually got his horns back by hiding below the water and pretending to be Coyote's reflection. Hunter pointed out that the story displayed Coyote's vanity.

Outside, the voices had started again. Some were close. Some farther away. They added an eerie background to the old man's stories, to Gabe's mind, giving the legends depth, texture, and even some credibility.

"Coyote is not good. Coyote is not evil. Just as a man is not born good or evil . . . But we have the choice to *do* good or evil. Men say Coyote chooses evil when he steals from a man's herd.

"In Coyote's eyes, all creatures are equal. If a man owns a flock of sheep, that man says he has dominion over these animals. To Coyote, no creature can own another. When Coyote steals a lamb, it is to feed himself, and he offers thanks to that lamb's spirit. But Coyote owes nothing to the man."

"So what you're saying is Coyote is a pest."

"Not at all. Coyote has great capacity for good. It was Coyote that led man from the fourth world to this world. When the fourth world flooded, all the men and women were saved because Coyote built a ladder and led them through the *Sipapu*, the place of emergence. Coyote thinks of men as his children.

"As any parent, though, Coyote sometimes walks among us to remind us to behave. As any parent, Coyote can help us, guide us, if he chooses.

"The opposite is also true. Coyote can be vain and greedy. And always the Trickster, sometimes he plays his jokes on us because he can't help himself.

"It is said Coyote made a home in a great cave and decorated it with many beautiful things. But because Coyote was lazy, he never made these things himself. He stole them from others. He stole some of the stars from the Nine Black-Faced Gods to give his cave light. He stole half of the rainbow from the Rain God to give his cave color. Mostly, though, Coyote stole things from men because men can be tricked so easily.

"He still steals things. Sometimes Coyote steals small things like a baby's rattle or a child's kachina doll. Sometimes he steals larger things like a finely woven blanket or a sand painting that has taken many days to create.

"Coyote is at his most wicked when he steals things of great value. Once he stole a village's entire supply of seed corn. The people in the village were forced to steal from others so they would not starve. He stole the peace pipe smoked at Shiprock when the United States made the first treaties with the Navajo. He even stole the Great Chain of San Lorenzo, given to the Navajo people by the viceroy of New Spain after the Pueblo Wars."

"What was the Great Chain of San Lorenzo?"

Kim had been sitting quietly, half listening to, half ignoring Hunter's Coyote stories. She had heard them all when she was growing up. She was disappointed in Gabe's innocent fascination with the topic. To her, it was like spending an evening with Grimms' fairy tales. When Gabe asked about the Great Chain, she jumped at the chance to discuss actual history.

"When the Spanish moved into New Spain, what's now

New Mexico, they were very fervent about making Christians out of the native tribes. This went on until the 1670s, when the tribes rose up in revolt. The rebellion, which lasted almost twenty years, was led by the Tewa and Towa Pueblo people, but they were joined by the Navajo and other tribes in the area.

"When the Spanish finally regained control in the 1690s they were a little more accommodating. As a token of goodwill with the Navajo, the viceroy sent craftsmen to teach our fathers how to work raw silver into fine jewelry. He also gave our people the Great Chain, a necklace about thirty feet long, encrusted with turquoise and obsidian. For two hundred years our craftsmen used the chain as a pattern to teach younger generations how to work the silver. The chain somehow disappeared about a hundred years ago."

"Yes," Hunter agreed. "Coyote stole it. I was taught that as a child. Our master craftsmen kept the chain in a secret place and only Coyote could have devised a trick to steal it."

"It's probably in some private collection somewhere," Kim insisted. "Hunter is right about one thing. A man, even a red man, can choose to do evil. . . . Some poor reservation Navajo probably traded it away for a bottle of cheap whiskey."

Gabe thought about Kim's claim and the death of his own father. He tried not to take her statement personally, but it was impossible to shake the image of his father passed out drunk on the sofa. *Even a red man can choose to do evil.* Did his father really steal five thousand dollars from the clan's building fund? Gabe tried to bury his thoughts by asking more questions. "Why did Coyote come back?"

Hunter also seemed to be offended by Kim's remark. His disapproving frown softened a little when he again spoke of Coyote. "I asked the Holy Men why Coyote has returned. They said, if indeed Coyote has come back, it is because the people have forgotten his power. A whole generation now lives who only knows about him through stories. He walks among us now to show that he is real and to remind us that we must follow the traditional ways."

"How long will he stay?"

"Who knows?" Hunter shook his head. "Coyote is Coyote. He comes and goes as he pleases. When he is satisfied his children believe in his power, perhaps then he will go away."

It was nearly midnight before Hunter left. Kim and Gabe stood on the front steps and watched Hunter's truck rattle down the dirt road to the highway. With the moon nearly full, it was easy for them to see their breath in the chilly night.

"What is your fascination with this coyote stuff?" Kim asked. "You're like a kid who's been told his first ghost story. You now know why things go bump in the night and you can't get enough of it."

"Have you ever listened to the coyotes?"

"I grew up a hundred yards down the road. I've heard coyotes all my life."

"But did you ever *listen* to them? Try to figure out what they were saying?"

"Those are just howls, Gabe. Yips and howls made by wild animals, and that's all they are."

"I take it you're not overly committed to the Navajo beliefs."

"Does the Virgin Mary hear every prayer you make?"

"I'm not convinced anyone hears our prayers. At least, no one has listened to many of mine."

Kim smiled. "Spoken like a true Navajo. Like you keep saying—this is all new to you. When the newness wears off, you won't be so mystified. I believe in the Navajo way only to the extent that it keeps my culture . . . our culture and our people, alive. But Hunter's Coyote is no more real to me than Santa Claus and the Easter Bunny."

An unexpectedly loud howl burst from the hill behind Kim's house. Both jumped at the sound. When each saw the other's reaction they started laughing.

"Someone doesn't care much for your beliefs."

"I guess not," Kim admitted. "From now on I'll keep my opinions to myself. . . . Let's go inside," she said, shivering. "It's cold out here."

"Good idea." He followed her inside and closed the door.

"How was the sofa last night?"

"About a foot too short."

"Well, you're the one who volunteered for guard duty."

"Yeah, I know. I guess it beats trying to sleep in a patrol car."

41

LANSING JUMPED AT THE GENTLE TOUCH OF A HAND on his shoulder.

"What? What?"

"I'm sorry to disturb you, Sheriff," the soft voice said. "But it's after midnight."

Lansing looked up at the young nurse. He was only vaguely aware that he was in a hospital.

"I thought you might like to get some rest. Those chairs can get uncomfortable."

Cliff realized he was still holding Margarite's lifeless hand. Reluctantly, he laid it next to her on the bed.

"Yeah, I guess I should go." He stood stiffly. "Listen, I'm staying at the Super Six Motel. . . ."

"Yes, sir," the nurse said. "We have that on Dr. Carerra's information sheet. You gave it to us earlier. If there's any change in her condition, we'll call you. I promise."

"Oh . . . Okay."

Lansing picked up his Stetson from a side table as he rubbed his eyes.

"Are you going to be all right?" the young nurse asked, touching his arm to steady him. She sounded genuinely concerned.

"Thanks. I'm fine. A few hours sleep, I'll be as good as new."

Lansing walked down the corridor weaving side to side a little. He hoped no one was watching. The chilly night air helped revive him and he made it to the motel without incident.

His last thought before oblivion was that he had forgotten to tell Margarite good night before he left.

42

WHEN 5:30 ROLLED AROUND, LANSING'S INTERNAL clock sounded. His first thought was about his coffeepot. He couldn't remember if he had loaded it before he went to bed. His second thought was that he was in a motel room and there was no coffeepot. The clock on the nightstand read 5:31. Lansing realized it was Sunday. There were no horses to feed and he had nowhere in particular he had to be.

He closed his eyes. He would get up in a minute, go find a newspaper, and enjoy the morning.

Suddenly someone was pounding on his door. He jumped up. "Who the hell is up at this time of day?" he muttered. He glanced at the clock. It now read 10:00.

"Damn!" He swung his feet onto the floor. He couldn't remember the last time he had slept so late. His visitor pounded the door again. "Just a minute!" he yelled.

He grabbed his trousers from a chair and slipped them on. He peeked through the peephole before turning the knob. He wasn't happy at what he saw. Letting out a weary sigh, he opened the door.

"Can I help you?"

"I believe you're out of your jurisdiction, aren't you, Sheriff?" Special Agent Hobson asked. Agent Williams stood behind his partner, sporting a frown.

"I suppose if I were trying to arrest somebody I would be." Lansing yawned. "Now, if that's all you wanted to know, good-bye. I'm going to take a shower."

"Not so quick." Hobson stuck his foot in the door to keep it from being shut. "I thought we explained to you last week that the SBI had taken over the Tallmountain investigation?"

"You did."

"Then why are you in Farmington asking a lot of questions about him?"

"I'm conducting an investigation into a shooting. A good friend of mine was almost killed. She may still die. If I asked any questions about Walter Tallmountain it was only because the cases might be related."

"Where did this alleged shooting take place?" Williams asked.

"Why would you guys care?"

"Professional curiosity," Hobson said, backing up his partner.

"Spider Woman Rec Area." Lansing watched to see if that information would get a response. Both agents remained impassive.

"So how does this rec area tie into the Tallmountain case?"

"It probably doesn't. I heard he sometimes went there. That's all."

"I see." Hobson sounded skeptical. "Why is it you requested copies of the autopsy report and our investigation findings?"

"The dead body ended up in San Phillipe County. I'm required to keep files on things like that."

"Well, I've got news for you, Sheriff. We're not permitted to release anything from an ongoing investigation. Once we're finished, you can have copies of anything we find . . . in triplicate. Until then, I'm afraid you're going to have to return those files."

"Highway Patrolman Hernandez said there wasn't any problem with the SBI releasing that file."

"Hernandez was given those papers by mistake. We have a new secretary in our office. She's not completely familiar with bureau policy yet. You know how that goes."

"Yeah, sure."

"Just hand over the file. Once the investigation is over, we'll give you anything you want."

"If that's the way it is," Lansing said, shrugging, "then that's the way it is. I'll put everything in the mail to you as soon as I get back to Las Palmas."

"Why can't you hand the stuff over to us now?"

"Because I don't have it. The file is sitting in my office somewhere. I'll probably have to scrounge around and see if I can find it."

Lansing could see Hobson gritting his teeth.

"All right," the agent finally said. "We'll look for it in the mail. . . . But let me make one thing clear. This is our investigation. The bureau will take a dim view if you interfere in any way. Do we understand each other, Sheriff?" Hobson almost spit the last word out.

"Perfectly."

Hobson held his foot in place a few moments longer, as if to emphasize his power over a local law officer. Lansing waited patiently until the agent tired of the game. When Hobson finally removed his foot, the sheriff slammed the door in his face.

"What a jerk!" Lansing muttered. He headed to the bathroom for a shave and shower.

"Was he upset because I asked to come out and talk to him?" Lansing asked. "After all, it is Sunday."

"Not at all," Sheriff Spence said. "I explained you were

over here from Las Palmas and didn't have a lot of time. I said you were trying to get most of the investigation done over the weekend."

Spence pulled his car into the large driveway.

Lansing couldn't help but be impressed with the Spanish hacienda motif. Every house in the upscale neighborhood looked large and expensive and, Lansing guessed, well out of his financial range.

He let his counterpart lead the way up the stone walkway. When Spence rang the doorbell, Lansing had to admit even the chimes sounded lavish. A man in his mid-thirties, dressed in expensive, casual sportswear, opened the door.

"Ah, Sheriff Spence. Come in."

Spence made the introductions. "Thad, this is Sheriff Lansing from San Phillipe County. Cliff, Thad Berkeley."

Lansing shook hands with his host.

"Come on in," Berkeley said, leading the way to a solarium toward the back of the house. "Jenny's off with the kids somewhere, so we can talk in peace."

When they reached the sun-drenched room Berkeley indicated they should make themselves comfortable. Lansing found himself surrounded by hanging ferns, potted trees, and flowering tulips. A dozen white wicker chairs with thick cushions were casually distributed around the room, giving the area a feeling of spacious comfort.

"Can I get either of you a drink?" the lawyer asked. "I'm going to have a gin and tonic myself."

"None for me," Spence said.

"No, that's all right," Lansing declined. "I don't want to keep you very long."

"No problem." Berkeley smiled, fixing his drink. "I'm glad you caught me early. I have a tee time at two-fifteen."

"The reason I'm here," Lansing began, "is I wanted to talk to you about Walter Tallmountain."

A pained look crossed Berkeley's face. "Walter, huh?

You don't know how badly I feel about that whole mess. I don't know if you know this, but I was out at his place last Sunday." He stopped mixing his drink for a second. "Damn," he said, retrospectively. "I'll bet I was one of the last persons around here to see him alive." He looked at Lansing. "Are you involved in the Tallmountain investigation?"

"Indirectly," Lansing confessed. "I'm actually here on a separate case. I don't even know if they're related. I'm just asking a few questions here and there to see if I can get some direction."

"Ask away." Berkeley made himself comfortable in a nearby seat.

"Exactly why did you go out to see Tallmountain last Sunday?"

"Tribal business. I work almost exclusively for Tribal Councilman Edward Hania. I handle his business affairs, I handle his personal affairs, and I do a lot of consulting for the tribal council."

"Am I stepping on any toes if I ask what kind of tribal business you were discussing?"

"I don't think so," the lawyer said, shaking his head. "It had to do with a council vote on a logging proposal. As a matter of fact, I had gone out to Walter's at his request. I don't know if you've heard about any of this, but Walter and his group of supporters had been trying to block any timber cutting on reservation land. They're on some big ecology kick. Mr. Hania has supported the proposal all along. It really is a good deal for the Navajo Nation. The timber is going to bring in a lot of revenue and the project will put people to work. That's just what they need on the reservation. That's all tribal politics, though. It really doesn't affect me.

"Anyway, Walter had been trying to block the proposal and he knew he was running out of time. He asked if I could arrange a delay in the council vote. He said he had more data coming in."

"What kind of data?"

"Oh, I have no idea. He just said he was waiting for a report."

"What did you tell him about the vote?"

"I said I would talk to Mr. Hania, but I really have no control over what the council decides. Like I said, I'm only a consultant."

"Did Tallmountain tell you he was going out of town?"

"Yeah. He said he was going camping for a few days. I told him to give me a call when he got back. If the council changed its mind I'd let him know."

"I see," Lansing said thoughtfully. "Did you happen to tell anyone else that Tallmountain was going camping?"

"Sure. Mr. Hania. I was there as his representative. I told him everything we discussed."

"Anyone else?"

Berkeley knitted his brows in thought. After a few seconds he shook his head. "No. I can't think of another soul."

"Can you remember when you told Mr. Hania about your conversation?"

"That afternoon. I was already out on the reservation. I went directly to Mr. Hania's after my visit with Walter."

Lansing nodded, looking at the floor. He sat quietly for several seconds before looking up. "I can't think of anything else." He stood. "I really do appreciate your time."

Spence and Berkeley stood at the same time.

"I hope I've been some help," the lawyer said. "If you have any more questions, please feel free to call. I'm in the book."

"Thanks."

"Yeah, thank you, Thad," Spence added.

Berkeley led them to the front door. As he stepped

through the doorway Lansing turned back to the lawyer. "Why did you go to Tallmountain's place on Tuesday?"

"What do you mean?"

"Tallmountain told you he would be gone for a few days. You told him to call you when he got back. I was just curious why you went out there if you knew he wouldn't be home."

Berkeley eyed the sheriff coldly. It took a couple of seconds for him to reply. "I had gone down to Coyote Summit with a survey team that afternoon. Walter's was on the way back to town. I simply stopped by to see if he had gotten back yet."

"Why?"

"I was going to tell him the council hadn't made a decision on when they would vote. Anything else?"

"No." Lansing smiled pleasantly. "That should do it. Thanks again for your time."

"It looked like you struck a sour note with Thad back there," Spence observed.

"About what?" Lansing asked.

"When you asked him why he was at Tallmountain's on Tuesday. He didn't look too happy about answering."

"Really?" Lansing said innocently. "I hadn't noticed."

Spence gave his friend a sidelong glance. "Humph . . . You want to stop off and get something to eat?"

"Thanks, but I had a late breakfast. You can just drop me off at the motel . . . and I need to get those directions again to Kimberly Tallmountain's place."

"SHERIFF LANSING." KIM GREETED HIM, HOLDING THE door open for him. "It's a good thing you called first. Gabe and I were going to take a motorcycle tour of the area this afternoon."

Lansing entered Kim's small house, removing his hat.

"Sheriff Lansing," Gabe said from the sofa.

"Hi, Gabe." Lansing noticed the pillow and blanket stacked next to his deputy. He hadn't known Gabe for very many months, but his respect for the young man immediately increased. Gabe's motives for staying at Kim's appeared to be more honorable than Lansing first suspected. "How's the sofa?"

Gabe grimaced. "Too short and too lumpy . . . and the television reception out here really stinks."

"He's doing it to himself, Sheriff," Kim said with a laugh. "I like his company, but I'm not sure I need a bodyguard."

"You probably don't," Lansing agreed. "But since he's doing this on his days off, I don't have any input."

"Since the kitchenette is the only place big enough to hold three people, why don't we sit at the table?" Kim suggested.

"Fine with me."

Kim took the sheriff's hat and hung it on a peg next to the door. "Can I get you something to drink? Iced tea?"

"Yeah. An iced tea sounds good." Lansing took a seat at the table.

"I'd like a refill," Gabe commented, getting up from the sofa.

"You know where the refrigerator is," Kim said. "The sheriff's a guest."

"What does that make me?" Gabe asked, coming up next to her.

"Since you signed on for guard duty, you're nothing more than hired help." She nudged him in the ribs.

"Thanks."

Kim joined Lansing at the table. "What was it you wanted to talk to me about?"

"Your father. Did you know he was in Santa Fe last Monday?"

"No, he wasn't. He went camping."

"Oh, I'm convinced he went camping," Lansing agreed. "But before he did, he went to Santa Fe. I got a copy of the preliminary investigation into your father's death. They have statements from three eyewitnesses who all agree they saw your father there. Two of them even talked to him."

"They're lying," Kim insisted. "They have to be."

"Maybe . . . but I don't think so. Special Agents Hobson and Williams, the ones you first met in Las Palmas, showed up at my motel this morning. They were very anxious to get that file back. They gave me some cock-and-bull story that this was an ongoing investigation and the State Bureau of Investigation wasn't allowed to release any preliminary findings."

"Did you give them the file back?" Gabe asked.

"No. I hadn't really looked at the witnesses' statements yet. I told them the file was in my office and that I'd have to mail it to them."

"Do you have it with you?" the deputy pressed.

"I didn't want to get caught carrying it around," Lansing

admitted. "I stuffed it under the mattress in my room. After the Hardy boys left, I did take a closer look at it. Aside from the screwup about not checking for cocaine on Tall-mountain's clothing, I couldn't figure out what they were trying to hide." He looked at Kim. "The three people who positively ID'd your father all work at the state's Bureau of Natural Resources."

"We work with those people all the time. They probably would have recognized him. But why did he go there?"

"I was going to ask you the same question," the sheriff said. "Did he tell you he was going there?"

Kim shook her head. "No. I would have remembered something like that."

"Can you think of any reason why he would have gone there?"

Kim's face was a blank. "We worked on almost everything together. . . . I can't think of any reason why he would go there."

Lansing nodded thoughtfully. Maybe he was wrong. Maybe the statements didn't mean anything. He racked his brain to remember what else was in the file. Did he miss something? Or . . . maybe there was nothing to miss. Maybe Hobson and Williams simply wanted the file back because they were a couple of bureaucratic assholes.

"Do you think anyone would have killed your father because of the upcoming council vote?"

"Of course not." Kim sounded shocked at the question. "I mean, there were a lot of people who didn't agree with my father and his views . . . but not enough to kill him."

"The Navajo tribe could make a lot of money from that timber. I keep hearing it's going to generate jobs here on the reservation. Don't you think there are some people who would really like to see that proposal go through?"

"Sure there are."

"Just who is going to get the revenue from the timber?"

"The tribe . . . as a whole. It's all spelled out in the contract. I have a couple of copies here, as a matter of fact. Would you like to see one?"

"Sure."

Kim dug though a stack of papers on the table in her living room. Eventually she returned to the kitchenette with a large manila folder. She handed the sheriff a thick document produced on legal-size paper. The package had a blue cover with large letters that read CONTRACT PROPOSAL BETWEEN THE NAVAJO NATION AND ROCKY MOUNTAIN RESOURCES.

Lansing opened the folder and began browsing. The document was filled with legal jargon that confused the issue for the sheriff more than it clarified it. Kim walked him through the different sections.

"Section one simply specifies who the parties involved are: party of the first part is the Navajo Nation; party of the second part is RMR." She flipped to the next page.

"Section two talks about what resources are being assigned to RMR. . . . It says here 'RMR, party of the second part, will be solely consigned, granted, and in all matters licensed the rights to develop, utilize, exploit, and extract natural resources to include, but may not be limited to, timber, plants of medicinal value, mineral, solar, wind, hydro-related occurrence, i.e., artesian springs, hydrothermal energy, et cetera, of said tracts of lands so specified in section three, subsections A through D, inclusive.' As confusing as this all sounds, even the tribal lawyers said this is standard stuff."

She flipped through a few dozen pages. "Section three outlines the specific tracts of land that would be logged: Coyote Summit, Hooker Springs, Flat Mountain. . . . It's all laid out in geographical coordinates.

"Everyone feels section four is the important one. It talks about compensation to the tribe and who will be allowed to do the work." She looked over one page, then turned to the next. "Okay. Page twenty. It says only members of the Navajo Nation may be employed by RMR and its designated management firm . . . along with the typical escape clause about 'qualified' workers. Page twenty-one has the stuff about compensation. Basically, it says the tribe will be paid current market price for all lumber extracted from the reservation. Electrical energy developed by solar, wind, or hydrothermal sources will be returned to the reservation at no expense to the tribe. Of course, we have to build the power lines. If they find water, it has to stay on the reservation for tribal use. Otherwise, RMR retains 'all other obligations incurred/assets derived.' "

Lansing was almost sorry he asked. He had hoped a single individual might be named as a special beneficiary of the deal. "Do you mind if I keep this copy? I'd like to read through it some more."

"Go ahead. There are plenty of copies floating around."

The sheriff thought for a moment. "I keep hearing about this Edward Hania. He's leading the push for the logging development. What can you tell me about him?"

"You mean Gabe's uncle?" Kim asked.

Lansing actually felt his jaw drop. "What do you mean 'Gabe's uncle'?"

Gabe nodded. "I just found out Friday . . . but yes, evidently, Edward Hania is my uncle." He looked embarrassed. "It's a long story."

Lansing could tell Gabe wasn't interested in talking about it. He looked at Kim. "Could you fill me in?"

"Edward Hania is a self-made businessman. I don't know if he's a millionaire, but he's got to be close to it. He made a fortune outside the reservation. He has something like five car dealerships, a couple of grocery stores, a construction company. He does a lot of real estate deals."

"What's his big interest in this timber deal?"

"He's a tribal councilman. He's going to push for anything that raises revenue for the nation. That's how councilmen get reelected."

Lansing thought for a moment. "This contract didn't say anything about milling the lumber."

"The newspaper said RMR was looking at a site northwest of Farmington," Gabe offered. "It wasn't on the reservation."

Lansing's face brightened. "How much you want to bet we already know the name of the person who owns that property?"

Kim looked at the sheriff. "You mean Councilman Hania?"

"It would take two minutes to look that information up at the county assessor's office," Lansing said. "I can do that in the morning."

"What if he does own it?" Gabe asked. "What does that prove?"

"Maybe nothing. But right now we're trying to prove Miss Tallmountain's father—"

"Kim . . . please," the young woman asked.

"All right. Kim. We're trying to prove Kim's father wasn't dealing drugs. To do that we have to offer another reason for why he was killed. The only thing remotely possible so far is the council vote. And the one name that keeps popping up is Edward Hania.

"Hania knew your father was going out of town camping. His lawyer told me that earlier."

"So you think my uncle killed Kim's father?" Gabe suddenly felt defensive.

"I didn't say that, Gabe. But it would look suspicious if he was pushing for the timber vote and was going to make a tidy little profit from a side deal when it went through. Don't you think so?"

"Yeah. Maybe," Gabe said without a great deal of commitment.

"Men have been killed for a lot less," Lansing said pointedly. He noticed the hurt look on his deputy's face and decided to change the subject.

"Kim, were you here when Hobson and Williams showed up with their search warrant?"

"No. I was at work. They came out here with Sheriff Spence and Lieutenant Hawk. The lieutenant stayed until I got home. He told me what happened."

"Did they search your house too?"

"No. Just my father's. They broke in the front door."

"Where did they find the money?"

"In his toolshed out back."

"So you don't know if they looked there first or started off with the house."

"No."

Lansing thought for a moment. "Did they take anything besides the money?"

"Lots of things. All of his papers, the phone book . . . Lieutenant Hawk gave me an inventory of what was taken." She went over to her refrigerator and pulled a paper from beneath a magnet. "Here." She handed the page to Lansing.

The sheriff looked over the property list. The fifty thousand dollars was broken down by denominations. The inventory went on to list medications, personal files, rock samples, address books, bank books, telephone books, calling lists, computer disks.

"What are these rock samples listed here?"

"Who knows?" Kim admitted. "Dad was an amateur geologist. He was always dragging home rocks with precious stones embedded in them, fossils, turquoise. He always cataloged whatever he found and then sent it to Window Rock to the museum."

"How about these medications?"

"I guess they figured he made pills out of his cocaine and then kept the stuff in his medicine cabinet." There was more than a little sarcasm in her voice.

"Okay. How about his personal papers? Do you have any idea what was in those?"

"They say those are personal papers. They all had to do with his work. He didn't have much of a life beyond his job. Kind of like me." She gestured toward the stacks of books and computer printouts strewn around her living room.

"So it's possible there's something in that paperwork that explains why he went to Santa Fe."

It was Kim's turn to brighten up a little. "Yes, there could be . . . but the SBI has all of his things."

"They can hold it as evidence, but there's nothing to keep us from examining it."

"Even if it's an ongoing investigation?"

"We can get a court order if we need it. That's something else we can do tomorrow, Gabe. Try to get hold of those papers."

"What's this 'we' stuff? I thought I was on my own time?"

Lansing let the smallest of a smile escape. "I'll officially put you back on the clock . . . if you come up with anything."

Gabe gave his superior a sour look. "You're an awfully hard man, Sheriff."

"I have to be. It comes with the territory." Lansing stood. "You know what? We may be chasing up a box canyon, but at least now we're chasing something."

Kim stood as well. "Are you leaving?"

"Yeah." Lansing walked toward the door and retrieved his hat. "We have our work cut out for us tomorrow. I think I'll take a little time off and visit a sick friend in the hospital."

"God, I forgot," Gabe said. "How is Dr. Carerra?"

"Resting quietly," Lansing said solemnly. "And that's about it." He opened the door. "Give me a call at the motel in the morning. We'll figure out then where we want to get started."

44

AS LANSING'S TRUCK STIRRED DUST DOWN THE NAR-
row road leading to the highway, Kim turned to Gabe. "I'm
ready for that motorcycle ride."

"Great," the deputy said. "Any place in particular?"

"Yes. The chapter house. I want to check my dad's office.
Maybe he kept some papers that explain his trip to Santa
Fe."

It was already late afternoon when Gabe parked his motorcycle in the empty parking lot. He held the bike steady
as Kim climbed from the rear.

"What'd you think of the ride?"

"I'm glad you made me wear a jacket. It got a little cold
back there."

"You haven't seen anything until you've driven in the
rain."

"I can hardly wait." Kim sounded unconvinced.

The doors to the chapter house were locked and Kim had
to use her key to get inside. There was barely enough light
from the sun for them to find their way down the hall. When
Kim reached her father's office she took out another key. As
she pushed the key into the lock the door swung open.

"We always keep our offices locked," Kim said warily.
She reached through the opening and switched on the

light. The room was a shambles. Desk drawers were pulled open. The file cabinet had been emptied. Papers were thrown everywhere.

She hurried down the hall to the next office door . . . her office door. When she turned on the light she found her room in the same condition.

"So you have no idea what could have been taken?" Lieutenant Hawk asked.

"No." Kim was a little surly. She had called the tribal police as soon as she discovered the break-in. It had taken the lieutenant an hour to respond. "We didn't keep anything of value here."

They were standing in Walter Tallmountain's office. Neither Kim nor Gabe had touched a thing.

"When was the last time you were in this office?" the officer asked.

"Friday . . . Saturday . . . Saturday, I guess. I had other things on my mind that morning. . . ."

"Yeah, I know," Hawk said apologetically. "I was here."

"I grabbed the mail from our box in the reception office and dropped it on the desk. Those were the only papers laying out." She raised her hands in helplessness. "And now this."

"What about your office?"

"Same thing."

Hawk shook his head. "I don't know what to tell you. I checked the other offices. They were fine. Do you have any idea what they were looking for?"

"No." Kim knew that was a lie. She had a guess about what might be missing. At that moment there were only three people she trusted: Hunter Niyol, Sheriff Lansing, and Gabe Hanna. During the hour wait, she had already told the deputy what she thought. She was grateful her friend didn't contradict her.

"Okay," Hawk said, closing his notebook. "That's all I can do tonight. I'm sorry it took me so long. I appreciate your waiting."

"Sure," Kim said.

The three walked out of the building together. It was already dark outside. Kim double-checked to make sure the front door was secure.

"Good night," the lieutenant said as he got into his Jeep.

Gabe waved at the officer. "Good night." He turned to Kim after Hawk drove away. "Why didn't you say anything about that report?"

"Because I don't know if there was a report. Dad said it was supposed to come in either late in the week or Monday. It might not even be here yet." She looked around nervously. "I don't want anyone to know about it. Especially if it's as important as my father thought . . . but I'm convinced that's what they were looking for."

"I guess we can assume it wasn't in the mail you dropped off Saturday," Gabe pondered. "They would have taken it off the desk and no one would have known."

"Or," Kim suggested, "they took it off the desk, then tore up the office to make us think they were looking for something else."

"Boy," Gabe said, shaking his head, "you really know how to mess up a perfectly sound theory."

"Or"—Kim smiled weakly—"it hasn't come yet."

"You're just making it worse." He picked up his helmet from his motorcycle. "It's almost a full moon. Is it too dark for a tour?"

"Yes," Kim said, climbing onto the back of the cycle. "And it's too cold. Let's go back to my place. I'll fix us something to eat."

"That's the best offer I've had all day." Gabe turned the ignition and fired up his bike. A second later they were heading south for Kim's house.

45

LANSING OPENED THE DOOR TO HIS MOTEL ROOM AND flipped on the light switch. The lamp next to the phone illuminated. As he surveyed his sterile cubicle he only became more depressed. He had avoided hanging around the hospital all day. He had hoped, if he stayed away long enough, there would have been a change in Margarite's condition. That didn't turn out to be the case. When he arrived she was as lifeless as the first time he saw her in the bed.

He had spent the late afternoon holding Margarite's hand, telling her about the Tallmountain case. He talked about the visit to Berkeley's house and the trip out to Kim's place. He apologized for not having anything more concrete to report. All he had to go on now were hunches and second guesses. He told her he was positive the SBI files held the key to Tallmountain's murder . . . and her getting shot.

The more he thought about the witnesses' testimony, the more he realized the SBI didn't ask one very important question: Why did Walter Tallmountain come to their offices in the first place? That was something else he and Gabe would do in the morning. Contact the witnesses and find out what business Tallmountain was conducting at the Bureau of Natural Resources.

Lansing held Margarite's hand until he ran out of things to say. Then he held it longer, trying to will her into consciousness. Even when he realized he was failing as a healer, he continued to hold her hand just so he could touch her.

It was dark when he finally left the hospital. He hadn't eaten since breakfast, but food didn't seem to interest him. He went directly to his motel.

As the door clicked shut behind him, Lansing realized he had left the contract Kim had given him in his truck. What the hell, he thought. Lawyers get so wrapped up in how they say things, maybe someone was missing *what* was being said. He had all evening. He decided to read it through again.

As he reached for the doorknob, someone gave his door a gentle rap. Without thinking, he swung the door open. Special Agents Hobson and Williams stood on the walkway, guns drawn and pointed at the sheriff.

"Back away from the door, Lansing," Hobson ordered. He used his gun to motion the sheriff to one side.

As Lansing backed away from the door, the two men entered the room. Williams blocked the doorway. Hobson moved farther inside, taking a position at the foot of the double bed. Lansing was still in his uniform, complete with holster and belt. "Now I want you to reach across with your left hand," Hobson instructed, "and remove your gun from your holster."

"What the hell is this all about?" Lansing demanded, keeping his hands clear of his gun.

"You're under arrest, *sheriff*," Hobson said.

"Under arrest! For what?"

"Obstruction of justice, for starters."

"You two are out of your gourds," Lansing snorted.

"Oh, yeah?" Hobson reached under the mattress and pulled out the Tallmountain file. "You were ordered to return this today and you didn't." He threw the file onto the bed, then grabbed a paper bag from the niche that served as a closet. He dumped the burnt contents onto the bed as well. "And if this stuff has anything to do with the Tallmountain case, we also have you for withholding evidence."

"You're full of it, Hobson. I'm an officer of the law conducting a legal investigation. How did you know about that stuff, anyway?"

"After you left this morning we had a talk with the manager. We told him a suspected felon posing as a sheriff might be staying in this room. He was more than willing to cooperate. He let us in."

"Did you have a search warrant?"

"No." Hobson didn't seem worried.

"Your charges will never stick."

"The murder charge might."

"What are you talking about?"

"We did a little checking around. Your girlfriend was hit by a bullet from a forty-four caliber weapon. Isn't that what you have strapped to your side there . . . a forty-four Magnum? If she doesn't pull through, it could look awfully bad for you."

"It's a three-fifty-seven," Lansing snapped. "And all of this is bull. I'm making a phone call." He quickly turned and grabbed the phone sitting behind him on the nightstand.

Before either agent could react, he yanked the heavy device from its cord and threw it at Williams. The agent dove for the floor, squeezing off a shot as he did. The bullet went wide.

Lansing knocked the lamp from the nightstand, extinguishing the only light in the room. Hobson, momentarily distracted in his concern over his partner, fired his gun twice at the spot where Lansing had been standing. To the agent's left, a dark figure filled the doorway, then disappeared into the courtyard beyond.

Running for the door, Hobson stumbled into Williams as he tried to get up. They had to untangle themselves before they could take up pursuit.

Lansing's room faced the interior courtyard, which contained the guest pool. The pool was flanked on all four sides by buildings. Access to the parking lot was through a breezeway a couple of doors down from the sheriff's room.

By the time Hobson and Williams reached the parking lot, Lansing had already backed his truck from its parking spot. Williams ran for the passenger door, his fingers just touching the handle as the truck surged forward. Hobson fired two shots at the fleeing vehicle, but their quarry kept going.

Lansing barely missed an approaching car as he skidded onto a side street. Instead of heading for the main road through town, the sheriff pointed his truck toward the south and the desert beyond.

"Now what?" Williams asked.

"Go call Sheriff Spence. Tell him Lansing resisted arrest and fired at us. We want an APB. Suspect is armed and dangerous. Looks like he's heading south on Highway 371. Tell him we're in pursuit. Use the phone in the manager's office. I'll pull the car around."

"I WAS WONDERING," GABE PONDERED AS HE LET HIS motorcycle idle in front of Kim's house. "Did your father have any secret hiding places in his house? A loose board or a safe behind a picture . . . someplace where he kept valuables?"

Kim was still perched behind him on the bike. "Yes, he did. I forgot all about it. There's a loose stone in the front of the fireplace. He kept a metal box in it with his personal papers, you know, like his marriage license and birth certificate."

"Want to take a look and see if the SBI found it?"

"What for?"

"Maybe there would be something in there that explains why he went to Santa Fe."

"It's worth a shot." She got down from the back of the cycle. "Let's grab a flashlight just in case his lights aren't working again."

"What's wrong with his lights?"

"It's the fuse box," Kim said from her steps. "It was the very first one Thomas Edison made, I'm sure of it." She let herself into the house. Turning on the interior lights, she dug through a kitchen drawer. A moment later she appeared at the door, flashlight in hand.

"Let's go," she said, taking her position behind Gabe.

"You're not going to turn off your lights?"

"Naw. We'll be back in a few minutes."

Gabe gave his engine some gas and thirty seconds later they were stopped in front of the adobe house Kim's father had called home. Flashlight in hand, Kim tried the wall switch inside the house. A single bare bulb, suspended in the middle of the ceiling, no more than thirty watts, came to life. Gabe couldn't help but think the nearly full moon outside gave off more light.

"Are there any more lights in here?" the deputy asked.

"Yeah. How's this?" Kim switched on a desk lamp. The room brightened considerably.

"Much better." Gabe nodded. "Now, where's this hiding place?"

"Over here." She was standing next to a floor-level hearth that was built into the wall. Ashes under the metal grate indicated her father had used it recently during the colder nights. Kim took a metal fire poker and tapped two of the large, flat stones that made up the floor of the house. One tap produced a *plink* sound. The second tap sounded more like a *plunk*. Kim indicated the second stone. "This is it."

She knelt and tried to force her fingernails into the crack surrounding the stone. After three tries she took the poker and used it to pry up the stone. Once she got it started it came up easily. The interior of the hole was dark. She reached inside and felt around. "I don't feel anything . . . Could you hand me the flashlight?"

Gabe picked up the flashlight from the table. When he did, he happened to glance outside. A set of headlights turned from the highway onto the dirt road leading to Kim's house. As soon as the headlights were pointed toward Gabe, the driver extinguished them.

The deputy immediately turned off the desk lamp, then the overhead light.

"Hey!" Kim protested. "What are you doing?"

"Someone's coming down the road."

Kim got up, brushing off the knees of her jeans. "So what?"

"They don't want you to know they're coming. Look." He pointed toward the highway. It was easy enough to see the dark vehicle in the bright moonlight. It contrasted especially well against the lighter-colored dirt road. The driver seemed to be approaching cautiously, as if he didn't want to alarm anyone by his arrival.

The vehicle stopped two hundred feet short of Kim's house, Gabe guessed, then slowly turned around so it was pointed toward the highway. From its silhouette the deputy thought it looked like a Suburban, or possibly a Ford Bronco. It was black or dark green; but whatever the color, it was a single tone.

Instead of continuing toward the highway the vehicle stopped and the driver got out. He left his door open. Walking to the back, he reached inside the open gate window and pulled out two items. Then he turned and started walking toward Kim's house.

"What's he doing?" Kim whispered.

"I don't know," Gabe admitted. "We're going to have to wait and see."

The lights from Kim's house produced two square patches on the ground in front. With Kim's truck parked on the gravel drive the little house looked occupied.

The stranger continued his approach, keeping Kim's truck between himself and the house. When he reached the truck he stopped. He leaned something against the truck. A second later he lit a match. For a moment it looked like the man's right hand was on fire.

Gabe realized it wasn't the man's hand. He was holding something . . . a bottle with a burning rag dangling from its mouth. The man continued toward the house, stopping short of the lit squares on the ground. As soon as he stopped he threw the lit container through the kitchen window.

Both Gabe and Kim heard the glass break when it hit the floor. Kim pressed her hand against her mouth to keep from screaming. Gabe threw his arms around her for support.

The arsonist calmly walked to the truck and picked up the item he had placed there. Gabe could see him cradling a rifle as the stranger calmly leaned against the truck and lit a cigarette. The deputy guessed he was waiting for Kim, just in case she chose not to burn to death.

"Come on," Gabe said, still whispering. "We have to get out of here."

"What if he sees us?" Kim whimpered.

"That's a risk we'll have to take. He may be planning on burning this place next. We're not going to wait around to find out."

Gabe sent Kim out of the house through the bedroom window. He then checked the front door. The arsonist was still smoking his cigarette, enjoying the growing blaze.

Keeping a low profile, he scrambled to his motorcycle. Pushing the bike off its support stand, he quietly pushed it to the far side of the adobe house, where Kim was waiting.

Before he started his engine he wanted to know which way they should go. "The only road into here is where that guy is parked," Kim complained. "The rest is sagebrush, rocks, and gullies."

"Sounds like fun to me," Gabe said grimly. "Hold on tight."

He started his engine and turned the bike so it was pointed toward the dirt road. The only thing they had going for them was the element of surprise . . . and speed.

The motorcycle roared beneath them. The tachometer read 3000 rpm when he kicked it out of neutral. The motorcycle leapt forward like a charging beast. With the high rpm set, Gabe immediately throttled through second and third and into fourth gear. He hit sixty miles per hour in six seconds.

The arsonist didn't even see the bike until it was almost even with him. By the time the man had the rifle to his shoulder Gabe had passed the parked vehicle. It was definitely a Ford Bronco, the deputy noted.

Gabe heard two shots. They seemed too far away and too late to do any harm. He could still feel Kim clutching him tightly when they reached the highway. For no particular reason, when they reached the asphalt he pointed the motorcycle south.

He ventured one glance behind him. The Bronco's lights were now on and he suspected the chase was about to begin. He kept his own lights off, hoping he and Kim would be swallowed by the night. He couldn't help but curse the bright moon. Speed was their only ally now. He hoped it would be enough.

47

"SHERIFF LANSING," MAY WILLARD EXCLAIMED, "HOW is Dr. Carerra? I've been asking around, but nobody seems to know nothin'."

"She's still in the hospital in Farmington," Lansing said, sounding a little distracted. "She's still in a coma."

Lansing couldn't believe he had gotten as far as he had. Just before Highway 371 exited town, he had taken another side street and doubled back.

At the first pay phone he found he called long distance to Las Palmas and talked to Deputy Cortez. He reported there was a death threat against Margarite and that Cortez was to call the San Juan County Sheriff's Office to request twenty-four-hour protection at the hospital. Lansing told his deputy he didn't have time to explain why he couldn't do it.

Cortez asked if Lansing was still at the Super Six Motel, in case he needed to be reached. No, Lansing lied. He was calling from the Westward Motel in Gallup and would be going to Santa Fe first thing in the morning. He'd call in sometime the next day.

After the phone call, Lansing followed the side streets to the eastern end of Farmington. He expected there was an APB out on him and he wanted to stay off the main highways as much as possible. He had to get rid of his truck.

When he finally got on the highway he held his breath every time a set of headlights approached. The one thing he had in his favor was that it was Sunday night, when most patrols were at a minimum. He figured if he could make it to his own county he stood a chance of buying himself some more time . . . after he dumped his truck. He wished he could dump his uniform as well.

"Lordy, lord." May shook her head. "Well, that poor woman certainly has been in my prayers these past two days." She casually looked over Lansing's shoulder to her gas islands out front. "I didn't hear you pull up. Where's your Jeep?"

"I've been using my truck the past couple of days. . . . Now it's starting to give me fits. Mechanical problems. I parked in back of your store."

"You need a ride to town? I close up here at eleven. That's only thirty minutes from now."

"No, no. That's all right. I saw that Dr. Carerra's truck got brought from the rec area. I'll just use it. Do you have the keys?"

"Sure. Right here." She opened her cash register and produced Margarite's key chain. "When Jeffy drove it in, he said it was kind of low on gas."

"Oh," Lansing said, a little disappointed. He didn't want to waste any more time than necessary. "I guess I'd better fill it." He produced a twenty-dollar bill from his wallet and traded it for the truck keys. "If anybody asks, tell them I went home to get some rest. If they need me, I'll be at the office in the morning."

"Sure thing, Sheriff."

Lansing went outside and disappeared around the side of the grocery store. A few minutes later he pulled Margarite's truck up to a gas pump. To May, he looked impatient while the tank filled. As soon as the pump quit running, Lansing hung up the nozzle. May checked the pump gauge next to her cash register. She owed the sheriff two dollars in change. As she rang up the difference she saw Lansing get into the truck and drive off . . . toward Farmington.

48

TEN MINUTES AFTER THEY HAD TURNED ONTO THE highway, Kim tried to yell something to Gabe. With the roar of the engine, the rush of the wind, and his own helmet blocking the noise, Gabe couldn't understand her. He shook his head and tapped his helmet over the earpiece.

Kim then pointed toward a dirt road they were quickly approaching. Gabe could see that it snaked off into the hills in the distance. In the bright moonlight, he knew they would be spotted from the highway, even if he had gained five minutes on their pursuer.

Gabe wasn't sure why Kim wanted to take that particular dirt road, but he knew they didn't want to stay on the highway forever. He slowed a little to survey the terrain. A mile down the road, perhaps two hundred yards to the left, a small outcropping of rocks jutted up. They could hide there until they were certain the coast was clear.

He checked his rearview mirror. Since passing the last hill two miles back he hadn't seen any sign of headlights. If they were going to take an evasive maneuver, now was the time to do it.

He slowed even more, turning onto the stony, rutted path as Kim had requested. The only sign of civilization was a lonely mailbox perched on a weather-beaten post. Gabe couldn't help but wonder where the owner lived.

The moonlight Gabe had cursed minutes earlier, he was now thankful to have. He didn't miss all of the rocks, but he missed most of them.

When he thought he was far enough down the road, Gabe turned off the worn path and started negotiating his way between tufts of sagebrush and miniature boulders. He found the ride bumpy, uncomfortable, and a little dangerous. He was certain Kim was miserable.

Once they reached the safety of the outcropping, Gabe shut off the engine.

"I don't know why you wanted to stop here, but that was fun!" Kim exclaimed. "Are you going to teach me how to drive one of these?"

Gabe shook his head. Somebody had just burned down her house and was probably trying to kill her, and Kim was having fun. The deputy climbed from the bike, then walked over to the rocks. Kim followed.

"Why did we stop here?"

"I don't know how much of a head start we had, but with this moonlight you can see ten miles down that dirt road. I didn't want him to spot us. We'll wait here for a while."

Gabe peeked over the rocks. The highway was still empty.

"How fast were we going?"

"I couldn't see the speedometer, but I had it wide open. Probably a hundred and fifty."

"No wonder we got here so fast."

"Where is 'here'?"

"This is the road to Hunter's place. We must have gone twenty miles in ten minutes."

"At least . . . . First thing we're going to do when we get to Hunter's is call the reservation police."

"I wish we could. He doesn't have a phone."

"Great." Gabe looked toward the highway again. A set

of headlights popped over the hill. It was too far and too dark to identify the type of vehicle, but it was traveling fast. To Gabe, the lights appeared to slow down slightly as it reached the turnoff for the dirt road. If the vehicle had slowed, it was only momentarily. It quickly resumed its high speed, the taillights disappearing into the distance in a matter of minutes.

"We'd better get moving," Gabe suggested, "just in case he decides to come back. How far is it to Hunter's from here?"

"Fifteen miles, maybe."

"He must not care for visitors much."

"Oh, he loves visitors. He just hates having neighbors."

Hunter nodded, quietly puffing on his pipe, as the two young people described the events of the evening. The small adobe hut was chilly and he sat in a rocking chair with a blanket across his lap. "And you have no idea who this was who burned your house?" he asked.

Kim shook her head.

"Do you think it was the same person who broke into the chapter house?"

"It could have been," Kim admitted. "But we don't know who did that, either." She was silent for a moment. "Maybe it had something to do with Dad going to Santa Fe."

"Santa Fe?" The words seemed to perk the old man up. "When did your father go to Santa Fe?"

"Last Monday, before he went to Spider Woman. Sheriff Lansing said he read statements from witnesses who saw him there . . . at the Bureau of Natural Resources."

"Yes, yes, yes," Hunter said, suddenly standing. "Why is it an old man can remember from fifty years ago and forgets yesterday?" He hurried over to his kitchen cabinet and retrieved an envelope. "This came in my mail yesterday. I didn't open it, because it is not mine." He handed it to Kim.

The envelope was addressed to Mr. Walter Tallmountain, Care of H. Niyol, RR #4, Shiprock, NM. The preprinted return address said State of New Mexico, Bureau of Natural Resources.

"Why would he have them send me a letter for him?"

"I don't know," Kim said, hurriedly opening the envelope. She unfolded the letter. "This is from the Assay Office. It's dated last Wednesday. Let me read it to you:

" 'Dear Mr. Tallmountain,

" 'As you requested, this office expedited its analysis of the three ore samples you delivered on Monday. Without a larger sample size to work with it was hard to make a full determination, but we estimate purity at 01.56 percent. Our conservative assessment places extraction rate at approximately five hundred ounces of silver per ton of raw ore.

" 'Additionally, fissuring in the samples indicates the existence of a major vein that could yield significantly higher levels of pure metal per ton extracted.

" 'If this office can be of further assistance, please feel free to contact us.'

"At the bottom there's a cc with Hunter's address."

Kimberly's hand was trembling when she finished reading.

"I can't believe this. Why didn't my dad tell me about the silver?"

"Probably for the same reason he didn't tell you he was going to Santa Fe. He didn't want you to get killed," Gabe said. "This is the report he told you about. The one that would stop the logging."

"It's not going to stop the logging. They'll chop down the trees and when they're finished they'll dig up the ground." Kim threw the letter down. "It doesn't change a damned thing!"

"It's got to change something!" Gabe insisted. "If it didn't, they wouldn't have killed your father."

"What would it change?" Kim argued. "If the tribal council thought they were going to make a fortune mining silver, every last one of them would vote for the proposal."

"I don't know," Gabe said, shaking his head. "I guess you're right. Geez. Five hundred ounces per ton." He sat down in a chair and leaned over, resting his elbows on his knees. "You know, a ton isn't very much material. I worked construction one summer. One day I had to haul twenty wheelbarrows of sand from one end of the building site to the other. When I got finished the foreman told me I had moved two tons. I guess ten wheelbarrows would be about one ton." He thought for a moment. "What's silver worth?"

Kim shook her head. "I don't know." She sounded defeated. "Compared to gold, not all that much. Five dollars an ounce. Something like that."

Gabe did a few quick calculations in his head. "Damn. That would mean each wheelbarrow load would be worth over two hundred dollars. That could add up really quick." He thought for a moment. "How much would the tribe keep out of that?"

"I don't know. I really don't care," Kim admitted. "Whatever the contract said."

"I don't think the contract said anything about silver."

"Don't be silly. Lawyers think of every angle, just in case something happens that they didn't predict. That way they have their butts covered."

"I listened to what you were reading this afternoon. One of the sections talked specifically about what the Navajo Nation would get from RMR."

"Yeah," Kim said, trying to remember what the contract

did say. "Something about current market price for the lumber. And the tribe got to keep all of the electricity generated. Any water they found had to stay on the reservation. RMR got to keep everything else. . . ." Kim's face lit up. "Dammit, that's it! RMR keeps anything else they find! We'd signed over the rights to the minerals and they wouldn't have to pay us back."

"RMR . . . or somebody, knew about the silver," Gabe theorized. "So did your father. No one would vote for that contract the way it reads now. RMR knew that too. That's why your father was so secretive about the assay report. He was afraid RMR would try to stop him. The camping trip was a cover for his trip to Santa Fe."

"But they did stop him!" Kim snapped.

"No. They may have killed him, but they didn't stop him." Gabe picked up the Assay Office letter. "They sent two reports. One went to your office. . . . Your father figured if they found out what he was up to, they'd intercept the report—at his house, at your house, or at your office. That's why he had a duplicate sent here."

"Okay, I'll buy that. But why tear up the offices? Why burn down my house and try to kill me?"

Gabe held up the letter. "This is a photocopy of the original. Somebody already has the original. They knew a second copy was mailed. They were trying to find it or destroy it any way they could."

"But why would they think I had it?"

"The report came in Saturday's mail. They figured that out when they broke into your office. Hunter was with you Saturday. They figured he gave you his copy then." Gabe hesitated before starting his next sentence. "Maybe that's what my uncle thought . . . that you had the report. That's why you turned down his twenty-five thousand dollars. This piece of paper is worth millions to someone."

"Yeah. I'll bet it is." It was Kim's turn to sit. "It doesn't make sense. When the council finds out there's silver, they're still going to chop down the trees. What's worse, they're going to tear up the land with their mining. In a strange sort of way, my father is helping them. This is going to go against everything he ever believed in."

"Maybe, little one, your father believed in more than one thing," Hunter said thoughtfully.

"What do you mean?"

"It is true Walter believed in preserving the land and the resources for our children and our children's children. The Great Spirit created five worlds and this is the last one. When it is gone, there will never be another.

"But your father also believed in preserving the Navajo people. For hundreds of years the white man killed us, stole from us, forced us to live on lands he did not want. Now he comes again, trying to trick us into giving him our silver without his paying for it. Your father loved the land. But he loved his people more. He would not stand for such an outrage. He was willing to give his life to keep that from happening."

Gabe watched the tear trickle down Kim's face. "I wish I could have met your father," he said softly.

"You would have liked him." Kim sniffed.

The three sat in silence for several minutes, contemplating the unfairness of the past week's events and of life in general. It was Hunter who finally said something.

"So you have this piece of paper now. What are you going to do with it?"

"I'm going to take it to the council on Tuesday and block the vote," Kim replied.

"What if they don't believe you?"

"Why wouldn't they believe me? This is an official letter from the State of New Mexico."

"It is a copy of a letter with the copy of a letterhead on

top. It could have been made from two different letters. That is what some people might say."

"It might be enough to delay the vote until I can get another letter."

"Maybe." The old man nodded. "But it might be better to have proof of what the letter says."

"What kind of proof?"

"Rock samples. Like your father took to Santa Fe. Then the council would know the letter is true."

"I'll bet those were ore samples that the SBI took," Gabe guessed. "We could try to get them back from the state."

"Or," Hunter suggested, "you can get them from the same place Walter found them."

"That could take a week," Kim complained.

"You have one day," Hunter replied. He walked over to his bookcase and pulled out a sectional map produced by the Bureau of Land Management. He laid it on the floor so all three could see. Every house, every contour, every dirt road, every arroyo within a hundred miles of Farmington was displayed. He pointed at the end of a dirt road. "This is where we are." He then pointed to a series of peaks thirty miles to the south. "This is Coyote Summit. This is where they say they want to cut down the trees. This is where you will find the silver."

"I'm afraid they'll be looking for us on the highway," Gabe said.

"Hand me a pen from my table," Hunter said. "I will show you a way to get there without using the highway."

With the pen he sketched a route from his house to the peaks, pointing out the landmarks Gabe should use to find his way. It was after midnight when he finished.

"You two get some sleep now," Hunter suggested. "Tomorrow will be a long day."

MAY WILLARD'S SON, JEFFY, WAS IN THE PROCESS OF unlocking the pumps when the highway patrol car pulled into the parking area. Jeffy waved at the officer as he got out of his car and went into the store.

"Morning, May."

"Officer Hernandez," May said, sorting her cash for the register, "you're on the road awfully early. Especially for a Monday."

"Yeah, tell me about it. Is your coffee ready?"

"It just finished brewing. I'm sorry we don't have any fresh pastries. The truck doesn't get here from Bloomfield till about seven."

"That's all right," Hernandez said, filling a styrofoam cup. "All I need is something to keep me awake."

May broke open a roll of quarters and poured it into her tray. "I guess things haven't changed much with Dr. Carerra. Cliff Lansing said she was still in a coma."

The patrolman turned so quickly, he spilled his coffee all over the floor. "He did? When was this?"

"Last night. I remember, it was ten-thirty. I told him if he could wait half an hour I'd give him a ride into town."

"He was on foot?"

"No, he said he was having problems with his truck. He parked it around back and took Dr. Carerra's."

"Did he say where he was going?"

"As a matter of fact, he did. He told me, if anyone asked, he was going home to get some rest. He did say he would be in his office this morning."

Marty Hernandez had just come from Las Palmas. Lansing's house was locked and no one had seen him. Deputy Cortez said he had gotten a call from Lansing around 9:00 P.M. The sheriff said he was in Gallup and would be going to Santa Fe this morning.

Hernandez felt he knew Lansing pretty well. He didn't believe any of the charges being alleged. He assumed the obstruction of justice call was the SBI being overzealous in their duties. He couldn't believe Lansing had fired shots at another peace officer. And he thought the attempted murder charge was an out-and-out lie. Whatever the facts were, the sheriff was spreading as much disinformation about his whereabouts as he could.

"You sure he said he was going to Las Palmas?"

"That's what he said for me to tell folks. But he was acting awfully strange. He had to fill up the doctor's truck. When he finished, he headed right back down the road to Farmington. He didn't even come in to get his change. Now, don't you think that's strange?"

"Yeah." The patrolman didn't really. Under the circumstances Lansing was acting perfectly normal . . . for a man on the run.

Hernandez got a description of Margarite's truck, then took a look at the vehicle Lansing had left behind. The APB reported that Lansing was armed and should be considered dangerous. The truck had been cleaned out. The sheriff had left no bullets or weapons behind, which meant he was still armed.

Once he was back in his patrol car, Hernandez hesitated for just a moment. Lansing was a friend. He was a decent man and a damned good law officer. It didn't make sense that he was suddenly a fugitive. He also felt any charges being brought by Hobson and Williams were automatically suspect.

Despite his loyalty to Lansing, Hernandez reminded himself he had taken a pledge to uphold the laws of New Mexico and the Constitution of the United States. He was obligated to do his duty. If Lansing was innocent, like he hoped, there would be nothing to worry about. He picked his microphone up from its cradle.

"Bloomfield Center, Bloomfield Center. Highway Patrol Two Three. I have an update on an APB for a Lansing, Clifford A. How copy?"

Lieutenant Hawk parked next to an unfamiliar truck with faded green paint. His Jeep and the empty truck were the only vehicles around Peña Hogan. As he stepped from his Jeep, someone called him.

"Lieutenant. Over here, in the hogan."

As Hawk walked through the door he could see a shadowy figure at the far end of the round room. He heard the distinctive click of a gun's hammer being cocked.

"I appreciate your meeting me again. Now stop right there and drop your gun belt," the figure ordered.

"You sure you want to do this, Lansing?"

"I'm not going to hurt you. I just don't want you accidentally pulling your gun on me. I am a fugitive from justice. I'm sure you've heard that by now."

"We've seen a few things come over the wire," Hawk admitted. He carefully unbuckled his belt.

"Just toss it in the middle where I can see it."

The tribal officer did as he was told. "I'd feel a little better if you uncocked your gun. I don't want to accidentally get shot."

Lansing did as he was requested.

"Now, what is this all about?" the lieutenant asked.

"I need help."

"That's an understatement . . . but you sure have a strange way of asking for it."

"This has to do with Tallmountain's death."

"Which one?"

"What do you mean, 'which one'?"

"Kimberly Tallmountain's house burned down last night. I'm afraid she was inside when it happened. Her truck was parked out front."

"Have you found any bodies?"

"The ashes are still too hot to dig through. We were going to take a water truck out there this morning and douse the embers." He gave Lansing a curious look. "Why did you ask if there were *bodies*?"

"Because my deputy, Gabe Hanna, was staying with her, sort of as a bodyguard. Was his motorcycle there?"

"I didn't see any motorcycle."

Lansing reholstered his gun. "Then there's a chance Kim isn't dead. When I saw them yesterday afternoon, Kim said they were going on a motorcycle tour."

"I don't know about any tour, but you're right. I saw them last night at the chapter house. They were on your deputy's bike."

"Why did they go there?"

"You know, in all the confusion, I forgot to ask."

"What do you mean?"

"Kim called to report a break-in. Somebody had ransacked both her and Walter's offices. None of the other offices were touched. I did ask her what was taken, but she said she had no idea."

Lansing nodded thoughtfully. "She was going to go through her father's papers. She was trying to figure out why he had gone to Santa Fe."

"When was that?"

Lansing tried to summarize everything he knew as

quickly as possible. In the SBI file, eyewitnesses from the Natural Resources office placed Tallmountain in Santa Fe on Monday. The SBI wanted the Tallmountain file back. (That, in a nutshell, was why they tried to arrest him. Lansing was sure of it. At the time, he still had the file.) Someone didn't want it known that Tallmountain had gone to the Bureau of Natural Resources. Kim was trying to find a paper trail that would lead to Santa Fe.

"Walter Tallmountain's death had nothing to do with drugs. I'm convinced somebody planted that fifty grand in his shed. The drug business was nothing more than a smoke screen. Unfortunately, those yahoos from the SBI can't see that.

"I think we were getting somewhere with my investigation. We were going to get a lot done today," Lansing said, picking up Hawk's gun belt. "Gabe was going to read through the files the SBI took from Tallmountain's house. I was going to contact the witnesses and ask why he had gone to their offices." He handed the lieutenant his gear. "Now I'm on the run and both Gabe and Kim have disappeared." Lansing shook his head. "You know, I think we were really getting close."

"Maybe too close," Hawk observed, strapping on his gun belt. "Maybe the fire at Kim's house wasn't an accident. She might have found out why Walter went to Santa Fe. Someone was trying to silence her, just like they did her father."

"Yeah," Lansing agreed. "That makes sense. That's why she's hiding out."

"Now all you have to do is figure out where."

Lansing raised his eyebrows. "That old man that sat in the room with us Saturday . . . What was his name?"

"You mean Hunter Niyol?"

"That's the one. He seemed pretty close to Kim. Maybe he knows where they are."

"It's worth a shot." Hawk nodded.

"I need to find a phone book."

"Won't do you any good, Sheriff. Hunter lives way out in the sticks. He doesn't have a phone."

"That's just great. . . . Can you give me directions?"

"Better than that. I can take you there." Lieutenant Hawk's face suddenly clouded with concern. "You're the second person this morning who's asked for directions to his place."

"Who was the first one?"

"Some tall Anglo. I'd never seen him before. He said he had a delivery."

"Was he wearing a uniform?"

"No, but that's not unusual. Even the mailmen don't wear uniforms around here much."

"Can you remember what he was driving?"

"Yeah. A black Ford Bronco."

50

GABE SLIPPED HIS GEARS INTO NEUTRAL WHEN THEY reached the top of the rise. A series of three peaks jutted up from the dry desert floor. The slopes were covered with a thick forest of pine and juniper trees. "That's got to be where we're headed."

Kim pointed to a narrow dirt road approaching the peaks from the east. "That road comes in from the main highway. I've never seen this area from this angle, but the tall peak in the middle is definitely Coyote Summit. How long will it take for us to get there?"

"The ground looks fairly harmless from here. Fifteen, twenty minutes. Half an hour at the most."

"I can't believe we made it here without bringing Hunter's map."

"He told me last night what to look for," Gabe said. "The landmarks were easy to follow."

"Well, we're wasting time," Kim observed. "Getting there is just part of the battle."

"We're on our way." Gabe revved his engine and started down the gentle slope.

It was a forty-minute drive from Shiprock to the turnoff for Hunter Niyol's place. Lansing had left Margarite's truck behind, opting to ride with Noah Hawk. The lieutenant

COYOTE RETURNS   279

covered the ground as fast as he could, using his lights and siren to clear traffic when necessary.

Once they left the highway their progress slowed considerably. Lansing gritted his teeth whenever a rock slammed into the Jeep's undercarriage. Hawk seemed oblivious of the noise. He took bumps and turns at speeds Lansing thought were dangerously excessive. The sheriff couldn't help but admire the Navajo's driving skills. Except for one bump that sent the Jeep sailing through the air for twenty feet, the lieutenant pretty much managed to keep the vehicle on the road. It took them only twenty minutes to cover the fifteen miles from the highway.

They could see Hunter's hut sitting on a hill above the valley from three miles away. As they grew closer, they saw the old man's weather-beaten truck parked to the side of the adobe shack. There were no other vehicles around.

Hawk parked his Jeep and the two men got out.

"Hunter!" the lieutenant called, expecting to see the old man emerge from the house. There was no movement.

Hawk proceeded to the only entrance to the hovel. Lansing was right behind him. The lieutenant found the front door unlocked when he tried it. "Hunter?" he called again. Hawk pulled his gun, then slowly pushed the door open.

The inside of the shack was a shambles. The bookcases that Hunter kept neat and orderly were pulled from the walls and thrown to the ground. The kitchen cupboards had been cleared out, the dishes smashed against the ground.

"Look around," Hawk ordered. "See if you can find him."

The lieutenant carefully stepped his way through the mess until he reached the bedroom. He found it in the same condition as the rest of the house.

"Noah, over here," Lansing said. "Help me lift this." He was standing over a fallen bookcase. They carefully lifted the heavy wooden cabinet to an upright position. Stretched on the floor was the lifeless form of Hunter Niyol.

Lansing scooped up the old man and carried him to the bed in the next room as Hawk cleared the way. Hunter's face was battered and bleeding.

Hawk took Hunter's hand in his. "Hunter. Can you hear me?" The old man let out a faint groan. "Lansing, get me a towel and some water from the kitchen."

The sheriff did as he was asked. When he returned he handed the lieutenant the moistened cloth. The policeman gently dabbed Hunter's face. The action was enough to open the old man's eyes.

"No, no, no more," Hunter whimpered. "No more." He tried to push the lieutenant's hand away.

"It's all right, Hunter," the officer assured him. "It's Noah Hawk. I'm here to help."

"Hawk?" the old man said feebly.

"Yes. Lieutenant Hawk. Who did this to you?"

"Who did this?" Hunter seemed confused.

"Yes, who did this? Who beat you?"

"Beat me?" He thought for a moment. "A white man. A white man came. He was looking for my Yazhi."

"What's a 'Yazhi'?" Lansing asked in a whisper.

"That's Navajo for little one. Sort of a term of endearment." Hawk dabbed the old man's face some more. "Are you talking about Kimberly?"

"Yes, yes." Hunter nodded. "My Yazhi. I told him I did not know where she was. So he beat me. Still I would not tell him. Then I did a foolish thing. I saw the map on the floor. When he turned his back I tried to kick it away. He saw me do this and he picked up the map. He guessed the map would lead him to her. So he beat me some more. That's all I remember. . . ." He licked his lips. "Water . . ."

Lansing handed Hawk the glass he had brought. The

lieutenant held up the old man's head so he could drink. Hunter took a sip, then shook his head that he didn't want any more.

"Where did the white man go?" Hawk asked.

"Coyote Summit." ·

"Is that where Kim and Gabe went? Coyote Summit?" Hunter nodded yes.

"Why did they go there?"

"The rocks," Hunter whispered. "They have to find the rocks."

"What rocks?" Lansing asked Hawk. "What is he talking about?"

"I don't know," the lieutenant admitted.

"Where's Coyote Summit?" Lansing asked.

"About twenty-five miles southwest of here," Hawk said. "It's where they're going to do the logging." The old man let out another groan. "Hunter's in bad shape. We need to get him to the hospital."

"You take care of Hunter. I'm going to Coyote Summit. I'll use that old truck out there."

"All right." Hawk sounded disappointed he couldn't join Lansing. "Help me get him into my Jeep first."

51

GABE HAD INTERCEPTED THE DIRT ROAD COMING from the highway and followed it into the mountains. He and Kim continued along the road until it came to an abrupt end at a ridge of boulders. The tree line was still another hundred feet above them.

They immediately began searching the ground for any rocks that might contain silver. After scouring the area around the road, they began working their way up the mountain. They would stop and search a small section of the hillside. After determining there was no silver at that location they would move higher.

After an hour of fruitless searching they had reached the edge of the tree line. Kim sat down to rest.

"I'm thirsty," she announced.

"Yeah. Me too," Gabe admitted. "I don't know why we didn't think about bringing a canteen with us." He surveyed the mountain above him. It was heavily wooded with a thick carpet of leaves and pine needles. There was very little exposed rock. "I don't think we're going to find any rocks up there." He pointed at the pine forest.

"So what do we do?"

"Let's keep below the tree line, where the rocks are still exposed. Our chances of finding something will be a lot better."

"Isn't that like saying you dropped a dime across the street but you're looking on this side because the light's better?"

The deputy gave his companion a disgruntled stare.

"Okay," Kim said, slowly getting back on her feet. "Boy, I thought I was in better shape than this. I'm definitely going to start jogging again."

"Come on," Gabe said, smiling. "The sooner we find a rock, the sooner we can get down from here."

They dropped down from the tree line about thirty feet, then tried to parallel it. Every once in a while one of them would pick up what they thought might be a promising specimen. After closer inspection the stone would be tossed aside as useless.

As they rounded one large boulder, Gabe discovered a stony wash descending from the summit. It had been cut by the periodic rains that occasionally blessed the desert.

"You know what? This looks promising." Something pinged off the boulder next to his head, chipping a gouge in the rock. A second later came the sound of a rifle shot. Gabe immediately ducked, pulling Kim with him.

"What was that?" Kim blurted.

"Somebody's shooting at us."

Another piece of rock splintered above them, followed by another rifle report. Staying crouched, Gabe pulled Kim around to the far side of the boulder. Another shot sounded.

"How did they know we were here?" Kim wondered.

"I don't know, but we're not going to hang around and ask. . . . Come on." Gabe started scrambling for the dry streambed. Kim was right behind him.

Neither had spotted the gunman, but the boulder afforded them some temporary protection. The wash they were climbing was steep and the loose rocks made their footing precarious. Gabe would get two or three feet higher, then pull Kimberly up behind him. The deputy knew they couldn't stay in the streambed long. They were completely exposed. He kept looking for a path that would lead them into the protection of the trees.

Fifty feet above the protective boulder, Gabe spotted an animal trail. He pointed toward it. "We're going that way."

He climbed over the stony bank, then reached his hand down to pull up Kim. Another rifle shot sounded, ricocheting off the rocks behind her. Gabe gave a tremendous heave. The force of his effort pulled her up and on top of him.

As they untangled, another bullet dug into the earth next to Gabe's hand.

Gabe pushed Kim toward the trees. She started running. A bullet splintered a tree a few feet in front of her as the gunman tried to lead his shot.

"Keep going!" Gabe shouted, only a few steps behind her.

Kim did as she was ordered.

The path they were following had been made by deer and mountain goats, creatures more sure-footed than Gabe or Kim. The track had a definite tilt to it and both found it difficult to run and not slip. Every time Kim slowed even a little, Gabe would urge her on. "Keep going, dammit! Keep going!"

She wanted to snap at him and tell him she was doing her best. She knew that was a waste of breath. He was only trying to keep her alive.

It had been several seconds since the last rifle shot. Gabe was certain the gunman hadn't quit. He was probably climbing the same streambed they had used, looking for the trail they had taken.

The deputy refused to let panic overtake him. They were unarmed, but they also had an entire mountain they could use for hiding. They would put more distance between them and their attacker, maybe hide for a while, then double back for his motorcycle. It seemed simple.

Gabe's optimism vanished when he stepped on a loose rock and slipped. Panic grabbed him this time as he started to slide down the mountain. He locked his arms around a sapling, stopping his tumble.

"Gabe!" Kim yelled. She came back down the path looking for her partner. She spotted him hanging on to a tree ten feet below the trail. "Are you all right?"

"Yeah," Gabe puffed. "I think so."

Using a small tree for support, Kim carefully edged down the hillside as Gabe crawled toward her. They managed to lock hands and Kim used all of her strength to pull him up the slope.

Gabe didn't realize the damage he'd done until they reached the trail. He nearly fell when he tried to put pressure on his right foot. Kim caught him before he hit the ground.

"What's wrong?"

"I think I sprained my ankle."

"Can you walk at all?"

He tried putting his foot down and nearly collapsed again. "I don't think so."

Kim put his right arm over her shoulder. "Come on. You're going to have to lean on me."

"Forget about me." Gabe winced. "Get the hell out of here."

"We're in this together, whether you like it or not. Now come on," she ordered.

Gabe gritted his teeth and started walking. Every step with his right foot was excruciating. Kim tried to carry as much of his weight as she could.

"You're going to have to go on without me," Gabe insisted. "I'm not going to be able to go much farther."

"I see some boulders up ahead," Kim said encouragingly. "See if you can make it that far."

"I'll try."

The deer path emerged into a broad clearing, then continued into the forest on the other side. The clearing was bordered on one side by a thirty-foot-high cliff. Kim knew if they stayed on the trail the gunman would catch up with them. She searched desperately for a place to hide.

Dozens of bushes had grown up around the base of the cliff. They provided the only immediate cover. Kim dragged the limping Gabe toward the rock face.

"Where are we going?" Gabe asked.

"Since you've pooped out, we have to find someplace to hide."

Kim looked for an inconspicuous spot to seek cover. On the right side of the cliff face she saw what looked like a rabbit run leading through the brush. She helped Gabe to the entrance and eased him to the ground.

"Can you crawl?" she asked.

"That's about all I can do."

"Okay. Follow me." Kim got down on all fours and began crawling under the bushes. The path seemed well worn, but what surprised her was that she had plenty of room to move. Something bigger than a rabbit used the trail. She hoped they weren't going to come face-to-face with a bear. She pushed that thought out of her mind.

"Are you coming?" she whispered.

"I'm right behind you."

Kim expected the path to reach the base of the cliff, then snake its way into the forest. Instead, the trail ended at a split in the rock. The well-worn ground in front of the rock told Kim this was the mouth of a cave . . . a cave that had been used recently. The entrance was shaped like an inverted V, two feet wide at the bottom and three feet high.

Kim listened for any sounds coming from the recess, but everything was quiet. It was a den, she guessed, recently abandoned.

"What are you doing?" Gabe whispered, bumping into her.

"Shhh," she hushed him. "Follow me."

Kim entered the cave tentatively. The entrance was deceptive. The farther she went in, the larger the chamber became. Three feet past the opening she had enough room to turn around. She looked back to make sure Gabe was following. He was.

Kim felt like she could breathe a sigh of relief. They were safe, at least for the time being.

Lieutenant Hawk had hastily drawn a map. The policeman's scale was not very accurate, so Lansing had to rely on the odometer to measure out the correct mileage.

The sheriff had his doubts that he was going to reach the highway, let alone Coyote Summit. Hunter's truck was an amalgam of dents, Bondo, and rust literally held together with baling wire. The shocks and muffler had long since disintegrated, letting the driver enjoy the pleasure of every bump and pothole while he listened to the steady bang of five out of six cylinders.

On the highway, Lansing had to settle for fifty miles per hour. Above that speed the truck threatened to shake itself apart. Despite his doubts, he finally reached the dirt road that would take him to the summit.

Lansing had mixed emotions when he reached the end of the dirt road. He found what he expected, Gabe's motorcycle and a Ford Bronco. He was glad he found them. He was also scared to death he was too late.

With no one around, Lansing could only assume the owners had climbed farther up the mountain. He negotiated the small ridge of boulders, then stopped to survey the mountain above him, looking for any sort of movement.

Whatever his fears had been, they were amplified by the sound of a gunshot. The sound came from above him. He continued scanning the rock-strewn slope. Another shot sounded. It was above and to the right. He shifted his search.

Another shot. This time he saw movement, eighty feet above him and over a half mile away. It was a single person, but Lansing couldn't identify him. As Lansing started up the mountain, the man disappeared behind a boulder. The sheriff mentally marked the spot, then began struggling his way toward it.

Once Gabe was completely inside the cave, Kim crawled closer toward him. The floor was cluttered with loose debris, which she pushed out of her way. It was too dark to tell what it was. The naturalist in Kim told her the litter was animal bones from the den's previous occupants.

"You can sit up in here," she told her companion. There's plenty of room."

Gabe stretched out his right leg to relieve the pressure on his ankle. "Do we have this place to ourselves?"

"I think so. . . . How's the ankle?"

"It's throbbing a little. It's not too bad."

"Wait here," Kim instructed. She crawled back to the entrance and listened. She wasn't positive, but she thought she heard the sound of a man's footsteps. He was trotting. After a few seconds they seemed to disappear. She crawled back to Gabe.

"I think we lost him," she said. She didn't whisper this time, but she still kept her voice low. There was a slight echo in the cave, telling Kim they were in a chamber much bigger than she initially imagined. She crawled farther inside, pushing debris out of her way.

Ten feet past Gabe she still hadn't reached the back wall of the cave. She raised her hand above her head, expecting to feel rock. All she found was air.

She rose up on her knees, continuing to feel above her. There was still no ceiling. She cautiously stood up.

"What are you doing?" Gabe asked.

"Exploring."

"Why?"

"We might find another way out of here."

Kim walked carefully toward the entrance, finally locating where the ceiling sloped rapidly toward the floor. With arms stretched in front of her so she could feel the cave wall, she shuffled her feet sideways, trying to conduct a tactile survey of her surroundings. She moved her feet only a few inches at a time. She had no interest in falling into a bottomless pit.

As she moved along, she continually had to kick things out of the way. The dull light from the entrance provided her a point of reference but little else. She guessed she was thirty feet from Gabe when her hand bumped against something that moved slightly. She used both hands to identify the object. It was a jar of pottery sitting in a niche in the wall.

"You know what, Gabe? I think we found an old Anasazi cave. I just found some pottery." She carefully replaced the jar in its niche and continued her sideways search, being more careful about the litter she kicked out of her way. She scooted her right foot along the floor, kicking something that made the tinkling sound of metal on metal.

"Shhh!" Gabe ordered.

Kim could hear her companion crawling deeper into the cave.

The dim light of the cave entrance was suddenly darkened.

"Very clever, my friends," a man's voice said. "If that

trail hadn't dumped into a big field of flowers, I might still be chasing you." He was silent for a second.

"Oh, I know you're in there, all right. I do a lot of tracking. Mostly game animals, but there's always the occasional human. Your father was quite a challenge, Miss Tallmountain. Even after I shot him, he got away. Twice. I never did find him the second time, though I did hear a semi finished the job for me.

"I don't suppose either one of you wants to come out voluntarily. . . ." The gunman paused again. "I didn't think so. I'll give you a few minutes to think about it. In the meantime you can think about this."

The gunman fired his rifle into the cave. The bullet ricocheted off the walls a dozen times.

"Hit the floor," Gabe yelled. Kim did as she was told, flattening herself as best she could.

"Thanks for the confirmation!" the gunman shouted. He fired his rifle three more times, each shot at a different angle to get the maximum effect from the ricocheting projectiles.

When the pinging of the last bullet stopped, Gabe whispered softly, "Kim?"

"I'm all right," she whispered back.

"I suppose I could do this all day," the gunman pondered aloud. "Or I could just come in there. . . . No, that won't work." He paused to think. "I know. I'll be right back. You two don't go away."

52

AS LANSING ROUNDED THE BOULDER HE SAW A DRY creek bed leading farther up the mountain. There was no sign of any other people. He had to assume the others had used the wash at least for a while.

He continued his climb, stopping every ten feet to listen and to check either side of the dry bed for a possible path the others might have taken.

Forty feet above the boulder he heard a muffled shot. It seemed to come from his left, not much farther up. He held his breath and listened. Three more muted shots sounded in quick succession. He pinpointed the sound as coming from his left.

He continued up the wash, looking for a likely spot to enter the forest. Ten feet higher he found an animal trail. The heel mark from a boot had gouged a soft piece of earth. This was the path the others had taken.

Lansing climbed up the bank, then pulled his pistol. He didn't know how far ahead the gunman was and he wanted to be ready when they met. He heard no more shots, which worried him. If he was too late, speed didn't matter, surprise did. He moved down the path as quietly as possible.

Gabe crawled toward the sound of Kim's voice. "Are you okay?" he whispered.

"I think so."

"I guess I really blew it," the deputy apologized.

Kim reached out and touched his hand. "If you hadn't yelled, I would have stood there like a deer caught in head-lights. You probably saved my life."

"Yeah, but for how long?"

They could hear the gunman tromping around outside. He was breaking sticks and branches and rustling leaves.

"What do you think he's doing?" Kim asked.

Gabe crawled toward the opening for a better look. The gunman was blocking the entrance with dried brush. "I think he's going to try and smoke us out."

"No," Kim corrected. "The only way out is going to be blocked by fire. All he plans on doing is suffocating us to death." She stood and began feeling along the walls.

"What are you doing?"

"Maybe we can find another way out," she said defiantly. "I'm not going to just sit here and wait for him to cook us."

Gabe tried standing. His ankle was a little better, but it couldn't take too much weight. He began helping Kim with her blind search for another exit.

The cave was forty feet deep. Along the back wall they found a ledge six feet above the floor. Gabe lifted Kim up and she began feeling her way along, searching for a tunnel. It didn't help that the ledge was cluttered with all sorts of Anasazi bric-a-brac. It broke her heart to shove the price-less items to the floor, but she had no choice. In a matter of minutes they would become fodder for the fire anyway.

She tried standing. The ceiling was too low for her to stand completely upright. She hadn't completely explored the entire ledge when she heard the crackle of fire. The gunman had started his next assault.

The fire was being started on the outside of the entrance. As the flames grew the gunman would poke the fire farther into the cave. Smoke immediately began rising to the top of the cave. The top layer of air in the cavern was replaced by caustic fumes from burning pine needles, and Kim had to abandon her search.

Gabe helped her down from the ledge. The growing flames helped illuminate the cavern. Kim was partially right. The pottery she found was Anasazi. But there were many more things in the cave. It looked like a small museum. There were weapons and hide shields, blankets, pottery, tobacco pipes. Some items were Navajo, others were Tewa or Hopi. Some things even looked colonial Spanish.

Gabe got down on his knees and pulled Kim with him. "Forget about that junk," he ordered. "We have to keep low where there's still air. We can last longer." He got down on his belly, keeping his nose as close to the floor of the cave as he could. Kim did the same as more fire was being shoved into the chamber.

The longer it had been since the last shot, the more worried Lansing became. He quickened his pace, searching up and down the wooded hillside for signs of anyone.

The sheriff smelled the smoke before he saw it. Ahead of him was a rocky clearing. As he got closer he could see the small granite cliff. Smoke was billowing from its base. He stopped at the edge of the clearing to appraise the situation.

Fifty feet away a tall blond man was tossing a combination of dried leaves, sticks, and green pine boughs onto a small fire. After two or three handfuls, he would poke at the fire with a long stick, pushing it into a crack in the granite wall. Lansing couldn't tell the size of the hole, since it was blocked by low bushes. He tried to be quiet as he came up behind the man.

"A little early in the season for starting fires," the sheriff said. He had stopped thirty feet from the man, with his gun drawn.

The man immediately turned around. There was a look of surprise on his face. He tried to act casual. "You could scare a man to death, sneaking up like that." He noticed the gun and the uniform. "Is there a problem, Sheriff?"

"What's the fire for?"

"Oh, that. I trapped me a family of coyotes in there. I'm just trying to smoke them out. Twenty-five bucks a hide, you know."

"Kick it away from that entrance!"

"What?"

"You heard me." Lansing motioned with his gun. "Kick out that fire!"

"Hey," the man protested. "You can't tell me what to do. I have rights."

Lansing fired his pistol above the man's head.

"All right. I'm kicking. I'm kicking." The man started kicking at the fire.

Lansing moved closer to make sure the man was doing it correctly. "Use the stick to pull that fire out of the hole."

"All right." The man moved closer to the cliff face, giving him an angle to pry out the burning embers. He glanced at the sheriff, who seemed more interested in the fire. That was the distraction he wanted. He stuck the pole in the fork of a burning branch, then swung, lifting the bough from the hole and sending it sailing toward the officer's head.

Lansing saw the branch coming and ducked.

The gunman didn't wait to see the results. He dove for his rifle, which was leaning against the base of the cliff a few feet away.

When Lansing looked up, the blond already had his rifle in hand. It was the sheriff's turn to dive for the ground as the gunman squeezed off four quick shots. All four fell wide of their mark.

Lansing pushed himself up to a kneeling position and fired once, the same moment the gunman fired his fifth shot. Lansing's shot went high. The gunman's shot caught Lansing in his right forearm. The sheriff dropped his gun as he grabbed the wound.

The gunman took aim and pulled the trigger. The hammer fell on an empty chamber.

Lansing saw his chance. As the gunman desperately tried to chamber a shell from his belt, the sheriff closed the twenty feet between them and grabbed for the rifle.

"Those are shots out there," Gabe wheezed. "This may be our chance."

"How?" Kim coughed.

There wasn't time to answer. Gabe felt around in the smoky darkness for anything to use as a shield. He touched a piece of cloth. It was a blanket. Draping it over his head and hands, he crawled toward the fire. Burning leaves and branches had been stuffed three feet past the entrance. The fire filled most of the crawl space.

Gabe could feel the heat as he began pushing against embers. His bare hand touched a red coal and he flinched in pain, but he had to keep pushing. He was grateful for his leather jacket, which gave his arms and back protection.

There was no way he could guess his progress. His eyes were teared shut, and he coughed and gagged in the suffocating smoke. He kept pushing against the fire . . . pushing, pushing. His face and both hands were seared and he couldn't breathe. At the moment he was about to retreat to the interior there came a sudden rush of fresh air. He had broken through.

The gunman wasn't prepared for Lansing's assault. He was concentrating on getting the bullet into his rifle and didn't have a firm grip. Lansing grabbed the barrel and tore the weapon from the gunman's hand, throwing it out of reach.

The blond slammed his fist into the sheriff's stomach, knocking him backward. Jumping to his feet, he managed to connect another blow.

Lansing blocked the third swing with his left arm, then landed a right of his own. The pain in his own arm caught Lansing by surprise.

The blond saw the sheriff's hesitation. He dove headlong into the officer, knocking him to the ground.

With no power in his right arm, Lansing tried to wrestle his opponent, grabbing for the man's flailing fists. His adversary landed three quick punches to Lansing's jaw, dazing the lawman. Lansing's eyes focused just in time to see a large rock in the man's hands, poised to crush his skull.

Three tremendous blasts shattered the air. Lansing watched as the man's eyes widened in surprise, then fear. The rock fell harmlessly to the ground as the blond crumpled on top of him.

Lansing pushed the lifeless body away and looked up. Barely twenty feet away stood Gabe Hanna, the sheriff's gun still smoking in his hand.

53

KIM USED A PIECE OF CLOTH FROM THE DEAD MAN'S shirt to make a bandage for Lansing's arm. The bullet had gone completely through, leaving a deep gash that wanted to bleed. The bandage stopped the bleeding.

"How did you know where to find us?" Gabe asked.

"Hunter told Lieutenant Hawk and me where you were."

"Where's Lieutenant Hawk?" Kim asked. "Didn't he come with you?"

"I'm afraid Hunter's in pretty bad shape. That son of a bitch over there beat him and left him for dead. Hawk took him to the hospital." Lansing looked at the other two. "Do either of you know who he is?"

They walked over for a closer look. After just a few seconds Gabe nodded. "I met him at my uncle's house last Friday. I can't remember his name . . . something Norwegian. I think he worked for Rocky Mountain Resources . . . or my uncle."

Lansing walked over and picked up the man's rifle. "This is a forty-four carbine. It's the same caliber rifle used to kill your father, Kim. . . ." He studied the weapon quietly. "Same caliber used to shoot Margarite . . ." He took the gun by the barrel and beat the shoulder stock against a rock, splintering the wood. He was almost ready to throw it down the side of the mountain when he stopped himself.

"Better not." He smiled weakly. "We might want to get some ballistics tests." He threw the gun down.

"What the hell were you two doing up here anyway?"

"We were trying to find ore samples," Gabe explained. "Kim's father wasn't killed because of drugs or timber. It had to do with silver."

"Silver?" Lansing was surprised.

"That's why he went to Santa Fe. He took ore samples into the Assay Office. The report came in the mail Saturday, but no one checked the mail because of the funeral. When we thought to look Sunday, after you left Kim's, it was too late. Someone had broken into the office and stolen it."

Kim explained about the second report going to Hunter. That's why her house was firebombed, to destroy the second report. Fortunately, Hunter still had it. They had come to the summit to find more ore to present to the council.

"You were right, Sheriff," Kim said. "There was a clue in the RMR contract. The Navajo people were going to get paid for everything RMR removed from here except the minerals. Those bastards were going to keep everything they mined. That's why my father was trying to block the vote. To keep the Navajo Tribal Council from letting the white man trick us out of our wealth. According to the assay report, we're standing on a mountain of silver."

"We still might not be able to block the vote," Gabe admitted. "We never did find any ore samples."

"Is there some way we can make a torch?" Kim asked.

"What do you need a torch for?"

"We need to go back in that cave."

"What for?" Lansing asked.

"There are a whole lot of artifacts in there," Gabe explained. "But I don't know why we can't come back later."

"Humor me," Kim said. "I saw something in the cave that might help."

"What?"

"I'll show you inside the cave."

Lansing and Gabe stripped several green branches from nearby pines. The sheriff explained that the green needles could burn for several minutes before going out. If one started losing its fire, they could ignite another.

Kim entered first, pushing the burning branch in front of her. Once she was inside, she stood up. Lansing and his deputy were right behind her. The sheriff was surprised at the number of artifacts and works of native art spread around the cavern. He couldn't begin to guess the value.

"Okay, we're here," Gabe said. "Now what?"

"Look up," Kim directed.

All three looked at the ceiling. The roof sparkled like stars in the flickering glow of the pine branches. Wide veins of silver crisscrossed each other from one end of the cavern to the other. The two men were speechless.

"I saw it when I was standing on the ledge, when that man first started shoving the fire through the entrance. We can get all the ore samples we want in here. Sheriff Lansing, can I borrow your knife so I can chip some samples down?"

Lansing gave her his knife and Gabe lifted her onto the ledge. As Kim chipped at the ceiling, Lansing examined the artifacts strewn around the floor. At the base of the wall he noticed something shiny and tried to pick it up. What he thought was a ring turned out to be a single link in a necklace. The necklace had been buried under layers of dust, dirt, and trash dragged in by animals. The more he pulled, the longer the necklace became. He finally had to lay his makeshift torch down so he could use both hands to delicately extract the beautiful silver work from the earth.

When Kim was satisfied she had removed enough samples she had Gabe help her down.

"Kim, what do you think of this?" Lansing asked, holding ten feet of silver links with even more buried at his feet.

Kim came over for a closer look. "Oh my God," she gasped. She grabbed Gabe's arm. "It's the Chain . . . the Great Chain of San Lorenzo. . . . The one I told you about." Kim dropped to her knees and began digging out the rest of the chain, being careful not to damage any of the links. Lansing held on to the silver masterpiece as Kim fed it to him foot by foot.

Gabe looked around the cavern in wonderment. "Kim, you know what place this is?"

"What?" she asked, more interested in the chain she was uncovering.

"This is Coyote's cave. The one Hunter told us about."

"Don't be ridiculous."

"I'm not. Hunter said Coyote stole things and took them to his cave." He picked up a clay pipe. "He said some things were simple. Sometimes they were expensive. . . . Some of these things look like they've been here hundreds of years."

"I'm sure they have," Kim commented.

"But you said the chain only disappeared a hundred years ago."

Kim leaned back from her task and thought. "Yeah. I guess I did say that, didn't I?" She shook her head. "There's another explanation, I'm sure." Giving a little tug, she pulled the last of the chain from the dirt.

"Are we ready to get out of here?" Lansing asked. "I don't particularly like caves."

"Yeah," Kim said. "I'm ready." She started toward the entrance. "You coming, Gabe?"

"Yes," he said, examining something on the floor. "I'm right behind you."

Lansing and Kim emerged into the sunlight. The sheriff had lost track of time, but it was well past noon. He was tired and thirsty and hadn't eaten all day. He was ready to head back to civilization. For the time being the corpse of the gunman could stay where it was, for all Lansing cared. The sheriff wasn't about to drag it down the mountain. He'd ask Hawk to round up a recovery team.

Lansing was ready to leave and Gabe still hadn't come out of the cave. He stuck his head in the entrance. "We're leaving, Gabe. You can come along if you want."

"I'm coming," Gabe replied. He had been in the process of crawling through the short passage when Lansing called for him. He emerged from the cave carrying a rectangular object in his hand.

"What's that?" Kim asked.

Gabe stood holding the object so the other two could see. It was a leather pouch held closed by a heavy zipper. When he opened it, over a hundred bills in different denominations were revealed.

"There must be thousands of dollars in there!" Kim exclaimed.

Gabe pulled a white deposit slip from the pouch. "According to this, it's exactly five thousand dollars."

"Is there a date on that?" Lansing asked.

"Yeah. Thirty years ago—today." Gabe stared at the pouch for several seconds before slowly looking up. His face was a mask of painful realization. "This was the money they said my father stole."

54

BEFORE THEY STARTED DOWN THE MOUNTAIN GABE made a request that Lansing thought was bizarre. He wanted to put the Chain of San Lorenzo and the money pouch back into the cave. Kim thought the request was strange enough that the two got into an argument.

The Chain, Kim argued, rightfully belonged to the Navajo people. She was obligated to bring it back. Besides, someone might stumble onto the cave and disappear with it.

Gabe explained the Chain, the pouch, everything in the cave had been untouched for hundreds of years. What would one more day matter? If Kim came back the next day and everything was still there, then it was probably all right to take it. It would be with Coyote's permission.

"You really believe in those Coyote fairy tales, don't you?" Kim said, shaking her head.

"You're the one with all the scientific degrees," Gabe responded. "What's your explanation?"

"I don't have one yet," Kim snapped.

"Then, like you said earlier, humor me. . . . One more day. If Coyote doesn't move his stash tonight, then he's leaving it to the Navajo people with his blessings. Remember what Hunter said. Coyote would stay until he proved how powerful he was. What greater demonstration of his power than the contents of that cave over there? One more day, Kim."

"You're pitiful," Kim said. She looked at the Chain as if it would be the last time she would see it. "Here." She handed the intricate silver work to Gabe.

"Look at it this way," Gabe offered. "If there is no Coyote, everything will be here tomorrow." Still limping, he hurried back to the cave to return their booty. A minute later he emerged. "Let's go."

Lansing wasn't sure he wanted to know who this Coyote character was. Gabe mentioned items being in the cave for hundreds of years. Kim talked about fairy tales. The lawman decided he would keep out of the argument. This was the Navajo reservation and everything in the cave seemed to belong to the Navajos. Whatever Kim and Gabe decided was fine with him, though he was curious about the five thousand dollars.

As they walked down the mountain, Gabe told the story about his father and how he came to be kicked off the reservation. "I had it all figured out. It was my uncle who took the money. My dad got kicked out of the tribe just before he graduated from high school. . . . April is what I guessed. A few days after all the coyote business ended thirty years ago, my uncle opened his first car dealership. Five grand sure would have helped pay his start-up costs. I guess that's one thing I can't blame on him."

"What coyote business are you talking about?"

Gabe described what he had read at the library. Thirty years earlier there had been over a week of coyotes terrorizing ranchers and farmers. There seemed to be no way to stop them. It was like what had been going on in San Phillipe County recently. Then, suddenly, everything went back to normal.

"Hunter seems to think it's all tied in to Coyote returning," Kim said sarcastically. "Coyote is this mythical creature who can change shape and likes to play tricks on humans. Old men like Hunter and some of the feeble-minded"—she looked at Gabe for emphasis—"think Coyote shows up every once in a while to remind us of how powerful he is. He'll do some mystical trick, then disappear again."

"Yeah," Gabe said solemnly, "like steal the Chain of San Lorenzo from its hiding place—or five thousand dollars from a locked safe."

Lansing liked Gabe. He really hoped this infatuation with Navajo mysticism was a passing phase. "Kim's right, you know, Gabe. There is a logical explanation for that cave back there."

Gabe continued to limp along, wincing every once in a while when he didn't put his foot down just right. "Yeah, I know. There's always a logical explanation for everything. Sometimes, though, I wish there wasn't."

The deputy decided to avoid the subject. The "feeble-minded" remark from Kim had hurt. It reminded him about the gulf of education that separated them. Once everything was settled with the council vote, they wouldn't have anything in common any longer. He felt a sadness creeping over him that he couldn't shake. He wondered if letting Velma corner him in the men's room at the diner would ease his loneliness. He doubted it.

Coming down the steep slope below the tree line, Gabe's ankle started giving out again. Lansing put his deputy's arm over his shoulder to help him the last quarter of a mile to the vehicles. Kim walked in front, just in case either man should slip. Thirty yards from the ridge of boulders that separated them from the dirt road, they were stopped.

"Well, well, well. If it isn't our fugitive, Sheriff Lansing. I was curious who would be coming down that mountain."

All three looked toward the voice. Standing on the ridge were Agents Hobson and Williams, guns drawn.

"Miss Tallmountain," Hobson continued, "you will very carefully remove Sheriff Lansing's gun from its holster."

"You don't have to worry about this anymore, Hobson," Lansing said. "We found Walter Tallmountain's killer."

"Oh, yeah? Where is he?"

"He's lying dead up on the mountain behind us. He tried to kill my deputy and Miss Tallmountain."

"I see. You have everything tied up in a nice little package, do you?"

"Not everything," Lansing admitted. "Whoever that guy was worked for somebody else."

"But you don't know who?"

"I have my guesses. . . . Now will you put your guns away?"

"Who else knows about your killer up there?" Hobson gestured toward the forest above them.

"No one, yet."

"That's too bad." Hobson pointed his gun threateningly. "Miss Tallmountain, you haven't done what I asked. Get the sheriff's gun." Kim hesitated and Hobson fired his gun, hitting the ground a few feet to her left. "Get it now!"

Kim pulled Lansing's gun from its holster, then held it up so Hobson could see.

"Now throw it away . . . well out of reach."

Kim obeyed the agent's order.

"What's going on?" Lansing demanded.

"You still don't have the big picture, do you, Sheriff?" Hobson snorted. "There are a hundred million dollars at stake here and all you've managed to do is screw things up for the rest of us."

"You son of a bitch!" Lansing growled. "You were involved in Tallmountain's murder!"

"Not involved," Hobson corrected. "Just paid to look

the other way. Steer the investigation in the wrong direction . . . You see, Williams and I got tired of holding the
dirty end of the stick. We got tired of politicians getting
big salaries and keeping budgets down using our pay raises.
We got sick of arresting fifteen-year-old drug dealers with
more money in their pockets than we make in a month. It
was our turn.

"Things were going to work out nicely. In a few days we
were going after a drug dealer with a nasty reputation. He
was going to resist arrest and we would be forced to kill
him. Fortunately, just before he died, he confessed to killing that Indian. Case closed."

"Too bad I've screwed things up," Lansing apologized
sarcastically.

"Not so much that it can't be fixed."

"We're not the only ones who know what's going on,"
the sheriff observed.

"You mean Lieutenant Hawk? He's the one who told us
where you were."

"He's not involved in this too?" Kim asked.

"No. Not exactly. We found Lansing's green truck just
outside Shiprock. Some kid said he saw Hawk driving off
with an Anglo wearing a uniform. Said he saw them heading south. Williams and I are good cops. On a hunch, we
decided to follow.

"We flagged Hawk down when he was driving north. He
told us where Lansing was and that he needed help. That's
why we're here."

"Hawk knows as much as we do," Lansing pointed out.

"I figured that. He said he would join us as soon as he
could. When he does, there's going to be a shootout and
you, Lansing, are going to kill the lieutenant. At least, it
will look that way. In the process, either Williams or myself
will have to kill you and our original plan will go as sched-
uled."

"What about us?" Kim asked. "You don't plan on killing Gabe and me. How would you explain that?"

"We don't have to explain it. We never saw you." Hobson looked above Kim's head. "That's a big mountain up there. Chances are they'll never find your bodies. . . ."

Hobson's dissertation was interrupted by a low growl. Williams turned to the sound. On the boulder behind the two agents stood three coyotes. The closest and largest had its canine teeth exposed by a vicious snarl. He emitted another growl.

Williams pointed his gun at the animal and fired. The bullet struck two feet in front of the coyote, chipping rock fragments into the animal's face.

The coyote flinched at the shot, but only for a moment. The yellow eyes glared at the man in a torrent of rage. Snarling savagely, the coyote bounded toward the agent, leaping for the man's throat. Williams fired twice more, his bullets catching the creature in midair. The animal fell to the ground dead, a foot short of its target.

"What's going on?" Hobson demanded.

"Goddamn coyote," Williams said in disbelief, kicking the animal to make sure it was dead. "Get out of here!" he yelled at the animal's companions.

The two coyotes on the boulder ignored the command and started snarling. From behind a rock ten feet to the right three more appeared. The new arrivals were growling, the fur on their necks and shoulders hackled in anger. These had their eyes trained on Hobson. They spread in a quarter circle, their heads lowered as if they were stalking prey.

Hobson was the picture of indecision. He kept his gun pointed at the three humans, but his eyes darted back and forth between his hostages and the threatening animals.

To the left of the agents three new coyotes appeared, growling and snarling, just as anger-driven as their comrades. One of the new arrivals made a run for Williams. The agent turned and fired, wounding the animal before it could leap for him. The poor creature let out a pitiful yelp as it collapsed, its spinal column severed by the bullet.

The two coyotes on the boulder took the opening Williams gave them. One jumped, locking its teeth on the agent's arm. The other started snapping at his ankle, finally managing to get a firm hold of his pants leg.

Hobson didn't wait for an attack. He turned and began firing at the three animals stalking him. All three lunged at the same time. Hobson killed two before they reached him. The third managed to snag the agent's coat sleeve. Hobson hit and kicked at the animal, finally pointing his gun and firing point-blank into the coyote's skull.

The two remaining animals pounced on Hobson from behind, knocking him to the ground. To break his fall, the agent let his gun drop. The two coyotes nipped and bit at his legs and face.

Williams was desperately trying to dislodge his two attackers, his screams mingling with growls and snarls. One moment he was trying to shake his leg free, the next he was beating on the snout of the animal clamped on his arm, all the time trying to keep from being dragged to the ground.

Hobson, protecting his face with his left arm, managed to grab his pistol. Rolling onto his stomach, he fired into the chest of the animal closest to him. As the animal fell, Hobson shot at the coyote chewing on his pants leg. The animal yelped. Wounded in its hindquarter, it let go of its grip.

Hobson leapt to his feet and started running in the direction of the vehicles. Four more coyotes appeared. Three gave chase to Hobson. The fourth joined in on the attack against Williams.

Hobson disappeared behind the ridge as Williams was

pushed closer and closer to the drop-off above the dirt road. The agent's legs tangled with the body of the third coyote and he lost his balance. Williams let out a final, chilling scream as he toppled over the edge, dragging his three attackers with him.

Lansing, Kim, and Gabe watched the horrifying event in frozen disbelief. When Williams fell, all three ran to the edge of the ridge. Hobson had made it to his vehicle. He fired his last bullet into the closest coyote, then dove into his car.

Lansing looked around for his gun, determined to stop the agent. By the time he found it, it was too late. Hobson had the car started and was already speeding down the dirt road.

With Williams it didn't matter. His lifeless form was crumpled at the base of the rock on which the three stood. Two dead coyotes lay with him. The third, surviving the fall, had disappeared, as had the last two animals that had given chase to Hobson.

Lansing glanced around at the carnage on the ridge behind him. There were five dead coyotes. A sixth, wounded in its back leg, was limping away in the distance. Still another, the one with the severed spine, whimpered in pain as it tried to drag itself to safety with only its front paws.

Lansing walked over to the suffering animal. "You'll be better off this way, friend." He pointed his pistol at the animal's head and fired.

"I've never seen coyotes behave like that. They must have all been rabid," Kim said. She shook her head in amazement. "Why didn't they attack us?"

"Maybe because they weren't supposed to," Gabe said, limping down the ridge toward the dirt road. Lansing and Kim looked at each other, unable to fathom his enigmatic remark.

The sheriff was a little disappointed but not surprised

that Kim didn't want to ride back to Shiprock with him in Hunter's truck. She said she preferred the motorcycle. It was quieter.

As Gabe's bike rumbled down the dirt road, Lansing glanced at the top of the boulder ridge. A single coyote stood staring down at him. The two studied each other for several seconds.

"I don't suppose you could explain to me what just happened up there, could you?" the sheriff asked.

As if in response, the coyote cocked his head to one side. To Lansing, the expression on the animal's face said: "I could tell you, but you'd never understand."

"Yeah," the sheriff replied. "I'll bet you're right."

He opened the truck door and got inside. Backing the vehicle around, he adjusted the rearview mirror so he could see the ridge top one last time.

It was too late.

Coyote was gone.

55

LANSING SAT IN THE EMERGENCY ROOM AS THE NURSE
tended to his wound. He wouldn't have gone if Kim hadn't
warned him that her doctoring skills would kill a healthy
horse. He, at least, needed a clean bandage.

Lieutenant Hawk had intercepted the trio as they
headed north toward Shiprock. Lansing displayed the body
of Special Agent Williams in the back of Hunter's truck
and said Hobson was on the run. Hawk asked them to
follow him into Shiprock so he could take their statements.

At the tribal police station the three described in detail
their encounters with the gunman on the mountain and
the run-in with the two agents. The lieutenant wanted
everything down on paper. After reading their statements,
Hawk finally asked who was masterminding the whole operation.

Lansing hesitated before replying. He finally conceded
that though there was no physical proof, everything seemed
to point toward Councilman Edward Hania.

The lieutenant balked at that answer. To accuse a tribal
councilman of conspiracy to commit murder and financial
malfeasance was to be on dangerous ground. Hania was
very powerful politically. Hawk admitted that if he arrested
the councilman and was wrong, he could lose his job. He

would have to discuss the matter with his superiors before he did anything.

It was already dark outside when they finished at the police station. Their next stop was the Farmington hospital.

"Where have you been?" Lansing asked as Kim walked into the treatment room.

"I went up to see Hunter. He was banged up pretty good and has a mild concussion, but the doctor says he'll be okay. They want to keep him under observation for a few days before they release him. . . . Have you had a chance to stop by Dr. Carerra's room?"

"No, not yet," Lansing admitted. "I'll go after they're finished with me here. . . . Did Gabe have his ankle looked at?"

"No. He said he didn't have time."

"What do you mean 'he didn't have time'?"

"He said he had to investigate a four-fifteen-F, whatever that is. The way he talked, I figured you knew about it."

"Four-fifteen-F," Lansing mumbled. "That means family disturbance. . . ." He looked at Kim. "How much you want to bet he's on his way to his uncle's house?"

"Why would he go there?"

"Because Lieutenant Hawk won't. . . . How long ago did he leave?"

"About thirty minutes."

"That's fine," Lansing said to the nurse, sliding off the treatment table. "We need to call Sheriff Spence."

"Gabe!" Hania exclaimed. "What a pleasant surprise. Come on in." The councilman held the door open for his nephew.

"Thanks," Gabe replied, stepping through the door.

"That's quite a limp you have there," Hania observed.

"Took a little fall off my motorcycle. It's nothing."

"Listen, son," Hania said solemnly. "I truly was heart-broken to hear about Kimberly."

"The fire last night?" Gabe asked.

Hania nodded. "She really was a lovely girl."

"Yeah." Gabe nodded. "I wish I had gotten to know her a little better."

"Come on in. Let's talk about happier things." Hania led his visitor into the den. "I believe you know my associates, Gabe. You all had dinner together just the other night."

Thad Berkeley and Samuel Elverson were standing next to the wet bar talking quietly. The deputy couldn't help but notice the surprised looks on their faces.

"Yeah. Hello, Mr. Berkeley. Mr. Elverson."

"Yes," the lawyer said almost too quickly. "Gabe, it's good to see you again." He hurried over to shake the deputy's hand.

"Would you like a drink, Gabe?" his uncle asked. "We're having a little celebration tonight."

"Yeah, I'll take a beer." He sat down casually. "What's the celebration about?"

"We canvassed all our votes today." Hania smiled, retrieving a beer from behind the bar. "Looks like the council will vote in favor of the timber contract tomorrow." He walked over and handed Gabe his beer.

"Oh, that's great." Gabe tried to show a little enthusiasm. "I know you've worked hard to push it through."

"You have no idea, son. I know there were a lot of tribe members against it, but they'll change their tune when the money starts coming in."

"I guess you'll do pretty well out of the deal, too, won't you?" Gabe took a sip of his beer.

"What do you mean?" The smile on Hania's face suddenly disappeared.

"When you sell Rocky Mountain Resources the land for

the sawmill," Gabe explained. "I'll bet you'll make a pretty penny off that."

"Who told you about that land deal?" Hania asked suspiciously.

"Uncle Edward," Gabe sounded disappointed, "with all the businesses you have around here, I kind of figured you were always looking for another deal to swing. Just because something's good for the tribe doesn't mean you shouldn't be allowed to make a little on the side."

Hania studied his nephew closely for a few seconds, then burst out laughing. "I thought you said you didn't have a head for business, Gabe. You see things exactly the way I do. . . . Yeah, I might be making a penny or two off the site for the sawmill, but I'm certainly not going to mention figures in this group. Old Sam over there might take back his offer if he thought I was gouging him."

Hania took a sip of his drink. "I'm impressed, Gabe. I really am. Have you thought any more about coming to work for me?"

"A little." Gabe nodded. He took another sip of his beer. "I was wondering if you were still going to let Kim Tallmountain make her presentation to the council tomorrow before the vote?" He glanced casually at the two Anglo businessmen. They were giving each other nervous looks.

"Kimberly's dead, son," Hania said. The older man's face clouded with suspicion.

"If she could have, would you let her?"

"The council would have to decide," Hania observed. "Not me. But to be perfectly honest, I can't think of a thing she could have said that would change a single vote."

"You must have worried she was going to say something. Why did you offer her twenty-five thousand dollars to shut her up?"

"That was a gift. Not a bribe. I felt sorry for her. I knew

she could use the money. There's no law that says I can't take pity on someone, is there?"

"Yeah, and there's no law that says you can't hide fifty thousand dollars on somebody's property, either. If the police decide it's drug money, well, that's too bad. Isn't it?"

"What the hell are you talking about? Are you accusing me of planting that money at Walter Tallmountain's place?"

"No, you didn't do it. You sent your lawyer."

"You're treading on thin ice, boy," Berkeley threatened.

"Am I? Sheriff Lansing said you stopped by Walter's after you went out with a survey crew. Kim's office handles all the surveys. There wasn't one on Tuesday. The only reason why you went there was to plant that money."

Berkeley shook his head. "Unless you have an eyewitness, your charges don't hold water."

"There's plenty more." Gabe turned to his uncle while he pulled something from his pocket. "All this talk about how much money the tribe was going to make from timber. All the great jobs you were going to help generate. How much were you going to make on *this* little side deal after you finished ripping off your people?" He tossed a shiny nugget on the coffee table.

Hania shifted his angry stare from his nephew to the rock on the table. He picked the nugget up for closer examination. "What is this?"

"Silver," Gabe snapped. "As if you didn't know."

"Where did it come from?"

"You know damned well where it came from. Coyote Summit."

"Fine detective work, Deputy," Elverson said, walking over to a briefcase sitting at the end of the bar. "Too bad you won't be around to tell anyone."

"What do you mean?"

Elverson pulled a gun from the case. "You Indians are all alike. Nothing but a big pain in the ass."

"What's going on here, Sam?" Hania demanded. "Put that gun down."

"Shut up!" Elverson ordered. "You were so greedy to make a few thousand bucks on real estate, you never bothered to look at what was going on around you."

"What are you talking about?"

"That nice little contract you railroaded through gives RMR all the mineral rights to Coyote Summit. Everybody was so concerned about the trees, they ignored what was underneath. Thad put enough double talk in the contract, it looked like the Navajos were going to make money no matter what we found.

"Tallmountain thought he had figured it out, but he wasn't sure. So he took a few ore samples to the Assay Office in Santa Fe. A company like RMR has to have contacts at all levels of government. Our snitch in the Assay Office gave me a quick call about Tallmountain's visit. We followed him to his little camping spot. Since he couldn't be reasoned with, we had to eliminate him."

"What about the drugs?" Gabe asked.

"That was an afterthought. A good one too. It would have worked out better if his corpse was found in the car. Evidently, there was just enough life left in him that he could open the door to his car and run off. All I can say is, thank God for eighteen-wheelers. Everyone was so busy chasing drug lords, they forgot about this little contract issue.

"Unfortunately, Miss Tallmountain started figuring things out too."

"You killed her?" Hania asked.

Elverson shrugged as if it was a small inconvenience.

"Why are you telling me all this?" Hania demanded.

"Because I'm going to shoot your nephew and you're

going to dispose of the body. Tomorrow you'll vote for the contract, because if you don't, I'll blow the whistle on you. I made sure every piece of evidence pointed in your direction."

Elverson raised the gun and pointed it directly at Gabe.

"No!" Hania screamed, throwing himself in front of his nephew.

Elverson fired twice, both bullets catching Hania in the chest. The older man fell backward, knocking Gabe to the floor.

The sound of police sirens wailed outside.

Hania's wife came running in from the kitchen. At the sight of her fallen husband she started screaming, "No, no, no."

Distracted by the growing commotion, Elverson fired at Gabe's head as he tried to push his uncle off him. The deputy's head jerked back.

"Let's get out of here," Elverson said, wrapping Hania's fingers around the gun.

"What do we tell the police?" Berkeley whimpered.

"Family dispute . . . We barely got out with our lives. Come on."

Sheriff Spence's car skidded to a halt as Elverson and Berkeley ran out the front door. Spence got out of the driver's side as Lansing and Kim climbed from the backseat.

"Thank God you're here," Elverson said breathlessly. "They're in there killing each other!"

Spence drew his gun. "You two wait out here," he said to the two men. He rushed into the house, followed by his two passengers.

They found the bloody Hania lying on the living room floor. His nephew lay lifeless underneath him. Gayle Hania was on her knees next to her husband, rocking back and forth. She clutched his hand to her bosom and was chanting a prayer in Navajo.

"Gabe!" Kimberly screamed. She ran to him and sat, taking his head into her lap. Blood oozed from a gash in his scalp. She started stroking his face. "Gabe. Gabe. Can you hear me . . . ? Are you all right?"

Gabe's eyes fluttered open. He looked up at Kim. "What are you doing here?"

"Oh my God. I thought you were dead. I thought your uncle shot you."

"My uncle . . . No. He tried to save me." Gabe sat up, woozy from the graze to his scalp.

The sound of car engines starting came from the front of the house.

"Who did the shooting?" Spence demanded.

"Elverson . . . One of those men that was just here!"

"They're getting away!" Lansing yelled.

"That's all right, Sheriff," Gabe assured him. "They won't get very far."

"What do you mean?"

"I poured two pounds of sugar in each of their gas tanks. They'll be on foot in less than a mile." Gabe smiled at his commanding officer. "Old Indian trick."

Gabe carefully scooted himself from beneath his uncle, then took his uncle's other hand. He looked up at the two sheriffs. "My uncle didn't know anything about the silver. . . . He didn't have anything to do with Kim's father getting killed. . . . It was those other two."

"Davy!"

Gabe looked down at Hania. "Yes, Uncle."

"Davy"—the older man's voice was hoarse—"of all the things I've wanted in life, I wanted you to come home the most. And you have. I can have peace." He coughed and closed his eyes for a moment. When he opened them he looked into the face of his wife. "*Ho-ushte-hiye*," he whispered, "*daltso hozhoni . . . Piki yo-ye.* Good-bye, my wife."

Gabe's aunt let out a wail as Hania closed his eyes for the last time.

LANSING HAD OPENED THE CURTAINS TO THE HOSPI-
tal room and stood staring at the full moon while he spoke.
He had started out by apologizing for not coming sooner.
It had been a long, eventful day. He described his night
on the run as a rogue cop and how he had joined up with
Lieutenant Hawk to track down Kim and Gabe. Then he
talked about the fight with the gunman, the two SBI
agents, and the attacking coyotes. Finally, he covered the
shooting at Councilman Hania's house and how they
caught Elverson and Berkeley trying to thumb rides on the
highway after their engines gummed up.

"And that deputy of mine . . . I swear his head is made
out of rocks. He survived a pool cue across the back of the
head Saturday. Then tonight he deflected a bullet. I told
him, I've got a horse just like him."

"That's all well and good, Lansing, but answer me one
thing—"

Lansing spun around from the window. "Margarite!"

"What ever happened to those fish I caught? I'm starving
to death."

GABE AND KIM SAT ON A BENCH IN FRONT OF WAL-
ter's adobe house. The full moon had just pushed itself
above the horizon and the night air was filled with the yips
and howls of countless coyotes.

It had been a busy day. The council vote was nearly
postponed because of Edward Hania's death, but supporters
of the logging issue pushed for the vote, maintaining Hania
would have wanted it that way. Then Kim dropped the
bombshell. She presented the photocopy of the assay report
and a half dozen silver nuggets.

The council lawyers who had been railroaded by Hania
and Berkeley covered their tails by explaining this was another example of the white man's duplicity. They would
have caught the oversight if the council hadn't been in
such a hurry to push the contract vote through.

Edward Hania was fiercely denounced. Gabe asked if he
could speak on his uncle's behalf, but he was told he had
no standing in the council and a questionable position in
the tribe.

Gabe knew he would fight for his claim to be Navajo.
It wouldn't be that day. When he was ready, he would. He
would also have his father's reputation restored now that
there was proof he didn't take the money.

That afternoon they returned to Coyote Summit along

with Lieutenant Hawk and several councilmen and elders. A great debate began immediately about the meaning of the cave. Everything Kim and Gabe had found the day before was still in place. Arguments went both ways: There was no Coyote, or there is a Coyote and he chose to give back what he had taken. Gabe knew what he believed. He stayed clear of the clashing philosophies.

"You ought to be happy the vote went your way today," Gabe said, brushing a moth from his face.

"I am," Kim said sadly. "But it's a hollow victory. They'll draw up a new contract with someone else, cut down all the trees, and then dig up the entire mountain. And there won't be a thing I can do about it."

"Maybe they won't cut down the trees," Gabe observed. "At least not all of them. Maybe enough to clear a road to the mine. But the whole idea of logging was to generate money for the tribe. They won't have to log if they're making money from the silver."

Kim's face brightened at the revelation. "Damn. You're right, Gabe. We can still strike a balance. We can leave the forest in place. We don't have to destroy an entire ecosystem." She took Gabe's face into her hands and gave him a kiss.

Gabe relished the kiss as long as she was willing to offer it. She let her lips linger for a long moment before she pulled away. When she looked into Gabe's eyes she realized he wanted more from her kiss than gratitude. At first she was surprised. He had never been anything but a gentleman to her, with no innuendoes or subtle winks to insinuate his romantic interest.

Yes, she was grateful. But Gabe was handsome and smart and brave . . . And yes, she could feel more for him than just gratitude. She pulled his face close and they kissed again . . . like two people discovering each other for the first time.

Lansing flipped the light on in the barn. He had left his horses under the care of a neighbor and he wasn't quite sure what sort of reception he would get.

He hadn't planned on spending all day in Farmington again. But now that Margarite was alert and recovering, he wanted to be with her. He had to tell her the Tallmountain story all over again. When he finished, Margarite commented on the fact that he held her hand the whole time he was talking. She liked it. Lansing told her it was a habit he had developed while she was in the coma. She laughed and said she ought to try comas more often.

"Well, horse, I'm back," he announced to his favorite mount.

Cement Head scolded his owner with a long, disapproving whinny, then turned so his backside faced the stall gate.

"Yeah, so's your uncle." Lansing leaned against the stable gate. "The SBI wants me to go down to Santa Fe for a few days and clear up this Tallmountain fiasco, so don't get too used to this tender loving care. . . . I got a job offer to work for the bureau down in Santa Fe. Somebody there seems to think I do good work. What would you think of moving that way permanently?"

The horse turned his head to look at his master before letting out a snort.

"Yeah," the sheriff agreed. "I guess I feel the same way."

Lansing walked over and lifted the top to the feed barrel. It was empty. "No wonder you're pissed at me. You're out of oats." He grabbed the hay fork next to the door. "Sorry. Everything's closed. I'll get you some tomorrow. Tonight you're stuck with hay."

Lansing walked out of the barn and headed for the hay shed on the side of the building.

"Stop right there and turn around!"

The sheriff froze in his steps and looked over his shoulder. "I figured you'd be in Mexico by now, Hobson."

"That takes money. I had to clean out a few bank accounts first." The former SBI agent stepped from the shadows, into the light from the open barn door. "Before I left, though, I had one little score to settle."

"Not with me, you don't," Lansing said, keeping his back to the agent.

"Like hell. If you had minded your own business, none of this would have happened and I'd be sitting in tall clover. Now I've lost everything. My job, my pension, my home, everything! Somebody's going to pay for that. And that somebody is you."

"You don't think maybe you should take a little responsibility here? I mean, you are the one who violated every oath you ever took as a law officer."

"Shut up! What do you know? You're nothing but a two-bit sheriff in a jerkwater town and you ruined my life. Turn around. I want to see the look on your face when I shoot you."

An ominous growl came from the shadows behind Hobson.

The agent turned halfway around so he could still keep an eye on the sheriff. Two yellow eyes glared at Hobson. The creature let another growl rumble from its throat. "Goddamn, Lansing. You breeding these things or what?"

Hobson turned his pistol and fired three times at the glowing eyes. The creature let out a snarl and started running at the now terrified man. Hobson continued to fire at the attacking animal.

Lansing saw his opportunity. He wheeled around and held the hay fork like a lance. He ran for the agent. "Hobson!" he yelled.

The agent spun to face the sheriff. Lansing ran the prongs of the fork deep into Hobson's chest, pushing him backward until he had him pinned against the wooden coral.

Hobson's eyes were wide with horror. Dropping his gun, he tried to grab for the handle of the fork but his arms had no strength. His hands fell to his side as he raised his head to look at Lansing. His mouth formed some unintelligible word, but the only sound to come out was a rattle deep in his throat. His head fell forward as his entire body went limp.

Lansing let the corpse fall to the ground.

He shook his head, as if he had just experienced a terrible nightmare. The coyote, he thought. The shadows were too dark. He ran into the barn and grabbed a flashlight. Returning to the spot where he had seen the eyes, Lansing flashed the beam on the ground.

There was no sign of a coyote.

No body. No blood. No tracks.

As if to answer the question forming in Lansing's mind, a coyote on a nearby knoll let out a long, soulful howl that sent shudders down his spine.

The image of the coyotes attacking the two agents flashed through his mind, followed by the specter of the lone animal staring at him from the boulder. He recalled every thought that had passed between them.

Coyote had been wrong.

Maybe he could understand.

"Are you sure you have to go back tonight?" Kim asked. The question was laced with loneliness.

"Yeah, I'm afraid so." Gabe swung his leg over his motorcycle. "Sheriff Lansing's been awfully good about giving me time off. The least I can do is show up to work when he asks me to."

"Have any idea when you might come back this way?"

"It won't be too long, I promise," Gabe said, slipping his

helmet on. "It's only a three-hour trip. As soon as I figure out my new schedule, I'll call."

"Why don't you call me tonight when you get home? That way I'll know you made it safely."

"I can do that."

Kim leaned forward and they kissed one last time. Reluctantly, Kim stepped away from the bike.

As Gabe reached down to turn his ignition key, he stopped and looked at Kim. There was a puzzled expression on his face.

"What's wrong?"

"Listen."

Kim listened intently for a few seconds, then shook her head. "I don't hear anything."

"I know. The coyotes . . . the voices . . . They've stopped!"

COYOTE TROTTED DOWN THE SHOULDER OF THE HIGH-way. The full moon shone brightly in the clear, cloudless night. Coyote alternated between keeping his nose close to the ground, then high in the air, sniffing for anything that might interest him.

He was satisfied with his visit. He had gotten to play a host of pranks, plus he had helped his children. He couldn't remember the last time he had done something like that.

Most important, he had shown how powerful he was. People would talk of this visit for generations. He had com-manded an army of his cousins. He had made believers out of agnostics. And the cave . . . the cave . . . the cave was not a loss at all. To begin with, it was too cluttered. The people now knew the legends were true. He had given them proof that he had walked among them. When he came back, he would start collecting things for a new cave.

Coyote checked the stars above him. Yes. He was trav-eling north. That was good. He wanted to go north. It had been a long time since he had tricked his Lakota children. They needed a visit.

As Coyote continued his steady trot, he suddenly re-membered something: Coyote was hungry.

Coyote was always hungry.

Match wits with the best-selling

MYSTERY WRITERS

in the business!

SUSAN DUNLAP

"Dunlap's police procedurals have the authenticity of telling detail."
—*The Washington Post Book World*

☐	**AS A FAVOR**	20999-4	$4.99
☐	**ROGUE WAVE**	21197-2	$4.99
☐	**DEATH AND TAXES**	21406-8	$4.99
☐	**HIGHFALL**	21560-9	$5.50

SARA PARETSKY

"Paretsky's name always makes the top of the list when people talk about the new female operatives." —*The New York Times Book Review*

☐	**BLOOD SHOT**	20420-8	$5.99
☐	**BURN MARKS**	20845-9	$5.99
☐	**INDEMNITY ONLY**	21069-0	$5.99
☐	**GUARDIAN ANGEL**	21399-1	$5.99
☐	**KILLING ORDERS**	21528-5	$5.99
☐	**DEADLOCK**	21332-0	$5.99
☐	**TUNNEL VISION**	21752-0	$6.99

SISTER CAROL ANNE O'MARIE

"Move over Miss Marple..." —*San Francisco Sunday Examiner & Chronicle*

☐	**ADVENT OF DYING**	10052-6	$4.99
☐	**THE MISSING MADONNA**	20473-9	$4.99
☐	**A NOVENA FOR MURDER**	16469-9	$4.99
☐	**MURDER IN ORDINARY TIME**	21353-3	$4.99
☐	**MURDER MAKES A PILGRIMAGE**	21613-3	$4.99

LINDA BARNES

☐	**COYOTE**	21089-5	$4.99
☐	**STEEL GUITAR**	21268-5	$4.99
☐	**BITTER FINISH**	21606-0	$4.99
☐	**SNAPSHOT**	21220-0	$4.99

At your local bookstore or use this handy page for ordering:

DELL READERS SERVICE, DEPT. DS
2451 South Wolf Rd., Des Plaines, IL. 60018

Please send me the above title(s). I am enclosing $ _____
(Please add $2.50 per order to cover shipping and handling.) Send
check or money order—no cash or C.O.D.s please.

D e l l

Ms./Mrs./Mr._____

Address _____

City/State _____ Zip _____

DGM-11/95

Prices and availability subject to change without notice. Please allow four to six weeks for delivery.